Bitter Truth

Bitter Truth

MEREDITH WILD
AND JILLIAN LIOTA

 Montlake

Text copyright © 2024 by Meredith Wild & Jillian Liota
All rights reserved.

Published by Montlake, Seattle

www.apub.com

Amazon, the Amazon logo, and Montlake are trademarks of Amazon.com, Inc., or its affiliates.

ISBN-13: 9781662524578 (paperback)
ISBN-13: 9781662524561 (digital)

Cover design by Caroline Teagle Johnson
Cover photography by Staci Brucks
Cover image: © Jackyenjoyphotography, © Michael Sugrue, © Pattadis Walarput / Getty

Printed in the United States of America

*For anyone trying to figure out who they are
when life doesn't go according to plan*

*For Jillian,
for your friendship and bringing your passion to the page
when I needed it the most*

Chapter One

MURPHY

The sign for Rosewood streaks by, the lights from my car illuminating it for just a moment before it disappears behind me with the fading sunlight.

Twenty more minutes until I'm home.

I sigh, wishing not for the first time that things were different.

That this wasn't the way things in my life were falling together.

Or, I guess, falling apart.

The eight-hour drive from Venice Beach hasn't been that bad, but once I crossed the bridge taking me out of San Francisco and into Napa, it felt like time sped up. The drive I had earlier wished would pass more quickly now feels like it's coming to an end far too soon.

Because the fact I'm heading back to my hometown is finally starting to sink in, and I wish I could slow time for a little while. Just long enough to figure out . . . well, to figure out a lot of things.

What I'm going to say.

What I'm going to do.

But most importantly, how I'm going to cope with the aftermath of what happened back in LA and what it means for my life.

I take the next exit and catch myself grinding my teeth, my jaw flexing with the anxiety that overwhelms me with each passing moment.

As I leave the freeway and begin the final stretch out into the country, everything I see is a reminder of why I left. All the reasons I couldn't ever imagine a life here beyond the one forced on me as a child, when I had no choice about where to live and what to do.

The truth is that I hated Rosewood the moment we arrived. I was just four years old when my father, my brothers, and I showed up with a carload of belongings and a truckload of emotional baggage.

I take a deep breath and let it out long and slow, hoping it will help ease the anxious energy beginning to build in my chest.

It doesn't help.

And then I make the turn onto Main Street, crossing the short stretch of downtown. Rosewood has one of those quaint downtown areas that doesn't seem to exist anymore. It's a stretch of road that hosts a bar, a restaurant, a café, a coffee shop, a bakery, and of course, little shops filled to the brim with every wine-related tchotchke a tourist might desire.

In the years since I left, I've come to realize just how different Rosewood is from so many other places. Though I haven't yet decided whether that's a good or a bad thing.

It's particularly different from Venice Beach and Santa Monica, my stomping grounds when I moved to Southern California. People everywhere, beachy weather, tattoo parlors, and weed shops. The grunge and grit of the place make it feel like a town that brought out the wild, slightly unhinged parts of people. The social niceties of small-town life wouldn't be a blip in the minds of anyone who stuck around there long enough.

Rosewood is . . . the exact opposite. Clean and quaint and perfect in a way that is also absolutely infuriating.

Which is why the idea of being back sits in my belly like a stomach bug, a nauseating feeling that has me cracking my window for a little fresh air as I come to a stop at the end of the street. The familiar smells of wine country—damp earth and grapevine—flood my senses.

Memories from my childhood rush in, some bad, some good. Like the shared stresses of a bad year for the grapes, or seeing my father, covered in debris and sweat in the middle of the crush.

"Five generations have worked this land," he'd say after another day of tireless physical work. "It's our family legacy. You should be proud to be a part of something as beautiful as this."

By *you*, he meant my brothers and me. We'd share eye rolls whenever Dad launched into one of his "family legacy" sermons. I often wondered if he was trying to believe the words himself, more than he expected them to mean something to us. After all, he'd left Rosewood as soon as he was eighteen, wholly uninterested in the family business or the pride of legacy, only to return with his tail between his legs after tragedy struck, two children and a newborn in tow.

I wince a little and rap my fingers against the steering wheel. Maybe we're a lot more alike than I thought, my father and me.

Not that I'd ever tell *him* that.

I finally turn off the main drag, which takes me down the long highway out to my family's vineyard and past the Rosewood High School football field and Chantry Winery—two landmarks of my younger years.

High school in a little wine country town didn't offer much. I wasn't popular, but I wasn't unpopular either—kind of falling into that middle space that most high school students are in. I was invited to some parties, went to some school activities, had some friends.

Come to think of it, my high school experience is basically a metaphor for my life as the middle child. Not too much attention, but not enough.

Maybe that's the real reason I left.

It sucks to feel like you're just noticeable enough to be intentionally ignored.

I'd rather believe I bounced from Rosewood because I wanted more.

More fun.

More people.

More experiences.

Definitely more men.

The guys of my youth were mostly consumed with the quest for the two Ps. As my friend Quinn would repeatedly remind me—and possibly herself—as we spent countless nights on her living room couch watching reality TV, "All they're after, Murph, is popularity and pussy. And if you can't give them either, you have nothing they want."

She had a point, and it only became clearer to me when I moved away just how true it was of pretty much every guy, everywhere. I can hardly remember a first date when the guy didn't seriously think he was going to get laid at the end. Or at least get his dick sucked.

Not my style. Sex has never been a bartering chip for me.

My entire body shifts at that thought. The emotional whiplash of what happened back in LA makes my stomach turn over.

And then, as if the universe has decided to gift me one final middle finger on this emotional journey home, I hear a loud pop and my car begins to bounce and shudder, the wheel tugging to the side in deference to what I can only assume is a flat tire.

Fuck.

I know that nobody ever really *needs* a car issue, but this is seriously the last thing I need right now.

Something wells up inside my chest as I continue driving, hoping my memory is correct that there is a one-pump gas station around this bend . . .

I take a shuddered breath when I see it, and my car hobbles its way off the highway and into the dirt lot before I roll to a stop next to a beat-up old truck.

It feels like a great effort not to burst into tears as I shove my door open and then slam it closed, my irritation and frustration getting the better of me. When I round to the back and take a look, I see that the back right tire is pretty much flat on the ground. Thankfully I didn't damage my rim in that final few hundred yards.

I haven't ever changed a tire by myself before, which makes me even more upset, especially since my dad *and* my older brother offered to teach me several times when I was in high school.

Rolling my eyes at the irony, I head toward the tiny shop, hoping that somebody can help me out.

But as soon as I push inside, I know I'm out of luck. The woman behind the counter looks to be in her seventies at least, and when I ask if there's a mechanic on-site, she gives me an empathetic smile.

"I'm sorry, honey. But I've got a landline if you wanna call somebody."

I give her a thin smile and shake my head, knowing I'm eventually going to have to resort to calling my brother. The amount of shit Memphis is going to give me . . .

Sighing in disbelief at just how bad my luck has turned out, I head back to my car, staring at the flat tire as if I'll be able to will it to inflate.

If this doesn't sum up my life right now, I don't know what would. Getting so close, almost there, and then having everything fall apart.

And then, it just all becomes too much. The dam breaks. My emotions rush in—a culmination of my return home settling into my soul on top of all the other bullshit I've been dealing with. I burst into tears, overwhelmed and broken. Dropping down into a squat in the middle of the dirt parking lot, I hide my face in my hands and just let it all out. All the sadness and frustration and disappointment.

"You okay?"

My sob cuts off in the middle and I look to the side, embarrassment coursing through me as I realize someone has been watching me have a breakdown.

I stand quickly, wiping at my face and staring studiously at the man's feet, not wanting to see his likely judgment of the woman sobbing in the gas station parking lot.

"Yeah, I'm fine, I—"

But my voice cuts off. I can't even force the fake smile and customer-service voice that I've perfected over nearly ten years. Instead, I start crying again.

"I'm sorry, I'm going through a lot," I say, looking back to my car. "My tire popped and I don't know how to fix it, and it has just been . . . the *worst* day."

My observer is silent for a long moment, and when I finally glance over at him, I feel a second wave of embarrassment. Heat prickles at the little places behind my ears and at my wrists when I see the concern evident across his brow.

"I might not be able to fix your horrible day," he says after a long pause, "but I can handle the tire for you. Get everything fixed up so you can head on your way."

I blink a few times, feeling a little off-balance at his offer. I've spent the past decade in LA, where nobody slows down for a moment, and definitely not long enough to help someone in a shit situation. I almost forgot people do that kind of thing.

I nod, thankful that the emotions previously welling inside me seem to be dissipating.

"Yeah, that would be great, actually."

"Don't suppose you have a spare tire in there, do you?"

I wince, wishing I could say yes and preparing to tell him the story of when I sold it to a friend for fifty bucks during tough times. But before I can, he dips his head toward his truck.

"No worries. I have a spare in mine."

And then he strides toward his truck and drops down to the ground, sliding underneath the bed and working at something for a minute or two before he tugs out a tire and shimmies back out, his shirt and jeans now covered in dust.

"I'll have this fixed up for you in just a few minutes," he tells me, looping one strong arm through the tire and hoisting it over to my car along with a couple of tools.

I watch for a few minutes as he works, twisting a wrench for a while on the lug nuts before lifting the car with the jack.

Now that my earlier overwhelm has eased, it's hard not to appreciate just how handsome this Good Samaritan is. I've never been one to give elevator eyes before, but I can't help it now. My gaze lingers on his broad shoulders and flexing forearm muscles as he works on removing my flat.

My mind briefly flitters over the idea of what else he's capable of with those hands, but I clear my throat and scratch idly at my cheek, trying to shove that thought aside.

"I really appreciate you taking the time to do this," I say, not wanting to hover awkwardly in silence.

He glances up at me and grins, his hazel eyes warm and kind, then looks back at the task at hand. "I'm happy to help. You feeling a little better now?"

My face flushes and I let out a laugh that surely betrays my embarrassment. "Yeah. Sorry about the tears. I was feeling overwhelmed."

"You don't have to apologize. Life is overwhelming sometimes." He looks at me again and shrugs. "I had a good cry just last week."

I purse my lips, trying to hide my smile. "Oh yeah? A good cry, huh?"

He nods. "And a nice long bubble bath."

Shaking my head, I can't help when my smile gets the best of me. "Sounds soothing."

"You should really try it out. See if it helps."

I tuck my hands into the pockets of my shorts and lean back against his truck. "I will definitely consider that. Thank you so much for the suggestion."

He chuckles and continues working for a few more minutes before hopping up and tugging the tire off and setting it to the side.

"This isn't a permanent solution," he says, his voice slightly strained as he shoves the spare into place. "You'll still need to get a regular tire put on here. But this should be good for tonight."

I nod, watching as he puts the lug nuts back on and begins tightening them, and when he finally drops my car back to the ground and gives the trunk a tap, I say the first thing on my mind.

"Can I buy you a beer or something? As a thank-you? There's a bar about a mile up the road."

He looks off to the side, in the direction of town, and seems to consider it for a moment. But ultimately, he shakes his head.

"Not really a bar kinda guy."

I lick my lips, my ego slightly bruised.

Any other night, I would have said *Okay*, thanked him again, and gotten on the road. But something makes me try again.

Maybe I'm not ready for him to go just yet.

Or maybe *I'm* not ready to go.

Either way, I want a few more minutes with my rescuer, even if it's just in this parking lot.

"Or maybe I could grab us some cheap wine coolers from inside?" I stick my thumb toward the gas station. "I don't want to ask for help again, but I'd appreciate it more than you'll ever know if you give me a reason not to go where I'm headed."

He grins at me, licks his lower lip just slightly, then nods his head. "You know, a cheap wine cooler actually sounds great."

I beam at him. "I'll be right back."

Then I race inside and hurriedly pay for two of the little bottles that I used to sneak back in high school.

"All right, I've got mojito or margarita," I say as I approach where he's seated on the dropped tailgate of his truck.

"I'll take the mojito."

"Good choice."

I hop up next to him, then pop the caps off our bottles with my car key.

"That was a neat little trick," he says, taking his drink from my hand.

I smile and clink my bottle against his. "Desperate times teach you some wild things."

He smirks and raises his drink to his lips, mumbling, "Isn't that the truth."

We both take a sip, and I wince immediately, the flavor not at all what I remember from my youth. "Oh wow."

"Yeah."

"That's terrible."

"So bad."

"I remember it being so much better when I was in high school."

"Everything against the rules tastes better when you're young."

We both laugh. I swing my legs and cast my gaze over to the sun that has dipped low on the horizon, enjoying the simplicity of the moment.

I know once I hop off this tailgate and make the short drive down the road to the house, all the stress is going to rush back in. But for now, the peace and quiet, and sitting next to this handsome man who was willing to take time out of his day to help me, is exactly what I need.

"Thanks again for the tire save . . . and for sitting here with me."

His leg, dangling next to mine, bumps me so lightly I'm not sure if it was accidental or on purpose. I'm partial to the latter.

"And sorry you're covered in dirt now. I hope you don't have somewhere important to go tonight."

Chuckling, he shakes his head. "Nah. And I figure you did me a favor. Now I have an excuse to take another bubble bath."

My lips turn up and he winks before taking another sip from his wine cooler.

I watch as he does, and I can't help the way my gaze drops to his lips for one long moment, wondering what it might be like to kiss a man like him. And when he looks back at me, I see his eyes dip as well. Just for a moment, for a quick, almost invisible glance, before he turns his head and stares off into the distance.

My hand between us is braced against the lip of the tailgate, and a shiver of anticipation slides through me when his hand does the same, the edge of his palm grazing against mine.

"So what was the deal earlier? It seems like you might have had more on your mind than just the tire."

I nibble on the inside of my cheek, trying to decide how to answer. I want to keep talking to him, but the last thing I want to do is share all my dirty laundry. Ultimately, I settle on vague truths.

"Change is hard, especially when it feels like you're not really in control of the course your life is taking." I shrug and take another sip from my bottle. "I think earlier was like . . . a dam breaking, you know? The tire was just the last straw on a very large haystack."

He bobs his head. "Yeah, I know what you mean."

Even talking about it brings the emotional magnitude up to the surface, and I bat away a tear that breaks free.

"Hey now." His gentle voice, warm like a blanket I want to crawl into, wraps its way around me. His hand reaches up and cups my cheek, his thumb stroking where another tear has fallen. "No more tears tonight, hmm?"

I give him a watery smile, my emotions calming again.

"You seem to be able to keep my tears at bay better than I can," I tell him. "Maybe I should keep you around."

His lips turn up at that. "Maybe you should."

The world fades away in that moment, when our faces are so close together, our thighs touching and the evening humidity making everything feel hazy and warm.

I feel a little drunk, and there's no way it's from the wine cooler that I've taken only a few sips of.

No, it's this man holding my face in his hands.

I'm intoxicated with everything about him, and what I do know is very little.

All I know for sure is that it's been a long time since I've been this interested in a man.

So I do the only thing that makes sense.

I lean in and press my lips to his.

He seems surprised at first, but that fades almost immediately, and the hand on my cheek slips around to the nape of my neck as his mouth opens against mine.

The taste of mint and lime explodes on my tongue, along with something else even more heady that makes me groan just slightly.

I shift my body so I'm facing him more, and my hands reach out, bracing against his strong chest. I love touching him, feeling the strength and warmth of his body beneath my palms.

The kiss doesn't last long, and he nibbles gently on my lower lip before we eventually pull back and look at each other, each of us with smiles on our faces.

"That was unexpected," I say, trying to keep the smile on my face small so he doesn't see how wildly incredible I feel. I'm sure I barely succeed.

"It was," he replies, his fingers stroking gently against the back of my head before he lets me go.

We sit there for another ten or fifteen minutes, taking little sips from our drinks and glancing at each other every so often with knowing smiles. It's the kind of magical night that I would have dreamed about back in high school, when I would have been up all night with a pen and a notebook, trying to capture the experience in lyrics.

When we finish our wine coolers, he hops down and crosses over to a trash can that butts up to the back of the gas station to chuck them.

"You think the tire will be enough to get you where you're going?" he asks as he walks back to me.

"I should be fine."

He nods. "Good." Then he takes my hand and helps me down, my feet kicking up a little bit of dust as I drop to the ground. His muscles flex as he pushes the tailgate closed, and the sound of it slamming shut feels jarring against the quiet of the evening.

The toe of my shoe skims over the dirt between us, and I wonder if I should ask for his number. Or if he'll ask for mine.

He watches me for a long moment, and my heart throbs rapidly in my chest, the anticipation of what he might say growing until it's a living thing inside of me. As friendly as he seems to be, he's also very hard to read.

"You know, in another life, I would be asking for your number right now," he says. "But things in my life are . . ."

My heart falls. "You don't have to explain," I tell him with a thin smile, not wanting to hear another rejection. "My life is messy right now too, so . . ."

I trail off, not knowing what else to say.

So . . . I wouldn't give you my number anyway?

So . . . we're better off leaving things like this?

Neither of those are really true, so it doesn't even warrant saying them.

"Thanks again." I take a step back, in the direction of my car.

His eyes skim over my face, and I can't help but imagine that he's trying to commit me to memory so he can remember me later.

Doubtful, though.

Instead, he's probably trying to figure out how to say goodbye and get on the road without having to talk to me anymore.

Oh, how quickly all my warm and fuzzy feelings have begun to fade.

"All right, well, have a safe drive."

I nod, and we both turn to get into our respective vehicles. I glance at my phone briefly, seeing a missed call and a text from my brother.

Memphis: Let me know when you're ten minutes out. I'll come help with your stuff.

I take a deep breath and send off a quick response, letting him know I'm just a few minutes away, then drop my phone in the cup holder and glance to my left.

My Good Samaritan is already gone, and I can see his taillights in my rearview as he pulls out onto the highway.

Part of me is glad he took off so fast. As fun as it was to give my mind a chance to create a reality where something more might have happened, I'm not in the market for that kind of distraction. I have too much on my mind as I prepare to face my family for the first time in nearly a decade.

They always disapproved of me leaving town in the first place, and I know they will have plenty to say now that I'm back.

I only have to drive a few minutes before I'm pulling off the highway and down the long dusty road to the house I grew up in, but my eyebrows scrunch in confusion when I see a familiar truck parked off to the side next to some of the other equipment.

When I come to a stop, I scan the area around the truck, trying to understand why that truck would be here.

As soon as I step out of my car, I hear a newly familiar voice.

"Did, uh . . . did you need something else?"

I squint through the dark, finally seeing the form of the guy from the gas station heading toward me.

My head tilts to the side, and I cast my eyes up to our house, trying to make sure I didn't pull into the wrong driveway.

But no, even with just the porch light, I can see the same dark-brown front door and the same silver door knocker that my younger brother, Micah, picked out from Home Depot: a circular grapevine with a stem of grapes dangling in the middle.

The man from the gas station is standing about fifteen feet away from me with his hands on his hips, looking at me like I've followed him home.

But before I can say anything—ask him what he's doing here, tell him I live here, or any other thing that would actually make sense—I hear my name.

"Murphy?"

I turn and look back to the house where the front door is open, the light from inside illuminating a tall, strong figure that I know without a doubt is my brother.

"That was fast," he says, walking toward me. "I didn't realize you really meant only a few more minutes."

"Yeah, I got a flat so I was at the pump when I texted you," I reply, then look back over to where the Good Samaritan is still standing near his truck.

"Hey, Wes." Memphis greets him briefly and then stops at the trunk of my car. "This is my sister, Murphy."

My eyes stay on him—on *Wes*—and I watch as his body language changes, the tense way he'd been standing relaxing just slightly.

"Nice to meet you, Murphy," he says, his voice tight.

"You, too." Then I turn to where Memphis is tugging my suitcase out of the trunk. "Just the suitcase. I only have a few other things and they can wait until tomorrow."

He shakes his head. "We can get it now. Wes, you mind carrying a box or two?"

I sigh, feeling awkward about having him help when I still haven't processed the fact he's here right now.

"So how do you two know each other?" I ask, assuming that Wes and my brother are friends or something.

Memphis pauses, eyeing us both. "Wes works here," he tells me, hoisting a box out and handing it to Wes, who is suddenly right in my space and still smelling deliciously of dust and sweat and the faint scent of mojito wine cooler.

"Doing what?" I ask, watching as Wes stands silently, looking just as shell-shocked as I feel.

"He's the chef of the new restaurant." Memphis tucks a box under his arm. "So he'll be your boss."

I blink a few times, all of his words hitting me at once. There's a restaurant? There's a chef? Both are news to me. But one thing stands out the most, and my voice grows tight as I glare at my brother.

"He'll be my *what?*"

Chapter Two

WES

"It's bullshit, Memphis!"

I wince, knowing I'm certainly about to involve myself in something that is very clearly a family dispute. Something that doesn't warrant my opinion.

Still, though, I wait outside the room, hoping to eavesdrop long enough to determine whether there might be a chance for me to swoop in and hopefully alleviate the tension between Memphis and his sister.

Fuck me . . . his *sister*.

"It's not bullshit, Murphy, it's progress. We've been talking for years about making changes to the vineyard to bring in more tourists. It's not my fault you haven't been around to be part of those conversations."

I know jack shit about the Hawthorne family drama, but it doesn't take a genius to know that they seem to have plenty of baggage to unpack.

"I could care less about the changes you're making," Murphy spits back, and I can just picture her glaring at her brother, those gorgeous caramel-colored eyes of hers glowing with anger. "I'm part of this family too, but now I'm the only one with a *boss*? What the hell is that about? You said I'd be in charge of myself."

"Yeah, well . . . things change. Circumstances change. So if you want to move home and work here, you'll report to Chef Hart on Monday morning."

"If I *want* to move home?" Murphy shrieks.

I glance through the crack in the door. On the other side, she's standing across the room from where her brother is probably sitting at his desk. Murphy's hands are in little fists at her sides, and even from here I can see her jaw is tight. Less than an hour ago, I was kissing her sweet mouth and arguing with myself about asking her for her phone number as we sat on the tailgate of the truck. I was not expecting to see this other very real side of her.

"I misspoke," Memphis corrects himself, his tone losing some of the bite. "Whether or not you can move home is up to Dad. But if you want to get paid and have a job, the job that's available is waitressing. And Chef Hart is in charge of the new restaurant."

There's a long silence before I hear Murphy's voice slice through the quiet.

"You know, it only took me fifteen minutes of being home to remember all the reasons I left."

Without warning, the door to the office flies open and Murphy comes storming out, halting as she notices my presence. But just as quickly as she comes to a stop, she's going again, leaving me in her wake as she heads down a long hallway and around a corner.

Memphis told me his sister was a handful when he mentioned she'd be working for me, but I hadn't expected . . . *this*. For her to be the gorgeous woman I thought I was helping out at the gas station. For her to be all kinds of fire and heat.

Why couldn't she have just been some girl? Any girl, really. Anyone other than Memphis's sister.

But with the way life seems to constantly beat me back, I guess it makes sense.

I drag my attention away from the corner where Murphy disappeared and knock gently on the doorjamb to Memphis's office. He glances up and then waves me in with a tight smile, and I step into the room that has become quite familiar ever since he hired me last month.

Even though most of my work is done in the restaurant on the other end of the property, I've been spending a few hours a week sitting across from Memphis at this desk, the two of us discussing big-picture items and shooting the shit.

He seems like a good enough guy, if a little high strung.

All I know for certain is that he's the man who hired me, and for that, I owe him.

"I'm sorry about that," he says, his voice gruff as he shifts papers around on his desk. "I wasn't expecting Murphy to have a complete meltdown."

I scratch the back of my head for a second before tucking my hands into my jeans. "She seems . . . spirited."

And sexy as hell, though I keep that part to myself.

"Spirited," Memphis repeats, then huffs out a chuckle. "That's one word for her. I've got about a million more, but I don't want to scare you off by detailing all her faults. I'm sure she's a lot easier to get along with when you're not her big brother."

I chew on the inside of my cheek, considering him. Memphis told me his sister was intense, sure, but he said it in an affectionate kind of way. A way that hints at normal brother-sister fights over two decades of growing up in each other's business.

That's the way I talk about *my* brother, anyway.

Ash has plenty of faults, and the two of us have gotten into some serious arguments and at least a few scuffles over the years as a result. But I don't broadcast those things to anyone outside of our unit.

The way Memphis is clenching his jaw and glaring at the paperwork he's sorting through, and his mention of *all her faults* . . . It just makes me think he and Murphy have a few old wounds that haven't healed.

It worries me a little bit, the idea that I might wind up at the center of some family drama that I have nothing to do with.

But with my background and all the toxic workplace drama I've experienced in my years working in kitchens, whatever little skirmish is going on between Memphis and Murphy isn't enough to have me jumping ship.

I need this job.

Desperately.

So if that means I need to put up with hearing about the problems between my employer and his sister, so be it.

"Is there something I can help you with?" Memphis glances up briefly before focusing back on the documents in front of him.

I freeze, though thankfully he seems far too distracted by whatever he's working on to notice.

I hadn't even thought about a reason why I'd stick around after putting Murphy's boxes in the hallway. Sure, I might be living on the northern perimeter of the property in one of the studio cabins, but this is the first time I've been over here so late. Memphis and his father told me I was welcome inside their home anytime, even if it was just to rummage through the fridge, but I haven't taken advantage of that generous offer just yet.

Normally, I stop in here and there to connect with Memphis and talk through any updates or changes to our plans for the restaurant, but the only true time I spend in the main house is when their aunt Sarah makes everyone dinner in the evenings. It's one of those old-world, employees-as-family things that I don't think is that common anymore. But it's a pretty nice benefit, and Sarah is an incredible cook.

Outside of my hours working, I've kept primarily to myself, wanting to enjoy my last nights of freedom before I begin the real hours as the head chef of a brand-new restaurant.

So sticking around during a family squabble on a Friday night is a bit out of character for me. I scramble to come up with anything I can think of for why I'm still here.

"Your dad told me your aunt usually keeps some killer desserts in the fridge for whoever might want them after hours," I say, remembering what Jack said to me when he gave me a tour of the house and the property.

Memphis glances up at me. "Got a bit of a sweet tooth?"

I nod. "A little bit, but especially when I'm running on an empty tank. It's been a busy day."

He sets his pen down and then tilts his head from side to side before pushing away from his desk and slapping his knees. "I could definitely use the break. I'll show you where Sarah keeps the goodies."

I follow in his wake as he leads me through the large ranch-style home and into the kitchen.

Tugging open the fridge, he rummages around for a second before pulling out two large white platters. One is filled with cheese, salami, and other charcuterie elements. The other has a bunch of bonbons covered in cellophane.

I reach immediately for the tray with chocolate and peanut buttery treats and pop one into my mouth. I've been a chef for basically my entire adult life. Ever since my teens, I've cultivated a very educated palate when it comes to just about everything culinary. But chocolate and peanut butter are two things that are universally delicious, and always more so together.

"Sorry again. About Murphy."

I look to Memphis, who is leaning back against the farmhouse sink, snacking on a piece of salami.

"You have nothing to apologize for," I tell him.

"I get that, but I also know what you're in for with her working for you." He shakes his head. "I don't want to scare you off, but like I said, she's gonna be a handful."

I lick some chocolate out of the corner of my mouth, trying to keep my thoughts about Murphy to myself.

"I've worked with plenty of really complicated personalities," I reply, deciding to stay as neutral as possible. "I'm not worried."

Memphis chuckles and then shoves another slice of salami into his mouth.

"Help yourself to as much as you want. Just make sure to tuck it back into the fridge once you head out."

I nod. "Will do."

He reaches out, and we shake hands before he heads back down the little hallway toward his office.

I swipe another bonbon and pop it in my mouth. I glance around the kitchen. I've been in here before, but never alone. Never with the ability to stare and take things in, unencumbered by the observations of others. So I take advantage, walking over to the photos scattered on the wall that separates the kitchen from the living room.

There are plenty of people in these pictures that I don't recognize at all, but I keep searching until I find what I'm looking for.

Who I'm looking for.

Murphy Hawthorne.

I spot a picture of her when she was much younger—maybe in high school—sitting on a stool playing the guitar, a bright smile on her face.

I've seen this picture in passing, having faced toward it on most of the nights I've been here eating dinner just a few feet away. Now, knowing who Murphy is, I study it harder, comparing the photo to my memory of the way her eyes watched me as we sat in the back of the truck.

Next to it is a family photo of a much-younger Murphy and Memphis, maybe in their teens, along with their younger brother, Micah, who works at the vineyard as well. Their father, Jack, and their aunt Sarah are on either side of the three siblings, with an elderly couple in the back.

Their grandparents, I'm assuming.

My attention drifts back to the photo of Murphy with the guitar. I reach out to shift it slightly, correcting the crooked slant of the frame on the wall.

Memphis says she's trouble, and I don't know enough to agree one way or the other. She seemed sweet enough, playful enough, back at the gas station. But being playful and teasing are things you show to the world. The erratic, frustrating, difficult parts of people tend to come out more with family.

I guess I'll just have to wait and see how the chips fall once we're finally working together, which apparently is Monday. That leaves only a few days before we're thrust together in the chaos of all the final preparations that come in the weeks before opening a restaurant. After that, I won't be able to avoid her even if I want to.

I spin around to grab another bonbon off the tray, but freeze when I spot Murphy in leggings and a loose tank top on the other side of the island, one hand on her hip, the other holding a chocolate confection that she's nibbling on.

I'm at a loss for words.

Not just because I'm surprised to see her, but also because she's even more gorgeous with her hair pulled up in a messy bun at the top of her head, a few wavy strands hanging loose around her face.

Effortlessly beautiful. That's what she is. The kind of woman who would look incredible gazing into my eyes next to me in bed in the morning. The kind of woman who makes you wish you'd asked for her damn number.

I shake my head and look away, trying to quiet the storm of thoughts beginning to take my mind hostage.

"Have a nice little chat about me with my brother?" She pops the rest of the half-eaten bonbon into her mouth.

I step forward, bracing both hands against the edge of the tiled island.

"No, actually."

She slows down her chewing, but I can tell by her slightly narrowed eyes she doesn't entirely buy it.

"Why do I find that hard to believe?" she asks, confirming that I read her correctly. "I can't imagine my brother missing a chance to paint me as the black sheep of our family."

"Are you? The black sheep?"

She shrugs one shoulder. "Depends on your perspective."

"I'm interested in *your* perspective."

Her eyes hold mine for a long moment before she answers.

"I don't buy into the black-sheep theory," she tells me. "It implies that one person's faults and flaws are worse than another's, when really it's a matter of preference. Of taste, if you will. My brother, for example, is a bossy asshole who treats his siblings like employees. But he gets praised for that because he's a man. I openly disagree with him about something, and I'm *a handful*."

Something about my facial expression must give me away because Murphy lasers in on it and she almost laughs.

"He used that word to describe me, huh?"

I shrug my own shoulder this time, not wanting to throw Memphis under the bus.

"*A handful* is the most common. *Intense* is another. *Aggressive. Bad-tempered.* He likes to pick words that dance around how he really feels, things that are just enough to hint that I'm *a problem* without being intentionally cruel."

"Sounds like you and your brother have quite a history if you're able to describe him this specifically," I finally reply.

It's getting harder to stay neutral when I can see so clearly that the way Memphis talks about his sister wounds her deeply.

"I haven't seen him in nine years. I'd just assumed he might be willing to give me the benefit of the doubt before jumping to conclusions about who I am."

I raise my eyebrows.

When he said his sister was moving home after living in Southern California for a few years, I hadn't expected it to be *nine* years. That's a hair bit more than a few.

I don't really know how to respond, other than to encourage her to talk to her brother if she's frustrated. But I'm not sure that's the right move, for either of them. It assumes they have a healthy relationship where they feel safe while they're being vulnerable.

And clearly, that's not at all the kind of relationship they have.

I'm also not her therapist. Hell, we literally just met. I don't need to be handing out any kind of advice.

"I'm sorry that things between you aren't . . . easier," I settle on. "Family relationships can be tough, no doubt."

Her shoulders soften, and it looks like all the wind has fallen away from her sails.

"It's been a long day and I'm beat, so . . ." She pauses, plucking another bonbon off the tray. "I'm gonna head to bed. I guess I'll . . . see you around?"

I nod, letting my eyes wander a half second more to take a mental snapshot of her before she heads off down the hallway. I watch her until she disappears, and I realize I've done that twice now, almost like she's a magnet and I can't help but follow her presence.

Once she's gone, I force her out of my thoughts and make quick work of putting Sarah's treats back in the fridge. I leave through the french doors that lead from the living room to the veranda that spans the back of the house and offers an impressive view of the vineyard under the moonlight.

Taking a deep breath, I soak in the scents around me. The sea-salt air that rolls in with the evening fog. The jasmine vines sprinkled along the sides of the main house with their delicate pink blooms. The chaparral sage edging the stone pathway that snakes through the center of the property.

I've been wandering through the vineyard at night, enjoying the quiet. Tonight, though, my mind doesn't jump to the same recurring problems that normally plague me.

The only thing plaguing me is Murphy. I can't get my mind off her.

When I first saw her at the gas station, I'd been struck by her beauty. After I'd paid for my gas and emerged outside, I couldn't not do something when I saw her crying.

But it was in our flirtatious exchanges that I felt hooked. I could feel a thread of connection between us almost immediately, and I'm not sure if I'm going to be able to just turn that off.

And that kiss was . . .

I nearly groan just thinking about it.

The fact she's a Hawthorne is just . . . I kick lightly at the mulch on the path. What kind of a small world is that? I guess not *that* small since we were at a gas station less than two miles from her family vineyard.

I don't know what kind of disruption working together will cause, or whether this attraction to each other is a small flame we can snuff out quickly. But she seemed pretty upset to find out she was going to be "reporting" to someone instead of managing things on her own, so I guess I'll just have to wait and see.

But one thing is for certain. This job is more important to me than my attraction to Murphy, and that's something I need to remember whenever I find myself too enamored by her golden eyes or perfect pink lips.

Eventually I hit the place where the path splits, leading off in several different directions: the brand-new restaurant building to the right, the cellars and warehouse down the middle, and the cabins to the left.

No matter what, I need to remember that I'm here to work, and that getting entangled with my brand-new boss's sister is *definitely* not the right path to take.

Chapter Three

MURPHY

I stay in bed until after eleven on Saturday. The familiarity of my old twin mattress and the room I grew up in lulls me to a state of comatose bliss I haven't experienced since high school.

Life in LA was go, go, go. Rapid pace, never stop, keep moving.

It had been jarring at first, but I quickly adapted.

I didn't realize just how much I would enjoy the chance to have a lazy Saturday after years of pushing myself without a break.

I crawl out of bed and mosey sleepily into the kitchen. I take out a pitcher of fresh orange juice from the refrigerator, knowing that my aunt Sarah likely made it, just like she used to when my brothers and I were little. I welcome the twinge of nostalgia as I snag a slightly stale bagel from the pantry and pop it in the toaster.

Beyond the big windows that face out to the vineyard, a few workers are scattered across the fields. If we were in harvest season, there would be dozens more to help prep the grapes for crushing. But we're in the offseason, which means the crew is much smaller. At least, that's what it was like growing up here. My grandparents, my father, my aunt, my brothers, and two other hands that lived in the cabins on the other end of the property, Diego and Clay.

I remember people coming and going all day long, the house feeling busy and alive no matter where I was. Diego was like another father to me, and Clay was the nicest guy. I used to love practicing my Spanish with them. Or listening to their stories when they shared our table for dinner after a long day of working the soil, or setting up netting to protect the vines from pests, or any of the dozens of other tasks it takes to keep this place up and running.

But everything feels different than it did when I was a child. That familiarity is gone now, and I don't recognize any of the faces I see outside, roaming the property. Three gentlemen I've never seen before are moving slowly through the lanes, pruning the vines with their little clippers and chucking the pieces they remove into buckets at their feet.

I don't know why I expected to see Diego and Clay after nine years away, but the fact they're not here makes my heart sad.

The door to the fields opens, and suddenly my father is standing in the living room off the kitchen, covered in sweat, his skin still the same deep tan that decades in the sun will do.

He stamps his dirty feet on the rug a few times, but then his head rises and he spots me. He pauses for a long moment, an unnamable expression on his weathered face, before turning away and walking down the hall. The only sound is the quiet taps of his work boots against the terra-cotta tiles.

When he disappears, the sadness in my heart grows.

I hadn't ever figured out what things would look like with my dad, coming back after all this time. But I didn't think he'd just look at me and walk off without a word.

"He'll come around."

I turn toward my brother's voice, spotting him leaning against the doorway with his arms crossed. "He just doesn't know what to say when his feelings are bigger than his words."

I cross my own arms, mirroring Memphis's stance.

"Sounds like a condition the Hawthorne men all suffer from," I reply.

His lips flatten into a tight grin. "That would be accurate."

Neither of us say anything as I cross the kitchen to put cream cheese on my toasted bagel, and Memphis begins pulling supplies from the fridge to make a sandwich.

Eventually, we're sitting together at the small kitchen table, silently eating our breakfast and lunch, respectively.

Part of me wants to apologize for leaving. Or at least for going radio silent after I did leave. But I can't bring myself to do it when I know it was the right decision for me at the time.

I'd felt so lost here, so unimportant, so confused about what any kind of future might look like if I stayed. And going to LA to pursue my dream . . . It felt like the right thing.

Nobody in my family seemed to understand my need for something . . . else. Something different than what a life here would provide.

I wanted a life where I wasn't invisible. And for that, I can't apologize.

So instead of sharing any of that, I just stay silent.

We both do.

I spend the majority of the day unpacking my suitcase and trying to rearrange a few things in my childhood bedroom.

I don't know why I'm shocked that everything is still here, almost untouched. I think I'd just assumed that someone would have rearranged things, made this into a guest room or set up a treadmill or something.

Instead, it just sat here, an unused memorial to my teen years.

My formal dresses are still hanging in the closet from homecoming and prom, right next to my graduation gown and choir robe. The clock radio next to my bed is still set to 101.3, the station I listened to every morning as I got ready for school. There's even a notepad with a half-written note and pen still sitting on top of my dresser.

Apparently before I left I wanted to *remember to call Quinn about Tuesday and . . .*

But the note to my childhood friend was left unfinished, so who knows what I wanted to talk to her about.

I don't like knowing that this room sat untouched while I was in LA. It means they always knew I'd be coming home. That I'd need somewhere to go at some point. That I wouldn't be able to make it on my own.

And that hurts in a way I wasn't expecting.

Once my clothes are in my dresser and closet, I begin unpacking the few boxes I brought home. I never really had excess money, so *stuff* wasn't a luxury I could afford to accumulate. But I did have a few cheap picture frames, candles, and movies. Basically anything I could snag at discount stores for a few bucks that served my needs.

My movies slide onto the shelf next to the DVD player and computer monitor I used as a TV, and my candles and photos get spread around the room in various spots. I look at the last photo I set out for a long moment before finally placing it on my dresser.

It's a photo of me and Vivian out to dinner the weekend before everything fell apart. She'd told me my world was going to change soon, and she wanted to make sure the two of us got to enjoy a dinner out without the paparazzi hounding us all night. I rolled my eyes so hard at that idea they nearly fell right out of my head.

The frame is crafted from Popsicle sticks and those little white letters from friendship bracelets. At the top it reads BEFORE SHE WAS FAMOUS.

A streak of pain lances through me, and I set the frame down on my dresser, wishing I had the nerve to chuck it in the trash.

But it was a gift from my best friend, so it stays.

I break down my cardboard boxes and take them out to the garage to shove them in the recycling bin, then grab the very last item still waiting for me in the entryway.

My mother's guitar is a vintage 1987 Guild acoustic guitar. It's not anything crazy special or worth more than probably a few hundred dollars. It's still my most priceless possession. When I moved to LA, I had the original case too, covered in stickers from shows my mom went to when she was in her teens and twenties. But about two years in, it got stolen while I was playing at an open mic night.

Which is wild because who steals a guitar case?

Thankfully, I was able to find a similar one at a thrift store for way cheaper than it should have been priced. But I've always regretted that I hadn't been more vigilant about my belongings. Especially something that belonged to my mother.

I lean the case against the wall in the corner at the foot of my bed, then take a seat on the carpet and stare at it.

I found it in the attic when I was ten, along with a bunch of my mom's other things. From the first strum of my fingers over the strings, I was hooked.

I took weekly lessons for years, learned to read music as fast as I could, and constantly downloaded free sheet music online. I was insatiable. I wanted to know how to play anything and everything, by sight and off the top of my head. All kinds of genres and moods.

And when I was about fifteen years old, I finally realized I wanted to sing professionally. I wanted that Hollywood break, the chance to perform and make music and wow the world with my talent.

Now that will never happen.

So part of my brain wonders if it's worth it to ever pick up that guitar again.

It's remained untouched for the past two months, which is so unlike me. Even growing up, I was always lugging that thing everywhere, whipping it out whenever something came to mind, trying to figure out the right chords or melody or lyrics to a song I was sure would be a hit if only someone could hear it.

Who knew my chance would get ripped away from me before I was able to get anyone to listen?

◆ ◆ ◆

"Murph, you comin', honey?"

I glance over at my aunt Sarah, who stands in the doorway of my bedroom with a sweet smile on her face.

As much as she looks like my father with her heart-shaped face and thick head of chestnut curls falling wildly down her back, she looks far more like my grandmother when she smiles.

Though that's where the similarities end.

My grandmother was petite in all ways. My father and Aunt Sarah take after my grandfather with their long, athletic physiques and broad shoulders, two traits that passed down to my brothers and me.

But I love seeing that bit of my grandma in her when she smiles, which is far more often than anyone else in the family.

"I made your favorite."

My lips tilt up at the sides.

"Sloppy joes?"

She nods. "You know it. I couldn't have my girl moving home and put out something stupid for dinner, like lasagna."

I giggle, taking in the sight of her and all the warm memories that come with having her back in my world now.

I was particularly picky as a kid, and I often sat at the dinner table, stone faced, glaring at the dish in front of me, refusing to eat. Unlike my father, who would glare at *me* with his own stone face and demand I eat or go hungry, Aunt Sarah was always concocting new things to see if she could get me to try something.

I *hated* lasagna. The idea of food stacked in multiple layers was something I detested. But I was willing to eat sloppy joes, which is basically just the same insides of a beef lasagna but with bread instead. And then, one time, she made a sloppy joe lasagna.

"I'm trying to break your brain," she told me then, grinning at me as I stared with wide eyes at my favorite meal wrapped in noodles instead of bread.

Thankfully, I've grown out of whatever weird food idiosyncrasies I used to have. But it makes me smile to think that after all these years, my aunt thought of something like this for my first night home.

"I'll be out in a few minutes," I tell her.

She nods and leaves me alone again.

I sigh, turning my head to stare up at the ceiling. I've been lying on my bed for the past hour or so, studying the plastic stars I put up there when I was in junior high. I never thought to take them down as I got older. But instead of reminiscing about my childhood or thinking back to the night Quinn and I put those stars up, I've been trying to decide how to talk to my father.

He looked through me this morning, like he didn't even see me.

Didn't say a word. Didn't make a face.

After nine years?

I mean, I know I've always been his least favorite child, but come on. He could have said *something*. Anything, really.

He could have yelled at me to get out of his house.

He could have given me an angry face or thrown something across the room.

But no, he just gave me a half-hearted glance and ignored me completely.

The worst part about it is that it reminds me so much of how invisible I felt growing up.

I sigh again, my hand coming up to wipe at the tear trailing toward my ear.

It's really easy to promise yourself something like *I won't let the man make me cry again* when you're living four-hundred-plus miles away and have nearly a decade of time to compartmentalize your anger.

It's a lot harder when you're staring your father in the face, still curious whether or not he loves you at all.

I puff out another long breath and roll off the bed, then tug my hair up into a messy bun and head out to the kitchen. I can hear the clanking of plates and cutlery, the scraping of wooden chairs along the tiled floor.

When I round the corner, I scan the group of people moving through the kitchen, piling their plates high.

There are two faces I don't recognize. These must be the year-round workers who I haven't met before, the ones who seem to have replaced Diego and Clay.

Other than the unfamiliar faces, there's Micah and my aunt Sarah.

I cross the room and wrap my arms around my baby brother.

"Missed you," he grumbles into my ear.

I grip him tighter. "You, too. I didn't think it was possible for you to get any taller."

A small smile creeps onto Micah's face, but it's only there for a brief moment. "Yeah, well. I got Dad's genes," he replies, matter-of-factly, before turning and grabbing a plate off the counter.

Memphis and my father are nowhere to be seen, and my shoulders begin to relax just slightly at the idea that maybe the two of them are off doing something work-related and might not make it to dinner.

But when I hear the front door close, I poke my head into the hallway. My eyes widen slightly as I spot my father in the entryway, not with my brother, but with Wes. The two of them are laughing over something, and my father reaches out and pats Wes on the back a few times. They chat for another moment before their feet begin moving in my direction, so I dart into the kitchen before they see me, realizing instantly that the move did absolutely nothing as the two of them are right there, in the kitchen, just a few seconds later.

I don't know how I should feel when I watch both of their smiles fall away at the sight of me.

Wes gives me a neutral look, the easy smile from the gas station hidden away somewhere, so I cross my arms and pin him with my own unfriendly look. I don't know what the hell his problem is, but I sure as shit can give some attitude right back to him.

But then my eyes stray to my father, and I'm a little unnerved by the fact he looks like he could shatter the dinner plate he just picked up from the end of the island.

"We've got sloppy joes, a fresh garden salad, and corn bread," Sarah announces to the room, though it seems a little redundant since most everyone has their plates or are moving through the kitchen collecting food already.

"Sorry we're late," my father murmurs. "Memphis told me to tell you he'd be stuck working tonight. I'm just gonna go change."

Aunt Sarah just smiles and shakes her head. "Don't worry about it." She waves him off, and my father exits the kitchen in the direction of his bedroom. Then my aunt plops herself into a seat near the head of the long table that's been a centerpiece in this kitchen for as long as I can remember.

Without looking at Wes, who is perusing the drink options in the fridge, I grab a plate and move quickly through the trays of food, then take a seat between my aunt and a woman I don't know.

"Hi, I'm Murphy," I say, giving her a friendly smile.

"Naomi," she says, smiling back. "We've actually met before, but it was a long time ago, so I don't expect you to remember."

"Really?" I feel a little embarrassed. Normally, I'm so good with names and faces.

Naomi pierces a cucumber in her salad with her fork. "It was right before you left. I was helping out that summer."

A vague image of a slightly younger Naomi claws its way out of my memory. "Oh yeah . . . You were part of the harvest crew."

She nods again and then chomps into her cucumber.

"It's good to see you again."

Naomi swallows her bite and then gives me a grin. "You as well."

Before I can turn and introduce myself to the guy across from Naomi, Wes drops into the seat across from me, and it feels like my words dry up. He's intensely focused on his plate of food.

An entire five minutes goes by—I know because there's a clock on the wall behind him—and he doesn't look at me once.

When my father takes his seat at the head of the table, though, it distracts me from Wes. My father is no different. He seems to be intentionally ignoring me as well.

"I'd like to propose a toast."

My body goes rigid when I hear my aunt say those words as she lifts up her glass of water.

"I'm beyond thrilled that Murphy is back home. It's been quite a while since you left, sweetheart, and this house hasn't felt the same without you."

My lips turn up at the kind sentiment, but before I can say anything in response, my father breaks his silence.

"You shouldn't be toasting her return, Sarah." His voice slices through the room as his eyes laser in on me. "Because she never should've left in the first place."

You could hear a pin drop it's so dang quiet. Nobody at the table is moving their cutlery or glasses. They're all just sitting in complete silence, waiting for what happens next.

"You might not want to hear it, Dad, but deciding to leave was the right choice for me, and I don't regret it." Then I turn to my aunt. "Thank you, Aunt Sarah, for the toast."

My voice might sound confident to those at the table who don't know me, but it's forced, and I know my dad can tell.

"If it was such an important thing for you to leave, I guess there was no real reason for you to come back, then."

I blink a few times, my jaw clenched tightly. "Trust me, if I'd had anywhere else to go, I would have gone there instead."

My father stands suddenly, his chair screeching loudly on the floor as it shoots out from behind him, the noise echoing through the kitchen.

"Thank you, Sarah, for the delicious dinner. I'm sorry it was soured by poor company."

My nostrils flare at his insult, but I don't say anything else, just letting my father leave the table. A few seconds later, I hear the front door slam, and I know he's probably going to eat his dinner on the front porch.

I stare down at my plate of food, my vision blurred by the water beginning to pool in my eyes. Then I feel a hand pressed against my back.

"He'll come around," my aunt tells me, her voice quiet and kind, as it's always been for as long as I can remember. "He's just a proud old fart, you know that."

I take a deep breath and let it out long and slow, trying to cool the anger inside of me as much as I can.

"I don't need him to come around." I shove back from the table, my plate of food still mostly untouched. "I won't be here long enough to need it."

Without another word, I storm from the room, needing to be alone.

I know I'm being immature, leaving the kitchen in a huff and not even taking a moment to clear away my plate and extras from the table. But god, he just makes me so damn mad.

Between my arguments with Memphis last night and my father today, the part of me that feels like I made a mistake trying to come home continues to grow. Continues to point out all the reasons why I was an absolute idiot for coming here.

Realistically, I could have stayed in Venice Beach. I could have continued my stupid waitressing job at the Italian place I still struggle to pronounce. I could have used that money to pay the exorbitant amount of rent I paid for a shared bedroom in a shitty neighborhood. I could have continued living the little life I created for myself far away from here.

But the realist inside of me knew it would be pointless after what happened.

My dreams of becoming a singer, of making it big, of seeing my name in lights, were officially and very dramatically dashed to hell.

So all the work I did, all the sacrifices I made, all the crappy jobs and side hustles and tiny gigs that were nothing more than glorified karaoke nights, were for nothing. They resulted in *nothing*.

Because that's what I am.

And even though my return home was supposed to be my way of escaping from that reality, it only seems to reaffirm it.

I'm nothing.

And now I know, my father thinks so, too.

Chapter Four

WES

"Hey, Mom. It's Wes." I pause, wishing I'd just hung up the phone when she didn't answer. "Just . . . checking in. Give me a call sometime. Love you, bye."

I click off and let out a frustrated sigh.

The fact that my mother didn't answer when I called her wasn't surprising, but there was still a part of me that hoped she might pick up. That things had gotten . . . I don't know . . . better.

Scrolling through my contacts, I find Ash's number and give him a call.

He, of course, answers on the first ring.

"Wes!"

My thoughts about Mom disappear momentarily at the sound of my brother's voice, at the smile I can hear through the phone.

"Hey, Ash. How are ya?"

"Doing real good," he tells me. "Really good. How about you?"

I bob my head even though he can't see me, my fingers fiddling idly with an empty straw wrapper I found in my pocket a few minutes ago.

"Doing good, too. I'm back in California."

There's a pause on the other end, and I can tell I've surprised him.

When I left San Francisco seven years ago, I'd made it clear to my brother that it was unlikely I'd be back. He had finally turned eighteen and was heading off to college, and I was free to finally let go of some of the responsibility I always carried, since our mom was never around.

I'm pretty sure I mentioned in almost every conversation we've ever had how much I never wanted to come back to California.

So it's unsurprising to me that he's a little stunned.

"No shit?"

"No shit."

"Well . . . shit."

At that, we both laugh.

"When did you get back?"

"I've been back a little over a month, just wanting to make sure everything was really settled with this new gig before letting you know."

It's the truth. My interview with Memphis had been great, and I was excited about taking on a head chef position, even if the restaurant was smaller than places I'd worked in the past. But there was something that felt uncertain about this job position. Like it might suddenly disappear.

And my brother is a sensitive soul, so if I told him I was back in California and then left again, I knew it could be pretty hard on him. I wanted to be sure, and after a month of managing supply orders, getting comfortable with the new kitchen, setting up my menu, and testing out recipes, I finally feel like I am.

"Oh yeah? Where are you at?"

"Rosewood."

There's no sound on the other end, but I can tell I've stunned him again.

"Dude."

"I know. But trust me when I tell you it was a coincidence."

He hums something that makes me think he doesn't believe me, but he doesn't outright say it.

"I'm the new head chef at a winery. They're adding on a restaurant."

"No shit? That sounds awesome."

I chuckle. "We'll see. Have to prove myself first."

My brother makes a scoffing noise. "You don't need to prove your-self to anyone, Wes. You're one of the best chefs in the whole damn country. This place is lucky to have you."

I roll my eyes, but don't address his *whole damn country* comment.

"Doesn't matter what your reputation is when you're starting a new job," I tell him. "You still have to show the boss that they made the right decision in hiring you."

"That's why *you* should be the boss. Open your own restaurant."

I nibble on my lip. "Maybe someday."

I don't tell him that I doubt that dream will be one I'll ever see come to fruition. That I fucked things up too bad for something like that to happen. The last thing I need to do is point out to my little brother all the ways I've screwed up. Not when he looks up to me like he does.

"Let me know when I can come see you," he continues. "I want you to meet Mira."

My eyebrows rise. "You met somebody?"

The way my brother laughs on the other end of the line . . . I've never heard him laugh quite like that. *Unabashedly* would be the word to describe it.

"Yeah," he says, his voice dropping. "I met someone. And I can't wait for you to meet her."

I blink a few times. "If she's special to you, I can't wait to meet her as well."

We talk for a few more minutes as he updates me about work. He's an artist, my little brother, and he's been pursuing his passion on the side while he works as a manager at a paint store. I can't help but smile as I listen to him share about the educational programs he's been put-ting together in conjunction with the community center.

He's a good man. I've done my best to be there for him . . . to help him as much and as often as possible so that he didn't feel the sharp sting of life the way I have. Though I know it wasn't enough.

Not nearly enough.

"Look, I gotta jet," he tells me a little while later. "I'm meeting Mira and her friends for brunch in a little bit."

"No, I got you. Head on out. Love you, Ash."

"Love you, too."

We hang up, and I stare at my phone for a long moment.

It blows my mind that neither of us are dead or crazy-addicted to drugs with the way we were raised. Better yet, I get to sit and listen to my brother talk about his life and his work like he does.

We're fucking lucky.

So fucking lucky.

I might be trying to pick up the pieces of my life right now, but as long as my brother is happy and healthy, I don't care what happens to me. Not really.

◆ ◆ ◆

After my chat with Ash, I swap my sweats for running shorts, figuring now would be a good chance for me to get out some of my anxious energy. I'm not a huge runner, but when everything fell to shit at the end of last year, I started dealing with anxiety attacks.

I would walk around the city at night, the long blocks giving me the space and time to process my thoughts. Then a few months ago, I started running, and it became an important outlet for me to deal with my emotions.

I'm sure something like therapy might help a little bit more, and I'll get there someday, but for now, I tell my stories to the road.

The midday sun pounds my shoulders for the entire four miles it takes to get from the vineyard into town, and I'm grateful when I make it all the way to Main Street.

I come to a stop outside of The Carlisle to catch my breath. I step into the alcove of the café's backyard patio, tilting my face up and enjoying the sensation and coolness coming from the misters.

"Can I help you?"

I glance over at who I'm assuming is a server, since she's holding an empty tray under her arm. Her eyes rove briefly over my shirtless, sweaty form.

"No, thanks," I tell her, my chest still heaving. "Just need a sec."

She doesn't say anything else, just continues to watch me. It's . . . irritating.

Normally, I don't mind when women look at me. I'm six feet three and my chest and arms are covered in tattoos. Obviously, I'm going to attract some level of attention.

But for whatever reason, I'm not enjoying her perusal.

Feeling like I've cooled down a bit and caught my breath, I lift a hand at the server and then step back out onto Main, into the sun. I look up and down the street, trying to decide what I want to do, eventually choosing to give myself a little breather before I run back to the vineyard.

So I stop in at the little shop next door, grab a bottle of water, and chug half of it before taking a seat at a bench on the sidewalk.

And for whatever reason, my mind strays to the beautiful blonde with the golden eyes who I can't stop thinking about lately.

Murphy Hawthorne.

I still can't believe she's Memphis's little sister. What are the odds?

Last night, in my cabin, I'd allowed myself a few moments to consider just how differently things might have ended up if my mind had been in the right place. If I wasn't feeling constantly distracted by everything else going on. If I'd been even a fraction of the normal flirt I can be when I'm out looking for someone fun.

Though that would have been disastrous as well.

No, it was better for us to have just said goodbye and then find out she was my boss's younger sister. That she was completely and totally off-limits.

But then, as if I've conjured her up with my thoughts, there she is.

Murphy steps out of her car parked along the main road. I watch her move almost in slow motion. She flips her long, thick hair over her shoulder as she turns her head to look one way and then the other, and jogs away from me across the street.

The part of me that's thinking with the wrong brain wants to follow her to wherever she's going. Bumping into her accidentally would allow me the chance to talk to her.

And I know she wouldn't be able to keep her gaze off my chest. Clearly most women can't.

But before I can follow through, she dips into the shadows, pulling the door open of what looks to be a bakery.

Any other time in my life, I would have walked across the street and followed her inside. Flirted. Asked her to dinner or to grab a Sunday-afternoon drink.

Back in the day, sleeping with a coworker wasn't ever an issue. It's part of restaurant culture to sleep around. Chefs, waiters and waitresses, hosts . . . Big personalities work in kitchens. Creative. Sociable. Sexy.

And while I'm not a person who sleeps with anything that moves, I've definitely enjoyed the company of more than a few beautiful women that have worked at the same restaurants as me.

Until I got involved with the wrong person.

Pursuing something physical with Murphy would have been all too natural in my past, but I promised myself I'd start making smarter choices if I ever got the chance to try to rebuild my career as a chef.

Sleeping with an employee—my boss's sister, no less—is a mistake I can't afford to make.

So instead of heading across the street, I walk down Main, veer off the main drag, and begin to jog again along a side street lined with little houses and white picket fences.

Something happening with Murphy Hawthorne is the absolute last thing I should be thinking about right now. And as I pound the pavement, picking up speed, I promise myself that I'll do whatever it takes to make sure she feels the same way.

◆ ◆ ◆

I spend the rest of my Sunday in the kitchen, trying to keep myself busy and focused on the many things still to do before we open. Unfortunately, my thoughts continue to stray.

I try to review scheduled orders and work on my stock list. But then I see I've miscounted half a dozen items and realize I shouldn't be doing anything that requires significant focus.

I switch over to working on the menu. I sit at the small computer that was set up in a tiny office directly off the kitchen and search through lists of wine pairings for ideas. But nothing seems to stick out, and I feel like I'm just wasting time.

So I eventually begin working on one of the salad recipes I've been trying to perfect. I know I have the ingredients right—arugula, peaches, and feta—but the vinaigrette isn't hitting yet. Something is missing, and I don't know what. So I play around with my dressing base and mix in various ingredients trying to figure it out.

More balsamic. Less balsamic. Lemon. Lime. Basil. Nothing hits right.

Abandoning the task of solving the recipe, I turn to my tried-and-true method for keeping myself busy.

Cleaning.

There isn't a chef in the world who doesn't despise a dirty kitchen. I start with scrubbing the counter, then move on to the sink, which then showcases all the dishes I just dirtied in my exploratory dressing disaster.

When I finally finish, the last of the daylight has left the sky, and I'm exhausted, which is exactly what I was hoping for.

The ringing of my cell phone as I'm locking up has me tugging the brick out of my back pocket. My jaw clenches when I see the caller ID.

Reluctantly, I accept the call and hold it to my ear.

"Hey, Mom."

"My sweet Wes."

I close my eyes, disappointment lancing through me at the sound of her voice.

She's drunk.

But she's always drunk, so I shouldn't be surprised.

Letting out a long sigh, I begin my walk back to my cabin, the ten-minute journey suddenly feeling like it'll take hours.

"How are you doing?" I ask, though I already know the answer.

"Oh, I'm doing great, baby. Really good. Sorry I didn't answer when you called. I was working."

My jaw tightens.

My mother hasn't had a real job since I was in middle school, at least not that I know of. What she really means is that she was working a corner in some capacity, whether that means she was begging for change or working for dollars, I'm not certain. But I try not to think too hard about it.

"You still in San Francisco?" I ask.

You never know with her. A few years ago she disappeared for six months and when we finally found her, she was squatting with some guy in an abandoned house on the outskirts of Oakland.

"Where else would I be?" Her tone is jovial and loose, likely from whatever bottle of vodka she's been drinking out of. "You know I can't leave my babies."

I roll my eyes at her nonsensical statement.

Ash and I haven't been her babies since before we were teenagers. So to hear her claim she stays around town for us is laughable, and doesn't even touch on the fact that I haven't seen her in person in years. Ash sees her from time to time, but he rarely talks about it. He knows how

I feel about her, and my attempts at reaching out to her are usually just my way of making sure she's still alive.

"What about you, Wessy? How's Chicago? Getting any snow yet?"

I nibble on the inside of my cheek in irritation. "It's April, Mom."

There's a slight pause on her end of the line before she giggles. "I know that, Wes, but I don't know what Chicago's like. For all I know it could snow year-round."

"Right."

Most likely, my mom didn't know it was April. Most likely, she won't even remember that we talked when she wakes up tomorrow, hungover and wondering where she'll get her next drink.

And it's only because I know she'll probably forget everything I say right now that I decide to tell her I'm back in California.

"I'm actually not in Chicago anymore, Mom. I'm back in town."

"You're in San Francisco?" What sounds like her genuine excitement fills the phone.

I know it's just the vodka talking because when my mother is sober, she hates me.

"Not exactly. I got a job working at a vineyard."

"Oh, that's great, baby. Let me know where and I can come visit you."

I choke back an unamused sound. The absolute last thing I'd ever tell my mother is where I work. I've done plenty to ruin my own reputation. I don't need her showing up, wasted and willing to steal anything she can get her hands on to make my life even worse.

"Look, Mom, I gotta go, okay? I have some stuff I need to work on."

"Okay, well, give me a call anytime, baby. Your mama loves you."

I grit my jaw.

"Love you, too."

When I hit the fork in the path, instead of taking it toward my cabin, I follow it toward the warehouse. Just beyond a small incline there's a bench that overlooks the entire property and the rolling hills in the distance. I've found myself out there on quite a few evenings since moving.

When I get there, I take a seat and look out over the long rows of vines, the nearly full moon casting light across the landscape.

I do love my mother. When I told her that at the end of our call, I wasn't lying. But our relationship is incredibly complicated. Drunk Sonia is loving and kind and forgetful. She's a mother who gushes about her children but can't remember what day it is. Sober Sonia is angry and unkind, and she resents her sons for ruining her life.

So I'm in this horrible place of preferring my mother when she's wasted enough that she forgets all the reasons she hates us. Because when she's sober, she likes to remind me that I'm the one who made her fat and ugly, that I was an ungrateful and needy child, and she likes to remind Ash that he's the reason she's alone.

Nobody should have to deal with a relationship as unhealthy as ours is with our mother. But the alternative is something I don't like to imagine, so we continue to listen to her blathering when she's half a bottle deep because it's the only kind of mothering we get.

I whip my head to the side at the sound of footsteps, and my eyes widen when I see Murphy coming up the path.

She stops when she sees me.

"What are you doing here?" My words come out far more irritated than I intend, but at the same time, she's truly the last person I want to see right now. Not after that chat with my mother. Not when I've tried to avoid thinking about Murphy all day.

Her head jerks back. "I came to sit on the bench. Same as you." She pushes her chin up and stalks toward me, almost like she wants to prove a point. "If you don't like it, you're welcome to leave."

Then she plops down beside me.

I let out a sigh that sounds more like a growl and push up from the bench.

"Fine. Take it."

Murphy snorts. "You know, you're a lot more charming when you're helping a woman in distress."

Once I'm a few feet away, I spin around and look at her, my frustration from the day boiling over.

"And you clearly don't seem to realize when your presence isn't wanted."

The stricken look on her face is only there for a moment before her eyes turn to stone, but it's long enough for me to realize that what I've said is incredibly unkind.

Even though I was only speaking about this specific instance, this one evening when I just needed a few minutes to myself, it's pretty clear that I've touched a deeper layer of pain in her.

I want to apologize. To tell her that I've just had a shitty conversation with my mother and that what I said was uncalled for.

But before I can, Murphy pushes off the bench and heads toward the path that will eventually take her back to the main house. Her gaze, filled with disdain, lances through me as she passes.

Her silence says more than her words ever could.

And as I watch her form disappear into the darkness, part of me thinks that maybe having her hate me will be better for both of us.

Chapter Five

Murphy

It takes everything inside of me to get up and ready for the day on Monday morning, my brief interaction with Wes still fresh in my mind as I get in the shower. It certainly made clear to me the type of guy he is.

Charming until he doesn't get what he wants.

It makes me reconsider our entire conversation at the gas station. Whether the easy banter and perceived connection were all just figments of my imagination.

It's a hard pill to swallow, but I choke it down as I rinse the shampoo out of my hair.

That bench at the top of the hill is a special place for me—a place I'd go when I was younger to talk to my mom and hope wherever she was, she might hear me. I'd often steal away unnoticed through the french doors that lead from my bedroom out to the veranda that stretches the length of our house to sit in the vineyard in the evenings. Sometimes I took my guitar and I'd strum without any kind of purpose, just imagining that maybe my mother was there, too.

Last night, though, I just wanted a chance to sit and think. Being back here isn't easy. There's an element of defeat I have to admit to in order to accept that I've really had to move home. And even though

I've always considered myself to be a person who can handle defeat with grace, this one stings.

But instead, I arrived to find Wes sitting on my bench looking gorgeous. I was there in my pajamas and my hair up in a messy bun, but I didn't even have a chance to feel insecure about it. His words were biting, as if interacting with me was a horrible inconvenience.

"What are you doing here?" he'd asked, his eyes narrowed and his voice hard.

I've been asking myself the same thing over and over since the minute I arrived in Rosewood Friday evening.

What the hell am *I doing here?*

I only wish I had the answer.

Once I've finished in the shower, I tug on a pair of black jeans and a light-blue button-up that I usually wear to things where I need to dress professionally. Showing up in my pajamas with drool on my face to my first day at work probably isn't the best way to get in my brother's good graces.

Though the devious part of me doesn't exactly mind being a thorn in his side.

I stop in the kitchen to snag a banana, then head out to the veranda and down to the path that cuts through the vines to other parts of the property. The mulch crunches under my feet as I stroll through the long columns of grapes in early stages of growth.

I take in a deep breath of the fresh air.

I hate to admit it, but there really is nothing like the smells of the vineyard. The recently tilled soil, the misty mornings after the fog has rolled in, the subtle changes in the vines that happen day by day. It's a special place, as much as I resent it.

It's hard to believe that these eighty acres have been in the Hawthorne family for five generations. My ancestors made it through incredible hardships—the Great Depression, Prohibition, and various weather-related calamities. And we're still here, carving out a livelihood off the land.

When I was young, my grandfather used to talk constantly about the life cycles of the grapes and the vines. About the Mayacamas Mountains to the east and the volcanic mountain soil unique to this valley. About the fog and microclimate, so many little things that make this patch of Northern California uniquely perfect for the craft of wine-making. Even though I never wanted to be involved with any of it, I still know quite a bit about this place and how things work.

Eventually, I make it to the restaurant. There used to be a small warehouse here, used for storing ATVs and some of the older harvest machinery that has fallen out of use. The outside looks the same, but the closer I get, the more apparent the changes become. The barn-style exterior has been replaced by floor-to-ceiling windows along the northwest-facing wall, and a large patio has been constructed with a handful of stone firepits. I'm assuming outdoor furniture will be placed there at some point, allowing patrons to look out over the property and enjoy the sunset.

It's a shocking sight, considering that my original conversation with Memphis a few months ago was about putting together charcuterie boards at wine tastings and scheduling bachelorette parties. This is . . . a completely different ball game.

Once I've gotten over my surprise, I venture inside, my eyes flicking around the room as I soak everything in for the first time.

And it really is beautiful.

The massive windows are framed by rustic wooden beams and line both of the western-facing walls, giving diners the ability to look out over the vines to the north and the rolling hills to the south as well. The interior feels rustic and charming, the other two walls made of distressed white brick, with wooden shelves and brass accents at the bar.

There's still blue tape in plenty of places, and I can see that work needs to be done on the fireplace and what looks to be a private events room. The outdoor furniture is stacked in a corner waiting to be set up and everything inside is still scattered about as if a floor plan hasn't been determined. But the building itself feels close to finished. I'm actually incredibly impressed with what my brother has come up with.

"There you are."

I turn at Memphis's voice as he emerges through the swinging door that I'm assuming leads into the kitchen.

"What do you think?"

I huff out a breath of laughter.

"What do I think?" I shake my head. "Memphis, it's massive. Are you sure we really need this much space?"

It's the first thing that comes to mind, because I do wonder whether all of this is really needed, or if it will really get used the way my brother is hoping.

Growing up, there weren't a lot of people who visited the vineyard. We didn't offer tastings, special events, or tours. My family just made wine and distributed it as well as they could. I'm not sure how things have changed over the years since I've been gone, but a full-scale restaurant of this size feels a little bit like overkill.

"I think it's going to be great," Memphis says, his tone curt and a bit intense. He scans the room, and then he says it again, almost to himself. "It's going to be great."

When the kitchen door opens again, my gaze shifts past my brother and lands on Wes, who's emerging, a half apron wrapped around his waist.

I turn away, feigning interest in the view out the windows, unable to look Wes in the face.

"All right, why don't we all take a seat and talk?" Memphis motions to one of three tables that are currently upright.

Each of us snags a chair from the row lining the edge of the room and brings it to the table. My brother comes with a stack of papers and a binder, Wes with a single notebook, and me with a forced smile.

"I guess it's time to really and truly kick things off since we've got"—Memphis looks at his phone—"just under four weeks until opening. Now that Murphy is here to provide some additional hands, I think we'll be able to really get things moving."

I want to roll my eyes at the "additional hands" comment, as if I'm some rando he's hired to work on extraneous projects around the property. But I force my eyeballs to remain where they are. The last thing I need to do is pick a fight with Memphis on my first day of work.

"Wes and I have had a chance to chat about a lot of this, Murphy, so I'll just take a few minutes to bring you up to speed."

At that, he opens the folder in front of him and pulls out a few documents in duplicate, and he hands each of us a copy.

"The plan is for us to provide lunch and dinner on Thursday, Friday, Saturday, and lunch on Sunday, along with wine tastings and private parties. Chef Hart has already been here for about a month. He's been curating a menu that will pair well with our wines, and as you can see, we're nearly done with construction and design."

I glance around again as my brother provides some highlights about each space—the kitchen, the dining room, the special event room, the bar—as well as some of the logistics about seating and serving.

"Any questions?"

I shake my head, because the only question I have is how he plans to fill this dining room with enough people to make the financial investment worth it.

Not that I'm a numbers girl or anything. Realistically, I have no idea what a place like this would cost to create, let alone put into business. Maybe I'm overreacting.

But I doubt it.

"Okay, so mostly we're meeting so you have a chance to review what your job responsibilities will be before things really get moving," Memphis says, drawing my attention back to where he sits on the other side of the table. "I know in our earlier conversations when you were still waffling about moving back here, we'd discussed you overseeing a kind of 'small events' program. My thoughts had originally been to have you put together charcuterie plates and decor for small parties and bachelorette events, stuff like that."

I clench my jaw slightly. My shoulders tense. I can already feel the direction this conversation is going. He made it clear on Friday evening that Wes was going to be in charge of this restaurant—a facility I didn't even know they were building—but he never further clarified what kinds of things he'd like me to oversee.

And with the way he's downplaying the *charcuterie plates and decor and stuff like that*, I can already tell he's approaching this with a very different mindset than he had before.

In our original conversation, Memphis made it seem like my return home would be a serious help. Now, his tone sounds a lot more like he thinks he's doing me a favor by giving me a job at all.

"With how the restaurant concept has grown, Wes will be overseeing all aspects of the kitchen and dining experience. Outside of the business pieces, of course, like finances, which will be on me."

I blink a few times, glancing between the two of them, and my eyes catch just briefly on Wes's arched brows before they smooth out along with the rest of his face.

"So . . . then what am I going to be doing?"

"Wes's background in restaurants of a high caliber is an indicator that he has the knowledge and experience to set things up in a manner consistent with those other restaurants. The way I see it, since you're just a waitress, that's the job I'll have you do."

The sides of my face flame red at his words and the realization that comes along with them.

Just a waitress.

I nibble on the inside of my cheek, considering him for a moment. I'm trying desperately to give him the benefit of the doubt, but I can't help the way my eyes narrow as he continues speaking, irritation beginning to bubble up inside my chest.

"Now, the intention isn't for you to waitress alone. Clearly, with the size of the space and being open for lunch and dinner several days a week, we'll need additional staff. A few servers, one or two hosts."

There we go. I'll at least be managing the front of house with a few employees.

"I'm going to be placing Wes in charge of the hiring and training of the serving staff since a primary responsibility will be selling the food and upselling the wine."

My vision grows fuzzy as I glare at the table between us, unseeing, and almost unhearing, my brother's continued speech about the restaurant. All the expectations and blah blah blah go in one ear and out the other.

This is absolute bullshit. Wouldn't it make more sense for *me* to hire and train the serving staff? After all, I have been *just a waitress* for nearly ten years.

But that doesn't matter. Not really.

This comes down to trust, and clearly, Memphis doesn't trust me with shit.

"Memphis," Wes says tentatively.

My eyes snap to him for the first time where he sits, turned slightly in his seat and facing my brother.

"I wonder if someone with more experience on the serving end of things would do a better job of determining the qualifications of a good server or host," he continues. His gaze flicks to me briefly before returning to Memphis. "I really think the responsibility should rest with Murphy to handle most of that."

My body begins to vibrate with frustration.

Now Wes is shoving off responsibility he doesn't want?

I scoff, my irritation boiling over, and both men look at me in surprise.

"Look, it's clear that a lot of these *plans* for the restaurant and how things are going to be organized are still fairly rudimentary and not well thought out," I say, my words cutting with the intention of wounding my brother. I stand from my chair and shove it back in under the table. "Give me a call once you know what the hell you're doing."

I stalk through the restaurant and out the door.

I'm so sick of men who make women feel small, who make *me* feel small.

I'm so tired of a world where people treat others as disposable.

Where some people are important and others are not.

And I've been living in that kind of environment for far too long, feeling the emotional whiplash of someone finding me important or valuable only to then drop me like a hot potato.

The same can be said for Memphis.

When I called him months ago to let him know things in LA were starting to crumble and I was thinking it might be time to come back to Rosewood, he'd fallen all over himself with platitudes about what things would be like if I returned, how I could help him with this new project.

Charcuterie boards and bachelorette parties was the vibe.

All he needed was a pair of hands and a hard work ethic, and even though I'm *just a waitress*, Memphis has always known that I bust my ass. I may not have a passion for the wine industry, but I'm a hard worker. We all grew up that way, after all.

To show up here now and feel like I'm some charity case, like I have nothing to offer, is absurd. With the already brittle way I've been feeling about being home, it's all a lot more complicated than what I know how to handle mentally and emotionally.

"Murphy."

I turn at the sound of my name being called, my fists already clenched hard when I spot my brother following me down the path.

What I want to do is turn my back to him and keep walking.

Leave him in the dust. See how it makes him feel.

But I don't. Instead I just stare out over the horizon, my arms crossed, waiting for him. Who knows? Maybe he's coming to apologize.

"What the hell, Murph?"

Nope. Definitely not apologizing.

"I can't believe you just stormed out like that."

I continue staring out into the distance, trying to cool my frustration before I smack my brother upside the head.

"We have things we need to get done, and I don't have time for your attitude."

"*My* attitude." I glance over at him. "And what about *your* attitude?"

Memphis's face scrunches up in something that looks like a mixture of disbelief and confusion. Of course he wouldn't have any idea that something he's said or done is bothersome or offensive. That's how it's always been, and I figure now, it's how it's always going to be.

"What are you talking about?"

"I'm your sister, Memphis."

My brother just stares at me, his expression unchanging.

"I'm your sister, not some part-time robot with no feelings."

At that, he rolls his eyes.

"You're always so dramatic, Murphy. I'm not treating you like a robot. I'm treating you like an *employee*."

"And you see nothing wrong with that?"

"No, I don't."

I turn my head away and stare back out at the vineyard. "Maybe *that's* the problem."

Memphis lets out a sigh.

"Look, if you want to talk in riddles and code, Micah's a better bet. *I* on the other hand have shit to do, and I don't have time for this. You have *no* idea how important it is that this restaurant be a success, okay? So for once in your goddamn life will you think about someone other than your own damn self?"

My entire body bristles, but I'm surprised by what I see.

Memphis rarely shows his emotions. He's one of those *put your nose down and work* guys and it translates into him being kind of an asshole on most days.

Right now, though, I see something I don't normally see on my brother's face.

He looks rattled.

He rarely lets anyone see him as anything other than one hundred percent in control.

I open my mouth, wanting to understand more instead of just being talked down to or bossed around. But before I can say anything, he speaks again.

"Look, either do what I need you to do in the restaurant, or feel free to lend a hand to Micah and the grounds crew. But what I need is a waitress. Let me know if you want the fucking job."

And then he stalks off, his entire body tight with irritation.

Something uncomfortable settles in the pit of my stomach. Something that tells me my brother is keeping some kind of secret from me.

And I don't like how it feels.

Chapter Six

WES

"Sorry about that." Memphis takes the seat across from me where Murphy was sitting just a few minutes ago. "My sister can be . . . a lot."

"So you've said."

He glances up at me, a pinch in his brow, but then reaches out for the stack of paper he'd been working his way through before Murphy put him in his place and left.

I wanted so badly to speak up on her behalf. Not only because Memphis's *just a waitress* comment was uncalled for, but because it's a little ridiculous that he's expecting her to be the lead waitress while also shoving the serving staff on me as a responsibility. She clearly has a lot of experience, and I don't have the time to handle the hiring and training of front-of-house staff when I have a kitchen to run and my own cooks to hire and train.

But I have to be careful about stepping in to defend Murphy or take her side. The last thing I need is for Memphis to catch wind of my attraction to his sister if I want to preserve a good working relationship with him.

Besides, I don't really know Murphy that well. For all I know, she *is* irresponsible and easy to anger and all the other ways her own brother describes her. Maybe it *would* be a huge mistake for her to take on more responsibility than a simple serving position.

Still, there's something telling me Murphy is actually a lot more thoughtful and responsible than Memphis gives her credit for.

"I've been really impressed with the food so far," Memphis says, drawing me out of my short reverie. "And I'm thinking it's about time we finalize the menu for the opening. I'd like to schedule a full menu tasting once front of house has been hired so that the entire vineyard staff can get a fairly good idea of what the offerings will be."

I puff out a breath, scratching my chin. "I'll be honest, Memphis. I'm only about seventy-five percent done with the menu."

He waves a hand, as if that's not an issue. "Not a problem. Why don't we schedule it for the weekend before the opening? That should be more than enough time for you to finish things up."

I swallow thickly, wishing I had as much confidence in myself as Memphis seems to have. He doesn't understand what goes into settling on a menu. At my last job, I was part of the team that launched several new restaurants, and it took us nearly six months to finalize menus, not mere weeks.

And while this restaurant is on the smaller side, that doesn't have any impact on everything that goes into recipe development. This is supposed to be about upselling wines. In this way, the entirety of the restaurant's success feels like it rests on my shoulders alone.

A door opening has us both turning to look, and my lips can't help but tilt up when I see Murphy walking toward us, her head held high.

"I'm sorry for leaving," she says once she's approached our table. "Being back here is . . . an adjustment."

I glance to Memphis, and I find him with a similar demeanor, his chin up as he watches his sister.

If only these two could see how alike they actually are.

"Take a seat, Murph," he says after a long pause. "Wes and I were just discussing an upcoming menu showcase for the family and employees."

She pulls the chair out next to me and sits down. I'm instantly hit with the scent of her perfume—something sweet and fresh and slightly peachy—the delicious aroma faint but no less seductive.

Instead of discussing whatever menu showcase he's hoping I'll be able to throw together in the next few days, Murphy steers the conversation back to the dining room and the hiring of waitstaff.

I can hear the tension between them, but I'm only half listening.

My attention is consumed by the gorgeous woman sitting just inches from me. Her scent, her smile, her thick unruly hair up in a wild bun at the top of her head and the little tendrils that have fallen free at the nape of her neck.

"What do you think, Wes?"

I blink, realizing I've completely zoned out and missed whatever they were talking about. Clearing my throat, I try desperately to rewind the bit of conversation I managed to hear, but I can't seem to figure out what I'm supposed to say.

"Sorry," I tell them, shaking my head and giving an embarrassed smile. "I was thinking about the menu. What was that?"

"I asked what you think about handing over the hiring to Murphy," Memphis says with an obvious tic in his jaw. "She seems to think it would be better for her to manage things, and you mentioned earlier that you might also see it that way. I'd just like to get your opinion based on all your *years* of restaurant experience."

He says *years* with a dramatic flourish, looking to Murphy pointedly.

I clear my throat again, realizing it doesn't actually matter whether I believe Memphis's opinion of his sister or not, whether I know her well or not.

"I do believe that a front-of-house person should be managing the waitstaff, from top to bottom and start to finish. You said Murphy's had nearly a decade of experience working in restaurants too, and in a role that would have a lot more understanding of the needs waitstaff will have." I shrug a shoulder. "I can do it if you want me to, but I think you're missing an opportunity to have someone with much more direct experience than I have handle it the way it *should* be handled. My official opinion is that Murphy should be in charge of not just hiring, but also training and scheduling. I don't doubt she's more than capable."

Memphis's expression tells me he doesn't like my answer, but I can feel Murphy shifting in her seat next to me. And when I glance over at her, I can't miss the upward tilt at the edge of her mouth.

Her eyes flick to mine, and I see gratitude there.

"Fine," Memphis says, his tone clipped. "Murphy, I'd like a detailed report from you on what your plans are for hiring and staffing by the end of the week. Opening night is just around the corner, so there's no time to fall behind. And, Wes, please keep me posted on the progression of the menu. I'll have some farms for you to visit soon for sourcing ingredients."

Then Memphis is rising from his seat and heading toward the exit, leaving the two of us behind, alone.

At the sound of the door closing behind him, Murphy and I glance at each other.

"Thanks for that," she says, her voice soft. "Sometimes Memphis is a great guy. But I don't tend to be on the receiving end of that very often anymore."

I can hear the hurt in her voice, and it echoes my own pain. I know only too well what it's like to wish familial relationships were different.

And I know how deeply those wounds can grow, digging in and creating roots that carve marks that feel impossible to heal from.

But as much as I'd like for this to be some kind of bonding moment with Murphy, some way for us to connect, I know that it's a smarter choice for me to keep her at arm's length.

So I stand, closing my notebook and clicking my pen.

"Just don't screw it up. I don't want to regret putting the weight of my opinion behind you if you can't hack it."

I can see the way my words hit her as if they're a physical thing. The disbelief in her eyes, the way her head jerks back in surprise, how she shoots out of her seat in anger.

"God, you're unbelievable," she grits out, standing as well. "Next time you think about defending me, just keep your mouth shut, okay? I don't *need* you to step in on my behalf. Especially if you're so worried about the weight of your precious opinion."

And with a final look that sears me where I stand, Murphy is turning on her heel and storming out of the restaurant again. It seems to be how she handles her anger.

But this time, I don't think she's going to come back.

I navigate my way into The Standard later that evening, raising a hand toward a group of guys I've been getting to know when I spot them surrounding the pool table.

There are a lot of things about restaurant culture that are incredibly toxic. But it's also an environment that makes finding friends a lot easier than other lines of work. Servers and chefs know how to put on a show, how to be friendly and accommodating, so it isn't surprising that I connected with a few of the other townie cooks.

Ross is a line cook at The Carlisle a few doors down from the bar, and Garreth works the counter and makes sandwiches at a sub shop at the other end of town. The third guy looks familiar, but I can't remember his name.

But tonight, I'm not here to hang out with them, as much as I'd like to. Instead, I take a seat at the bar, my eyes tracking the man behind the counter as he smiles and gives me a wave.

He's the reason why I did a double take when I saw a job listing in Rosewood. But he has no idea who I am.

"What can I get you?"

"Whatever IPA you recommend on draft," I answer, keeping my expression easy.

"Coming right up." He taps the bar top twice before turning to grab a pint glass and take it to the tap. He's back in less than a minute, resting my pint on a coaster. "You opening a tab or just the one?"

I tug my wallet out. "Just the one." I tug out a twenty and place it on the bar. "Keep the change."

He grins and thanks me, spinning around to the till and giving me his back.

When Murphy invited me out for a thank-you beer, I told her I'm not really a bar guy, but I wasn't being entirely honest. Mostly, I just didn't want to come to *this* bar. Because I've been coming to The Standard a few times a week since moving here and still haven't mustered up the courage to introduce myself to the man on the other side of the bar. Part of me wonders if I have the wrong guy.

But as I watch him in the old, weathered mirror against the back wall, I can see far too many similarities for me to be wrong.

According to my mother, Gabriel Wright was a decent father until he disappeared from our lives, leaving her a single mother to a five-year-old and a newborn. I believed that until I was in junior high, when I started understanding that my mother's addiction problems meant she'd often lie about things.

It made me wonder if she lied about him, too. If he really was a man who just up and abandoned us one day, or if that's not the whole story.

I've wondered about him for years, and when I was considering a move back to California and saw the job at Hawthorne Vines, a little part of me thought that maybe it was time to put myself in his path. Open the door to whatever might come from meeting him.

I planned it all out in my head, how I'd befriend him first before introducing myself. How I'd come in and sit at the bar and talk to him, learn about him first. It seemed like the best way for me to know for sure that I really wanted to tell him who I was.

But each time I show up and he's working, I can't manage more than a few words, my chest tightening at the idea of striking up a conversation.

Tonight is more of the same.

The longer I sit here silently, the less brave I feel. I watch him chatting with a guy at the other end of the bar, the two of them clearly friendly with the way they joke and laugh.

It makes me wonder if we might be able to joke and laugh that way.

Eventually, I take my beer and head over to play a game of pool with Ross, Garreth, and the other guy I don't know.

Maybe another night, I tell myself.

But it sounds like a lie, even to me.

◆　◆　◆

"You can't be serious."

I turn my head and let out a sigh when I see Murphy walking up the path toward the bench.

"I'm not trying to be a bitch or anything, but this is my bench. I've been sitting here since my father built it when I was in junior high, okay? So . . ." She pauses. "Please leave."

"Look, Murphy, I'm not in the mood tonight," I tell her, crossing my arms and staring forward.

The last thing I need is another confrontation with her. I'm not sure I can handle it. After I bombed out on talking to my father *again* at the bar earlier, I'd really like to just be alone and have a chance to think.

"Tough shit," she says, walking over and plopping down next to me, much like she did last night. "This time, you can't bait me into leaving. I'm staying, so if you have a problem with it, *you* can leave."

I want to laugh at how serious she's being, but I doubt it'll be received well, so I keep it bottled inside with everything else.

Then Murphy and I sit in silence together, just staring out at the vineyard and the rolling hills in the distance.

Unfortunately, her presence does exactly what I expect. Distracts me from the things I need to be thinking about—the restaurant, the menu, my job, what happened in Chicago, my father, my mother, my brother—basically anything other than Murphy.

I'm hyperaware of her, sitting just inches from me, that same light perfume wafting my way in the damp evening breeze.

I catch myself taking long, slow breaths, hoping to catch another hint of it on the air.

"Why do you even come out here?" she demands.

Turning my head, I find her watching me, her eyes narrowed in frustration.

Clearly, she's fuming, hoping to light me on fire with her eyes, oblivious to me silently sucking in her perfume like it's water and I'm dying of thirst.

Great.

"Probably the same as you," I finally reply. "To be *alone* with my thoughts."

She makes a face, and I'm assuming it's supposed to be an expression of irritation, but it might be one of the cutest looks I've ever seen.

This time, I'm not able to keep my laugh to myself.

"What? Why are you laughing?"

I shake my head, my laugh trailing off. "Nothing."

Murphy crosses her arms and glares at me, and part of me wants to kiss that fucking frown right off her face.

But I don't let myself give in to that idea, not that Murphy would be interested anyway.

"Look, clearly you don't want me here," she says, uncrossing her arms and turning her body to face me. "I don't want me to be here either, okay? So can you just . . . stop being such an asshole? I'm already dealing with enough as it is."

At that, my shoulders fall.

I want to tell her I'm not normally an asshole, but then that would require me to explain that I've been trying to build a cement wall between us, for both our sakes, and that's not a conversation I feel like having any time soon.

So instead, I just nod.

"Yeah, I get that."

She seems to take that as a victory, because she turns and settles against the bench, her gaze shifting out to the valley and the view.

We sit for a while like that, just the two of us, and eventually, I can feel the bristling frustration between us cool and then fall away completely.

I'm not sure whether it's a good idea, letting my guard down around Murphy Hawthorne. I have a feeling it's actually a very *bad* idea.

But the longer we sit there, side by side, enjoying the silence and the late-evening spring breeze and comfort of being alone, together, the less I can seem to muster up the ability to care.

Chapter Seven

MURPHY

When I moved to LA nine years ago, just twelve days after my high school graduation, I stayed for a few weeks with a friend of a friend while I searched for a job and an apartment.

I'd been saving every single penny I could manage from my part-time job waitressing at The Carlisle, babysitting, and working for a few hours each Saturday morning at the Trager family's veggie stand. But I still didn't have much, and I ended up answering an ad on Craigslist for a roommate.

The place was a one-bedroom, and my "room" for almost two years was a corner of the living room that had shower curtains hung over PVC piping to create a modicum of privacy.

It was a nightmare.

Eventually, I managed to make friends and get connected with three people who had extra space in their two-bedroom apartment. Still, four people in an eight-hundred-square-foot box is tight. I grew accustomed to wearing earplugs because my roommate's boyfriend spent the night fairly often and they were completely unconcerned with privacy.

And yet, I still think either of those situations would be preferable to returning home. If circumstances were different, if I thought I might have ever been able to figure out how to get things to work out in spite of what happened, I would have stayed. I would have continued waitressing, continued signing up for open-mic nights and trying to make connections to get a different agent.

But I knew—hell, Paul flat-out told me—there was no future for me in LA.

So I left.

The quickness of it was jarring. I went from celebrating my sudden success to grieving my rapid fall within such a short period of time.

It felt like whiplash, the pain of it still reverberating through me months later.

"Hey, sweetheart."

I look out to the pathway that leads up to the back patio, smiling when I see my aunt approaching. She's wearing a big hat that shades her from the sharpness of the early-summer sun, but the hard labor of a vineyard worker is still apparent in sweat on her flushed skin.

My aunt Sarah has been a mother figure for as long as I can remember, and when I lived in LA, she called me regularly to ask all about my life and hear how my pursuit of a music career was going.

She never talked about my father, though, and rarely about my brothers. Instead, she shared details about the vineyard *in general*, about her new quest to use dating apps to find love, and the different hobbies she picked up here and there.

I'm glad I had her to talk to when I was away. She allowed me to feel somewhat connected to my home without guilting me into returning. And for that, I'll be eternally grateful.

I haven't told her why I'm home, though. The only people who know are my friend Vivian and my brother Micah, and outside of them, I have no plans to share.

"I'm heading into town to run some errands. Wanna come?" she asks, dropping down into one of the other patio chairs and taking a long swig from her water bottle. "I've missed our shopping trips since you've been gone."

I think back to all the times she did this while I was growing up. She'd take me into town to do whatever she needed to do, then we'd stop at Rosewood Café and get coffees or ice cream or something. There, she'd get me to open up about whatever was going on in my life at the time.

I have a feeling today she'll try to get me to share why I moved home, and I'm not sure I have the strength to keep everything bottled inside.

So I shake my head.

"No thanks, but maybe another time."

She twists her lips, my answer clearly disappointing her.

"You know I'm here whenever you need to talk, right?"

I nod, and my voice comes out as a whisper. "I know."

I feel bad for turning her down, but I don't change my mind. I've been a people pleaser for most of my life. Most middle children are. It's something to do with the fact that we don't get enough attention, and my life is nothing if not a cliché example of a middle child wishing she felt more loved.

There have been only a few times I can remember doing things that intentionally went against others' desires.

One is when I left Rosewood.

Another is the reason I came back.

"See you at dinner," she tells me, that same soft smile on her face as she pushes up from her seat and goes inside.

I look back to the property spread out before me, the long rows of vines that stretch farther than I can see.

As beautiful as this vineyard is, I can't help but hate being back here.

I hate the interactions I've had with my brother and father.

And I hate that I have to add this whole mess with Wes into the mix.

It would have been so nice to keep that sweet memory of the kind, attractive guy who helped fix my flat and made my pulse race. Instead, that guy has been claiming my bench late at night, invading my space and my home and my life.

My heart nearly shoots out of my chest when my cell phone rings on the table in front of me. I take a second, my hand to my chest, to catch my breath.

Then I pick it up and look at the screen, my lips tilting up even with my sour mood.

"Hey, V."

"Don't *hey, V* me," I hear from the other end of the phone. "It's been five days since you left, and I've heard nothing from you. You could have died!"

At the sound of Vivian's theatrics, I break into a real smile.

"I only drove to the other end of the state, not Mars," I reply. "I wasn't going to die."

"Look, weird shit happens at gas stations in the middle of nowhere, okay? Trust me, I know."

I laugh at the accuracy of her words, thankful for her distraction from the bullshit going on in my life.

"So how is it being back at Hawthorne House?" she asks me, and I can just picture her sitting on her patio, overlooking the water, sipping from a glass of wine like we did on so many evenings together.

"It's . . . still here," I answer, not really sure what else to say.

"Yeesh, that bad, huh?"

I sigh. "I think I made a mistake coming home, V."

"My couch is always available if you want to bring your cute little butt back to LA."

"I couldn't do that to you two. Besides, you know Roger hates me and would never be able to get over me invading his space."

"Roger is a little shit who can suck it up," she replies, and I smile at the image of her aging cat's narrowed eyes every time I visited Vivian at the apartment she shares with her boyfriend in Santa Monica. "But really, M, if you want to be here, I can make it work."

My heart twists, because I know she's being serious. And if circumstances were different, I might have taken her up on the offer.

But Paul made it clear the last time we talked. There is no future for me in LA, and it doesn't matter that V is on the ladder to success. There's nothing she can do about it.

So . . . her couch isn't really an option. Staying in LA wasn't an option.

The only real option for me was returning home and giving myself a chance to figure out what's next.

"I appreciate it," I tell her. "I really do. But we talked about this, V. You know that—"

"I know, I know," she cuts me off. "I just wish things were different."

"Me, too."

We sit in silence for a long moment, neither of us saying anything, just enjoying the closeness, even though we're so far from each other.

"So show me the vineyard," she eventually says, breaking through the quiet. "You've been talking about this place for years. I'm gonna call you back on FaceTime because I want to see everything."

I laugh as the phone goes black and then lights up again, then I'm grinning from ear to ear when I see Vivian's beautiful face on my screen.

"All right! Show me everything. And I mean *everything*."

I flip the camera around and show her the view from where I'm sitting.

"Daaaaaaang, girl. I need to plan a trip up to wine country."

I take her on a phone tour of the area fairly close to the house, showing her the vines and the house and then walking her out to the bench so she can see an even more killer view overlooking not only our vineyard, but most of Rosewood.

The entire time, she oohs and aahs and makes comments about how amazing everything is.

It's a relief, talking to V.

She was the one true friend I made during the years I lived in LA. The one honest, good soul who I'm going to miss.

As much as I enjoy talking to her, there's something bittersweet about it. Because it's a reminder that I don't have anyone here to talk with. To tell my secrets to.

When I finally make it back to the porch and we say our good-byes, I stare at my phone for a long moment, wishing not for the first time that I could change . . . well, anything. I wish I could change anything.

But that's not how life works.

"Who were you talking to?"

I startle at the sound of Memphis's voice.

"God, you scared me," I reply, my hand coming to my chest again.

I didn't realize I could be so easily startled. First Vivian's call, now Memphis?

"Who were you talking to?" he asks again, leaning against a post and crossing his arms.

I roll my eyes, wishing he'd learn how to not be such a stern stick-in-the-mud from time to time. "A friend," I answer. "Why?"

He shrugs a shoulder. "Just wondering."

And then he walks off back into the house where I assume he came from.

I make a face after he's gone, though it immediately makes me feel like I'm ten years old. I've never understood why Memphis is so . . . inflexible. He's like a brick wall sometimes, and I wish he'd be like a tree instead. Still strong and firm, but able to bend and move with the wind.

When my eyes fall to the papers I have stacked on the patio table, I'm reminded of what I was working on before my aunt Sarah sat down a little while ago.

And the fact that I actually need to talk to my brother.

So I snatch everything up and go racing into the house, finding him just as he's settling into his desk chair in his office.

"Do you have a minute?" I walk in and sit in the chair across from him. "I wanted to talk to you about the staffing rotation."

"Look, if it's too much work you can probably ask Wes to—"

"Memphis."

My brother stops speaking at my interruption.

Seriously, the guy needs to learn how to not make assumptions.

"Thank you. What I was going to say is that I've finished putting together a preliminary concept for staffing, as well as a potential training schedule. Of course, this is dependent upon being able to hire for several different positions in the next week."

I pass over the itinerary I spent most of yesterday and today working on, as well as the staffing structure and completed position descriptions.

"I figured the best bet for training would be to move everyone through phases, so if you look at"—I tug out one of the sheets at the back of the stack in Memphis's hand—"this page, you'll notice there are knowledge areas that everyone has to complete before they can finish the training. There's a front-of-house section that includes things like wines, the physical menu, supplies, and serving basics. Then there's the back-of-house section that includes health and safety, ingredients and food, supplies, and kitchen basics."

Memphis looks over the documents I've shared with him for a few minutes, his eyes narrowed as he scans over everything.

Then he looks at me.

"You created these?"

My shoulders drop, and something in my face must fall as well because Memphis speaks again.

"I'm just asking because it's an incredible amount of work to get done in two days, Murphy."

"No, you're asking because you don't think I'm capable of creating things like this."

At my brother's silence, I know I've hit the nail on the head.

"Look, Murphy, I don't know what you expect from me, okay? I haven't seen you in nine years, and we've only talked a handful of times." He sets the paperwork down between us. "How am I supposed to know what you can and can't do?"

I lick my lips, tears beginning to prickle at the backs of my eyes and sting my nose.

"Nine years *is* a long time, isn't it?" I take in a steeling breath. "Did it ever occur to you . . . *ever* . . . to come visit me in LA?"

Memphis shifts in his seat but doesn't say anything.

"In all those nine years, in the handful of times we spoke . . . who called who?" I continue. "Did you ever think to reach out to me? To ask how I was doing? To see . . . fuck, if I was even still alive?"

At that, one of my tears falls, but I bat it away, unwilling to let crying derail this conversation—one that Memphis and I have needed to have for quite some time.

"I have been working my ass off for years, sometimes two and three jobs at a time, basically just sleeping and working, and fitting in performing my music where I could. And in all the years I was pushing for my dream, Micah was the only one to come visit me."

"I was working my ass off, too." Memphis shoves out of his chair and begins to pace around the room. "While you were off having fun and doing whatever the hell, I was here, taking care of our family and making sure the vineyard didn't go into bankruptcy."

I'm gearing up to respond to the *off having fun* remark when I hear the second half of his sentence, and my head jerks back in surprise.

"What?"

He looks out the window, the vines in the distance barely visible at this late hour, but we both know they're there.

"Memphis, what did you mean by that?" I ask again when he hasn't said anything a few minutes later. "Dad always said business was booming when we were growing up. Did something change?"

My brother is quiet for another moment before he speaks again.

"Dad doesn't always know what he's talking about."

He doesn't turn around and look at me, but he doesn't have to. Even with close to a decade of time having passed since we last saw each other, I still know him like nobody else.

Even though his shoulders are tight and his voice has grown loud, even though he was pacing this office and now he's staring out into the darkness, I still know my brother. I give it less than three minutes before he finally spins around and pretends like nothing is wrong.

"You can talk to me, you know?" I keep trying even though I know the outcome.

Because that's what family does. They keep trying.

Or at least, it's what you're *supposed* to do.

Sure enough, about two minutes later, he turns around and heads back to his desk, his face returning to that infuriatingly neutral expression that I've seen far too many times. Once he's seated again, he collects all the paperwork we'd been talking about, shuffles it into a neat stack, and then hands it back to me.

"This looks great, Murphy. Just run it all by Wes so you're both on the same page since it looks like he'll need to be running part of the training."

I sit across from my brother for a long moment, just looking at him, and wondering how big the burden is that he's trying to carry all by himself.

As irritating as my brother can be, he's also one of those people who will bend over backward for just about anyone.

Maybe he's more like a tree than I realized.

"You're not alone in whatever it is, Memphis," I tell him, my voice just loud enough for him to hear me.

His lips tilt up in a barely visible smile then. But it's one that has something sad, almost heartbreaking about it.

"Yes, I am, Murph."

We sit like that, in silence for a long time, before he turns around, facing his computer again, effectively dismissing me.

So I stand and make my way to the door, hoping that, eventually, he'll let me in.

Even just a little bit.

Chapter Eight

WES

As far away as the opening is, it still feels like it's barreling closer at a faster pace each day. And even though I've been working on the menu nonstop, it feels even more like an amorphous blob today than it did a few days ago when Memphis suggested the tasting dinner for the entire staff.

I think he's envisioning a soft opening, but for only the Hawthorne family and employees. The idea is great, but it makes the true opening feel like it's looming.

I spend a long day creating a grocery list for Memphis based on a menu that isn't complete yet because he wants me to start visiting local farms to source my ingredients. Afterward, I decide to wander the vineyard, like I have on so many other nights since moving here. I take one of the bottles of wine that I still haven't paired yet and begin the walk out to my favorite bench. Apparently it's Murphy's favorite bench too, and I do my best to convince myself it has nothing to do with why I'm here again.

I could be doing any number of other things, but this one place on the property keeps calling me back.

When I was struggling with anxiety during my last year in Chicago, I would walk the city in the middle of the night. People used to warn me about walking around in certain neighborhoods that maybe weren't the safest, but I did it anyway.

Not because I had anything to prove, but because something about walking empty streets at night helped to clear my head. I was able to think things through on the gritty sidewalks of the city in a way that little else could provide.

In Rosewood, I can either walk the vineyard or the highway, and I figure walking along a dark highway at night is a recipe for disaster. So I run the highway during the day, when it's warm and bright. And at night, I can make these vineyard pathways my new city streets.

I think about my father for a long while, my thoughts flickering back over the one or two memories I have from my childhood before he disappeared.

They're less like memories and more like feelings, I guess, shadows of a life that doesn't feel like it was mine. Someone big and strong tucking me into bed. Being wrapped in a warm blanket at a campfire.

I can't even be sure these memories are of the man from The Standard, or if they're even real things that happened. But there was something truly comforting about those memories—real or imagined—and I think that's why I'm here, in Rosewood. I'm searching for that safety again.

I exhale into the night, my breath visible in the cool air.

Gabriel Wright might be the reason I'm here, but he wasn't the catalyst for why I needed somewhere to go in the first place.

No, that was something a lot more disastrous.

Coming up in the culinary world, I never had grand dreams for myself and my future as a chef. Even though my mentor was Bernard Hines, one of the most respected chefs in the industry . . . Even though I'd won a James Beard Award as an Emerging Chef . . . Even though I had my pick of offers for where to work whenever I was ready to break out on my own.

It was hard to envision big, life-changing dreams, though, when I could barely afford my rent.

So when a high-powered couple began talking to me about becoming head chef at their new restaurant, I was ready to jump at their offer. Alejandro and Bridget Santiago were well-known restauranteurs. Working in one of their restaurants meant joining the ranks of others who'd launched their careers with them, with incredible success. The chefs who worked under the Santiagos were names I heard on TV and had authored more than a few titles on my bookshelf.

But more importantly, they were chefs with huge salaries.

And that's what I wanted.

More than *anything*, that's what I wanted. A chance to lift myself out of the hole that I was born in. A chance to pull my brother out, too. And the Santiagos represented that to me.

So I was shocked when my mentor warned me away from them.

"All I can tell you is that you have to set standards for yourself with every job you accept," he tells me. "And as promising as a job with the Santiagos sounds, they have completely different business priorities than you do."

I shake my head. "Of course they do. They're running an empire. I'm looking for my first big break. In any case, I can just work for them for a few years, and then take those connections and make my next move."

He looks at me with a grave expression. "They're well known, but they're surrounded by controversy. Wes, if you get in bed with them, they have the potential to ruin your career. Permanently."

God, how I wish I'd heeded his advice.

Instead, I'd been too shortsighted, too focused on the immediate gratification.

Because Hines had been right.

And I *did* ruin my career.

My mind is exhausted by the time I take a seat on the bench around eight o'clock. The only thing that buoys my spirit is the idea that I might bump into Murphy tonight.

It's been a few days since I've seen her. As much as I enjoyed the way our Monday evening turned into us sitting together in silence, enjoying the view and, to some degree, each other's company, I also felt like it shouldn't be something I let happen too often.

Tonight, though, I'm hoping that by sitting on *her bench* so late in the evening, I'll see her walking up the path.

I even packed two wineglasses, just in case.

Sure enough, a half hour later, I see her form in the distance.

She's heading in my direction but pauses when she catches sight of me. My night immediately improves when she carries forward again, her expression impassive.

Used to be that I was looking for a woman to devour me with her eyes. Now, I can't get enough of the way Murphy tolerates my presence.

That thought makes me laugh. How the mighty have fallen.

"I thought I told you this was my bench," she says as she takes a seat next to me, but I can hear the lack of true fight in her voice. Instead, there's a note of teasing. Something slightly playful.

"Well, I figured it could still belong to you, and maybe I could rent it here and there."

Her lips tilt up. "Oh, I doubt you could afford the rent on this bench."

"I'm sure. Which is why I've brought bribes."

At that, I lean down, pull the wine out of the bag, and begin to uncork it.

Murphy laughs. "You're trying to bribe me with my own wine?"

I raise an eyebrow. "What, you don't think it's good enough to use as a bribe?"

She rolls her eyes. I just smile, then yank the cork from the top with a satisfying pop.

"I hope you know that I abandoned my *drinking straight from the bottle* days back in high school."

I chuckle, enjoying the visual of Murphy sneaking off with a bottle from her family vineyard, maybe meeting up with some friends and getting drunk in the fields.

"That's why I brought"—I lean down and pull out the two glasses—"these."

Handing her one, I revel in how pleased she looks as I fill up first her glass, then mine. She lifts it to her nose, taking a whiff, before raising it to her lips and tilting it back to taste.

"The merlot," she says. "One of my favorites."

I grin. "Mine, too."

We sit in silence for a while, each of us taking occasional sips from our glasses while enjoying the light evening breeze. It's so much like the time we spent sitting next to each other on the tailgate of the truck that I smile to myself.

"This spot really is beautiful." I keep my voice quiet. Something about this moment feels like a secret we need to keep just between us.

Murphy takes a moment to respond, but when she does, her voice is warm with affection.

"My father proposed to my mother right here when they were just seniors in high school."

I raise my eyebrows in surprise. "No kidding."

"Yeah, they were pretty young, but"—she shrugs—"they were crazy about each other, I guess. My dad put this bench here a few years after she died. Said he liked the idea of sitting with his memories of her."

My heart pinches. I don't know all the details about the Hawthorne family, obviously, but I hadn't realized their mom had passed away. When I see a family without a parent around, I usually assume separation or divorce.

"I'm sorry, I didn't realize she'd passed."

Murphy gives me a sad smile.

"I was only four, so it's not a raw wound or anything." Still, pain glimmers in her eyes. "Memphis was seven, and he has a lot more memories with her than I did. But Micah . . . He was a newborn. He didn't know her at all."

A few moments pass before I find the right thing to say.

"I can understand now why this is your bench. I'm sorry for not taking that more seriously."

She shakes her head. "It *is* a special place, but it's important to share things that are special. They mean more that way."

I've never thought about it that way before, but I like the sentiment. It resonates with me as a chef, as a person who finds joy in sharing my love of food with others.

"Thank you for sharing it with me tonight," I tell her.

We sit in the quiet then, each of us lost in our own thoughts, enjoying the comfort that being together can bring.

"Do you—"

Murphy's question cuts off midway through.

I turn to look at her.

"Do I . . . ?"

Even in the pale moonlight, her cheeks color with a faint blush, which only increases my curiosity about what she was going to say.

"Do you ever wonder about the night we met?" she finally asks. "If we'd exchanged numbers . . . or if you weren't working here at the vineyard."

My stomach tightens.

Because hell yes, I wonder about it. On more than a few occasions I've let my mind wander in the shower, my hand traveling south as I imagine how everything could have been different.

If I'd allowed that kiss to grow into something more.

I fight tooth and nail not to indulge myself in those moments, but they come anyway.

Her blonde hair splayed on my pillows as I lick down her body.

The noises she would make as I pushed inside her wet heat.

Even now, the thought of those imagined moments sends a shiver racing through me that makes me want to tell her the truth.

But I can't.

Especially now that we're . . . doing whatever this is.

I can't sit on this bench next to her, at this late hour, if I think she's wondering about it, too.

So the best thing I can do is shut it down. With a quickness.

"No, Murphy. I don't."

My voice is firm, and when I glance over, I see the blush in her cheeks has grown.

It cost her something to ask me that question, and my response only proved to her that it wasn't worth the price.

"And you shouldn't, either," I add, hoping to drive the point home. "We're going to be working together, so there's no use in *wondering*."

Murphy nods, but she doesn't look at me again. And it isn't much longer before she finishes off her glass of wine, sets it gently in my bag, and tells me to have a good night.

Something inside of me says it was a mistake to cut her down like that.

But I don't allow that little voice any ground.

Instead, I shove it down inside with the memories of the last time I let things at work become something they shouldn't have.

And then the little voice is silent.

Even though it's late, I return to the kitchen after my conversation with Murphy. I pull out the half-drunk bottle of merlot and pour a small glass for myself. One sniff sends my mind back to the bench with Murphy. Then, slowly, as the tannins of the warm red slide across my tongue, another memory emerges of a holiday *years* ago.

Back in my early twenties, when I first started working for Chef Hines, he invited me to spend Thanksgiving with him and his family. My own experiences with holiday meals had been frozen dinners in front of the TV, or sometimes even plates of food from the homeless shelter if my mom was nowhere to be found.

That Thanksgiving spent at the Hines family table, with Bernard's husband and children, along with grandparents and cousins, all gathered around a massive, beautifully decorated table enjoying some of the most delicious food I'd ever tasted . . . It was life changing for me.

I'm sure plenty of people wouldn't understand how a single family meal—one that wasn't even with my own family—could be life changing. But it was the first time I felt that kind of warmth that comes along with holidays.

I'd seen it on TV, on old sitcoms that felt unrealistic and completely out of touch. Families sitting around together, sharing a meal at a large table, the mom cooking the turkey and the dad sitting at the head of the table with the carving knife. But I never truly believed that people did things like that.

So that Thanksgiving changed my concept of what I wanted my future to look like. From that moment on, I knew I wanted that warmth and familiarity. The easy conversation. The kindness and togetherness.

Being here at the vineyard gives me hints of that feeling, when Sarah is laying out dinner for all of us, or those fleeting moments when Memphis and his dad let their guards down. But Murphy . . . Sitting with her on that bench, enjoying the ease and flow of our conversation, I felt a warmth in my soul that mirrored how I felt that day at the Hines family table.

On just the few occasions Murphy and I have spent time together, I've seen more of her layers peeled back—the softness she hides under her family's dysfunction, and the fiery passion that seems to simmer below the surface, too. Which makes me want to know even more. And that quickly, the future I envisioned here at the vineyard has started to shift.

Because of her.

Thoughts of Murphy and Hines swirl around in my mind, along with an even more unexpected desire to bring her and her brothers around the table in a way that might start to heal some of the animosity between them.

I start to take notes about the dinners that made me feel that sense of home unlike I'd ever experienced before. The green beans, the turkey, the mashed potatoes. The cranberry sauce and pumpkin pie and dressing. Eventually, a dish begins to take shape. Turkey legs in a cranberry merlot sauce, maybe with butternut squash and garlic roasted green beans as a side. All of which would pair excellently with the vineyard's merlot. The woodsy nose and plum fruit taste, the modest tannins, would be a perfect contrast to the savory dish.

I jot down several notes, carefully listing out all the ingredients before hopping on the computer in the office to shoot off an updated list for Memphis.

I'm relieved to have figured out another dish, but even more elated that it's something truly inspired. I haven't ever created food inspired by a person before, and I'm shocked at the way it feels. As if I'm taking the best things I know and infusing them into my work.

It's an incredible feeling.

I work well past midnight, pulling out other bottles of wine that I've yet to pair, hoping that this sudden stroke of inspiration is something I can repeat over and over again.

Chapter Nine

MURPHY

My phone is next to me, face down on the carpet. It's been buzzing for a while, a group text from my friends in LA trying to make a girls' trip out of visiting the vineyard. Ever since I showed off the property to Vivian, she's been incessant about it, but I can't muster up the energy to respond.

Not when things for them are going swimmingly and I'm sitting on the floor of my childhood bedroom feeling like shit.

There's a sense of loneliness that I wasn't expecting to face. When I imagined coming home, the things I was most concerned with were my interactions with my family and figuring out what comes next. The idea that I might sit in my bedroom crying because I miss my friends wasn't anywhere on my radar.

I guess the relationships I created in LA were more important to me than I realized.

"Hey."

I can't help smiling just a little bit when I spot my brother Micah standing in the doorway of my room, his hands tucked into his pockets.

"Hi."

He leans to the side, his shoulder resting on the doorjamb as he scans the room.

I don't doubt he's assessing the situation: me on the floor with red eyes, my phone vibrating next to me, my guitar case untouched, but the rest of my stuff *everywhere*.

I'd thought that rearranging my room would be a good use of my Saturday morning, help me take my mind off . . . well, everything.

Instead it just highlighted to me how alone I was.

The last time I rearranged my childhood bedroom, I'd had Quinn's help. Hell, she helped me move the furniture around on an almost yearly basis, maybe even more often. There was something about changing a bedroom around that could make my teenage soul feel like a brand-new girl.

But that feeling wasn't anywhere to be found as I tried moving my bed to face the french doors. Instead, I pulled a muscle in my calf and slammed my finger in one of my dresser drawers trying to shift that around, too.

Now I'm sitting on the floor in the middle of a room and none of my furniture is in the right spot. And knowing I've fucked it up all by myself is the worst part.

"Want some help?"

His voice is soft, his eyes kind, and the magnitude of how much I've missed him seems to hit me all at once.

If Memphis is a bulldozer and I'm a tornado, Micah is a soft snowfall. Calm and quiet. Observant and thoughtful.

"No, it's all right," I tell him, pushing up from the floor and rubbing my sore hands against my jeans.

"You sure?" He glances at his watch. "I've got a few minutes before I need to meet Naomi and Edgar at the warehouse."

I glance around the room, my eyes welling again at the idea of trying to move everything on my own, not to mention that this is the first time I'm seeing my brother in a long while. Clearly I'm dealing with some emotional shit, because sobbing while shoving bedroom furniture around is clearly not the vibe.

"Yeah, actually. That would be great."

Micah claps his hands together and steps into the room, and after I take a second to explain where I want everything, he takes the lead.

"Sorry I disappeared right after you moved back," he says, bending down to pick up my dresser from the base. "I had to go to San Francisco for a few days. Memphis sent me to this wine and spirits conference."

My brow furrows as we lift my dresser and move it a few feet away, so it's now set against a different wall. "Memphis sent *you* to a conference?"

Micah gives me a half smile. "I told him it was stupid, but he promised me it wasn't about the networking. He just wanted information."

Micah is the most introverted of us, so I can't imagine how exhausting it was for him to not only go into San Francisco, one of the busiest cities in the country, but also attend a conference surrounded by hundreds, maybe thousands, of people.

"Information about what?"

"International wine distribution."

My hands come to my hips. "Are you serious?"

He shrugs. "He said he's trying to compile a list of potential ways we can expand the vineyard."

I roll my eyes. "The restaurant isn't enough?"

Micah shrugs again. "Bed now?"

Nodding, I move around to the other side of the bed. We both lift and scoot the headboard so it's up against the wall opposite from the doors that lead out to the veranda.

"I like it," he says once we're done, standing back to evaluate.

"I'm glad. Me, too."

"Hey, I gotta run out to the warehouse. Do you want to meet me out there in a little bit? I'm doing an inspection run, and I was thinking you could ride with me."

Gosh, it's been years since I've done an inspection run.

When I was a kid, I'd ride around in the ATV with Grandpa every month so he could collect grapes from different locations on the property—different vines, different rows, different types of grapes—and take them back to his lab for testing. I called it a lab, but really it was just an office where he had some fancy equipment.

The building where he used to do those tests is gone now, replaced by a large warehouse a few years before I moved away, but the testing is still a big part of managing our vineyard. I remember my dad, Diego, and Clay regularly riding around the property with labeled bags, pulling samples and marking them intently so that if they found any issues they'd know exactly which vine the grape came from. A little part of me is happy that Micah has taken up the task, and it's an even better chance to get to catch up with him now that he's returned from his trip.

"Sure, I'll come out. Memphis mentioned there's a new cellar out there now."

Micah nods. "Yeah, we finished construction about four years ago."

"I'd love to see it."

My brother gives me a smile. "Awesome." Then he looks at his watch again. "Setup for the inspection run should only take thirty minutes or so. See you then?"

I nod, and Micah steps forward, tugging me into a hug that eases something sharp and uncomfortable in my chest.

"I'm glad you're home," he tells me, his voice low. "I know you might not want to be here, but I'm glad I get you back for however long it lasts."

His words swell inside of me, buoying me up after my emotional morning.

Micah plants a kiss on the crown of my head, then leaves my room.

I glance around, taking in the newly moved furniture.

It *does* make my room feel different.

And having help to do it sure didn't hurt.

◆ ◆ ◆

Twenty minutes later, I've showered away my emotions from the morning and emerged feeling like a different person. I exit onto the veranda and walk into the vineyard, giving myself a chance to wander leisurely through the vines on the way to the warehouse.

But when I come to the fork in the path, I decide to make a detour over to the cabins. If I'm going to visit some of the property that I haven't seen in a long time, it can't hurt to see if there have been any changes to the handful of studio-style residences that our year-round staff live in.

I also can't lie to myself—part of me is curious about where Wes lives.

Of course when I come around a bend, my footsteps falter when I spot Wes sitting on the steps of cabin 3. He's leaning against the wooden siding, his head tilted up and his face to the sun, eyes closed.

I didn't expect him to actually *be* here, outside, in the middle of the day. Shouldn't he be back in the kitchen, getting ready for the opening?

I know I sure as hell should be.

It feels like I've stumbled upon him in a private moment, not to mention the fact that things between us continue to be sort of tense.

I quietly backtrack around the corner I just came from, hoping not to alert him to my presence. A few more steps and I'll be in the clear, but then Wes's eyes open and he looks directly at me.

"Hey."

It's all he says, but I can tell he's curious as to why I'm here.

"Hey, sorry, I was just . . ."

"Snooping?"

My brow furrows. "I wasn't snooping."

Wes grins, then closes his eyes and tilts his face back up to the sun again. "I was kidding, Murphy. It's your family's property. You can go wherever you want."

I nod, though he doesn't see the movement, his eyes still closed and facing upward, and then I turn back down the row I came from.

"I have to say, I seriously missed the California sun."

Wes's voice freezes me again, and I turn back around to look at him.

"You know, it gets warm in Chicago during the summer, obviously. But the sun feels different. There is nothing like California sunshine."

"In LA, the smog was so thick you could see it from the mountains," I tell him, the memory coming out of nowhere. "It gave the sun this weird hue when it was particularly bad."

"Sounds gross." He peers at me through one eye.

"It was."

We both just watch each other for a long moment until Wes taps the spot next to him. "Come on over. Soak it in."

I hesitate, knowing I should get to the warehouse to meet Micah.

"I promise not to be a jerk. Again," he adds, grinning at me.

The tease in his tone mixes with the temptation inside me. I walk over and drop down to sit next to him.

I rest my forearms on my knees and turn my face to the sky, closing my eyes and letting the sun hit my skin the way he was moments ago.

"You're right," I tell him. "This is pretty great."

We sit in silence for a while, but it feels different than our nights on the bench somehow. Wes feels different. More playful maybe. Less closed off. Then again, I thought that last night too, before he shut me down. I lower my head and try to purge the embarrassing memory.

"You know, I was thinking about what you asked me," he says.

I blink up at him, suddenly mortified that somehow he can sense my thoughts. I decide to play dumb. "Oh? What did I ask?"

Wes's lips tilt up. "You know."

I cross my arms and close my eyes again, thinking I should just save myself the humiliation of whatever he's going to say next and run off back to the path.

But instead, I wuss out and keep my eyes closed. "You mean about whether you think about the night we met."

Wes hums his agreement, and then I feel him lean toward me, his voice lowering, as if he's about to tell me a secret. "I lied," he whispers. "I *do* think about it."

I feel the pace of my heart picking up speed, but I keep my eyes closed.

"I had all kinds of thoughts that night," he murmurs.

"All kinds, huh?" My voice holds far more confidence than I feel inside. "Like what?"

I know I'm just messing with a hornet's nest by asking. The last thing I need to know is anything to do with Wes's *thoughts*.

"You really wanna know?"

At that question, I open my eyes and find him looking at me in a way that sends a flurry inside my stomach.

He looks almost hesitant, like he isn't exactly sure how he wants me to answer. So instead of speaking, I just nod, the movement so small I'm surprised he can even see it.

"I was thinking about what it might be like to keep kissing you in that parking lot, instead of stopping when we did."

I nip the inside of my lip, trying not to let it show that I'd also imagined the same.

"I thought maybe we could grab a couple more wine coolers to go. I could bring you here and walk you through the vines in the moonlight. And maybe we'd stop right here, on my stoop." He pauses a second, his eyes locked on me. "Maybe I'd press you against the wall to my cabin and lean in, lick up your neck, maybe leaving a little mark."

I close my eyes again, overwhelmed at the visual, wishing it were real instead of imagined. My mind briefly wonders what's different now than before . . . why he's sharing this little tidbit with me when he shut me down so swiftly before. But I shove that thought aside, choosing instead to just be here in this moment.

"Then I'd bring you inside. Play some soft music. Slip my fingers underneath your bra."

My lips part, and that's when I realize I'm panting just slightly, my chest rising and falling with deep, labored breaths at his words. At the picture he's painting of the two of us.

If he had any idea how much I'm enjoying this little fantasy, he might be tempted to make it come true.

But what's keeping him from doing that now? The way he's talking to me, our bodies inches apart, not much is stopping him from making good on all of it.

"Until you were desperate," he continues, his voice lowering as his mouth gets closer to my ear. "Until you were so needy, you would take control. Maybe shoving me back on the bed or the couch, straddling me and writhing against me."

His lips brush against my neck, or maybe it's his nose, I can't tell. All I know is that the small touch sends a shiver ricocheting through my chest and along my spine.

I am needy and desperate, I want to tell him.

But instead, I stay silent, hoping he'll continue this story, tell me what the night could have looked like if things had been different.

His shoulder brushes against mine, just lightly, just enough to know he's moved closer . . .

"Murphy?"

My eyes fly wide, the sound of my name like a bucket of cold water dumped over my head, and I spot Micah watching the two of us with a furrowed brow.

"Hey!" I say, my voice betraying the fact I was caught doing . . . whatever this was.

With Wes.

"When you didn't show up at the warehouse I figured I'd try to catch you on your way." His words come out slow and even, but his gaze is pinned on Wes. A beat passes before he looks to me again. "I'm glad I found you."

I glance at Wes, an odd expression on his face that surely matches mine. "I'll see you later," I mumble, before pushing off the stoop and walking toward where my brother stands with his hands on his hips. "Hey," I say again. "Sorry for being late."

It's not every day you're getting dirty-talked into a panting mess and your brother interrupts. I'd like for that to never happen again, please and thank you.

"That's okay." His voice is more like a growl, and I notice he's still watching Wes behind me.

I slip my hand in his and give him a tug down the path heading toward the warehouse. "So tell me about the cellar," I say. "And all the other changes on the property I might not know about."

His eyes are focused on the ground as we walk. "What's going on with you and Wes?"

I almost trip over my feet when he asks.

Unlike Memphis and me, who have grown up learning the art of avoidance from my father, my baby brother is much more direct. He might not be a big talker, but when he has something to say, he says exactly what he means.

"What are you talking about?" I respond, hoping that if I play dumb, he might, too.

But no such luck.

"Don't be an idiot. What was that back there?"

I shake my head, but no words come out.

That was nothing is what I want to say. *You must have misunderstood* is another option. But instead of either of those things, I just stay silent.

"Look, I don't think Wes is the kind of guy you should be getting involved with."

My eyebrows rise. "What do you mean by that?"

Micah lets out a long sigh but doesn't say anything else.

He's not ignoring me, I can tell. This is just one of his things. When he's unsure about how to share something, he goes really quiet, weighing things over in his mind like he's trying to decide what's most important.

I like that I know him well enough to recognize that telltale face, but don't like being on the receiving end of his careful contemplation to the point where he feels like he needs to be cautious with what he tells me.

"I just don't trust him," is all he finally says. I know he's being a protective brother, but I don't like the way those words settle like a sinking stone in my gut.

"Look, Micah. It doesn't matter, okay?" We come to a stop outside the warehouse. "There's nothing going on between me and Wes."

My brother narrows his eyes at me.

I know he can hear it in my voice. The lack of sincerity.

I'm not trying to lie to him. I'm honestly not. There *isn't* anything going on between me and Wes. And there won't be moving forward, because something about Wes really does shake me up inside. I just know that it's not a good idea to get entangled with him. And I don't doubt he feels the same way.

But even though those things might be true, there's something not entirely genuine about what I've said.

And Micah knows it, almost as much as I do.

"Really," I continue, hoping to drive the point home.

My brother lets out another sigh, his hands on his hips.

"All right, well, just know that you can talk to me," he eventually says.

I can tell he's choosing to drop the topic of me and Wes—or at least set it to the side for now. He nods in the direction of the warehouse's front door. "Let me show you around."

His big hand rests gently on my shoulder for a quick moment before he turns and leads me inside.

I love my baby brother. I'm four years older than him, so when I was little, it was usually Memphis that I played with and talked to. He's three years older than me, and I looked up to him a lot. Once Micah was old enough to talk, we grew a lot closer, though the truth is that all of us were pretty independent from each other.

The one thing I know for sure is that I'm thankful for who he has become in my life over the past nine years.

He's the only one in our family who knows what happened in LA, and he's the one who talked to Dad about me coming home. I know he probably had to go to bat for me in some way, and that he likely smoothed down some of my father's ruffled feathers about me suddenly needing to come back.

I'm not sure if I'll share the details with my dad or Memphis. Or even my aunt Sarah. As much as I truly do love my father and older brother and aunt, I just have no idea how they'll respond. How they'll react. Whether they'll see me as a failure or a fraud. What kind of judgment they'll heap on my shoulders.

And unfortunately, I'm feeling a little too fragile right now to take anything from them other than a job and a bed.

Someday, maybe things will be different. Someday, maybe we'll be able to pick up the pieces of our broken family.

But those pieces were shattered to bits before I ever left for LA, and part of me wonders if they've been lying broken and forgotten for far too long to be repaired.

Chapter Ten

WES

The rest of the weekend passes by without incident.

I go on another run, get some laundry done, and meet a supplier at the restaurant for a delivery of pots and pans that were supposed to arrive a week ago.

Which is how I find myself in the kitchen cooking up a butternut squash ravioli at eight o'clock on a Sunday evening.

Or that's the intention at least.

If I could only find the box of flour that I know for a fact is somewhere in this damn kitchen.

After twenty minutes of looking, I decide I have three options. Drive into town to get more flour. Quit making ravioli altogether. Or walk over to the Hawthorne house and snag the bag that I know is on the left side of the pantry.

Since I've had a few glasses of wine—the burden of being a chef forced to pair dishes with a wine list—driving into town is out.

So . . . Hawthorne house it is.

I knock on the front door first, still wanting to be respectful even though both Sarah and Jack said I was welcome in the house at any time. But when nobody comes to answer after a few knocks, I turn the handle and push inside.

I can hear a quiet hum from somewhere, maybe some light music, but other than that it's still. So I walk softly through the entry, down the hallway on the left, and into the kitchen.

I'm in the pantry in seconds, and when I spot the bag of flour exactly where I thought it was, I smile.

Plucking it off the shelf, I step back out into the kitchen and thunk it onto the counter. Taking just a little helping for myself seems like a better choice than making off with their entire supply.

I'm digging around in the cabinets looking for plastic bags when I hear a familiar voice from behind me.

"What are you doing here?"

I close the drawer and turn around, my mouth going dry when my eyes fall on Murphy, her hair wet and wrapped in a messy bun on her head. She's wearing a pair of tiny sleep shorts and a tank top that's a little too see-through for my liking.

Or exactly see-through enough, depending on where you're coming from.

I clear my throat and turn back to the cabinets, continuing my search.

"Borrowing some flour," I tell her. "I'll be gone in just a minute."

"You making something?"

I pause just briefly in my perusal of the contents of the top drawer next to the cutlery, considering the best way to respond.

"Ravioli," I reply, figuring I can go with one-word answers.

Be curt, but not unkind. That's my plan.

Though I can't say it was my plan yesterday afternoon, when I narrated my own personal erotic romance into Murphy's ear outside my cabin. My palms start sweating a little at the brief remembrance.

God, I'd had her on the verge of panting at just the idea of the two of us together, without so much as touching her . . . until her brother showed up and ruined it.

I can't even say she caught me at a weak moment. I hadn't been drinking, hadn't been feeling particularly emotional or in turmoil or any other certain way that might lead me to bad decision-making.

I'd just seen her there, looking fairly similar to how she looks right now—damp hair, tight shirt, fresh face—and couldn't push her away anymore the way I have been, when all I've wanted to do since the moment I met her was pull her close.

Part of me wonders if I crossed a line. Scratch that. I *know* I crossed a line. But I'm finding it difficult not to push the boundaries when Murphy is around.

I find the plastic bags in the next drawer and turn to where I placed the flour on the island, only to find Murphy resting her elbows on the marble, her tits squished together. And what's worse, I can tell by her body language that she isn't posing for me, so I can't even be irritated at her.

"I used to work at an Italian place that made the *best* butternut squash ravioli," she says, an easy smile on her face. "I swear I gained ten pounds working there because I kept ordering that dish to go after every shift."

I try to keep my eyes on the task at hand as I dump a healthy serving of flour into the plastic bag. Only once I'm rolling up the top of the flour bag do her words register.

"That's actually what I'm making," I say before I can stop myself.

Of course her eyes light up.

"Really?"

I nod.

"Are you planning to make enough to share?"

Honestly, I was planning to make a shit ton. I love to cook when I've had a few drinks, and I have this empty, shiny new kitchen that's still crazy clean and hasn't even really been broken in yet.

But I shouldn't be making Murphy ravioli, late in the evening, while she wears that and while my inhibitions are lower.

It reeks of all the trouble I told myself I wanted to avoid.

"No. I'm not."

Curt, not unkind, I remind myself.

Murphy's posture changes as she pulls back from the island so she's standing now. I can see her disappointment clearly on her face and in her body language, and I feel a lance of regret.

"I guess I *could*," I say, changing my tune with enough quickness to give me whiplash, clearly having another moment of weakness. "If you want some, I mean."

Murphy's lips twist, and I can tell she's not sure what to make of my response.

"It'll only add on a few extra minutes," I continue, suddenly wanting her to come with me to the kitchen so I can cook her a meal.

A favorite meal, at that.

She inclines her head in the direction of the hallway behind her. "I'm just gonna grab a sweater," she finally says, all signs of her earlier disappointment gone. "I'll meet you over there?"

I give her a small smile, a mixture of emotions brewing inside me. "Sounds good."

Twenty minutes later, I'm kneading dough on the stainless steel worktable while Murphy sits on the counter next to the sink, watching.

"How long have you been a chef?"

I glance over at her, my gaze traveling over her bare legs dangling off the edge.

"My whole life."

She lets out a small huff of laughter.

"You came from the womb sharpening your knives and kneading dough?"

I lift the dough in my hand and smack it down on the table, then begin pulling and stretching.

"Practically."

She gives me a big smile, which I return, feeling no regret for inviting her over. I'm enjoying her company too much. It feels comfortable and easy, and I'm already regretting that she'll have to leave after I feed us.

"I cooked a lot growing up," I explain. "My mom was always . . . She wasn't home really to make sure we had dinner and stuff, so I cooked for my brother and me a lot. When I was old enough, I got a job at a restaurant and just kind of worked my way up." I shrug. "It *feels* like my whole life."

"No college or anything?"

I glance over in her direction. "No, college wasn't for me."

"Yeah, me neither."

My shoulders ease, and I suddenly realize I was worried about if she'd judge me for that. Over the years, plenty of people have made the assumption that I'd never make anything of myself because I didn't go to college or get a degree. But not everybody is book smart. Not everybody wants what college offers.

Having Murphy get that alleviates the need to explain myself, and for that, I'm grateful.

"No college for you, huh?"

She shakes her head. "Nah. I knew if I went, I'd be committing myself to some kind of normal-person job. A teacher. Someone who works in HR. And that's not what I wanted."

"What *did* you want?"

I know she just moved home after living in LA for—what did she tell me—nine years? But whenever Memphis talks about it, he's cagey. Not that I thought to pry much before I actually met Murphy. But now, I'm curious.

"I wanted to be a singer."

My eyebrows lift, and the surprise must be evident on my face because Murphy gives me a bashful smile.

"I know, it's like a one-in-a-million thing, right? But sometimes you get the bug and you just have to really go for it or you'll always regret not knowing, you know?"

I nod my head, because I do know. I might not have gone after something as entertainment-esque as trying to make it in Hollywood, but I understand the idea that you have to pursue your dreams or you feel like you're suffocating.

My dream took me to Chicago for seven years and then spat me out like a rotten apple, a firm dismissal and a clear indicator that my dreams would never come true.

It's something I'm still coming to terms with, but hey, at least I tried.

"I'm assuming if you're back, things didn't work out so well?" I ask, wondering what happened in LA to send her back to her childhood home.

Especially when it seems like she so clearly doesn't want to be here.

Her face pinches slightly, just briefly, but then smooths over, and she gives me a smile that looks forced as hell.

"No, it didn't. But I figure there's always room in life to create a new dream, right? Just because one thing doesn't work out doesn't mean you can't try to find something else, something new that can still give your life meaning."

I watch Murphy as she stares at her legs, tugging on a loose string in the hem of her shorts, and realize that her pain is a lot more fresh than mine.

It's been almost a year since I left Chicago trying to figure out what to do in the wake of my downfall. I worked as a dishwasher at a Chinese restaurant and made sandwiches at a small deli during that time to pay the bills, but I also healed a little bit and let go of most of my bitterness and resentment about what happened.

It sounds like whatever crushed Murphy's dream is recent enough that the wound is still wide open and raw.

"There's always room for that," I finally say, and when she looks up at me, uncertainty on her face, I give her an encouraging smile. "And until you figure out what that is, there's always delicious butternut squash ravioli to make you feel better."

She breaks into laughter, and I enjoy the sweet sound of it far more than I should.

We talk of our mutual love of Italian food as I continue with the dough, rolling it out much flatter than I could do by hand. Eventually I slice it into long strips and funnel each piece through the pasta roller, leaving me with the ravioli casing.

I pull out the concoction I created before going in search of flour earlier. The butternut squash mixed in with ricotta, pecorino romano, and nutmeg is already giving off a delicious aroma that makes my mouth water in anticipation.

Explaining my steps to Murphy as I go, I slice the pasta into squares and dab the edges with an egg wash. Then I scoop out the filling and add a small amount to each square, finishing with adding the second piece of pasta on top, then pressing firmly to seal.

"Here's where the magic happens." I slide a pan onto the stove and turn on the burner. "The sage butter."

I hear Murphy hum to herself in eagerness, and I suddenly know I need to deliver the most epically delicious ravioli I've ever created.

I finish up the final steps—creating the compound butter, cooking the pasta, and mixing the two together—before plating and searching out forks and knives so we don't have to eat my masterpiece like cavemen.

For whatever reason, this feels like a dish to share, so I leave everything on one plate and set it next to Murphy.

"God, it smells so good," she says, her eyes glued to the pasta dish that I must admit looks pretty damn amazing.

"Let's see if the taste lives up to the aroma." I slice a piece in half, stab it with a fork, and pop it into my mouth.

I close my eyes for just a second, simultaneously evaluating and enjoying the fruits of my labor. But when I open them, I see Murphy watching me with a look in her eyes that I know well.

And that's when I realize how close we are, with her up on the counter and me standing next to her mostly bare legs.

I swallow the pasta, then before I can think better of it, I spear the other half of the piece I just cut with the fork and lift it up to Murphy's mouth.

She blinks, but opens for me, her tongue peeking out just slightly before she closes her lips around the tines.

Then her eyes mimic mine, closing briefly as she begins to chew.

I watch her, enraptured. Because never has someone else eating my food given me so much pleasure before.

She nods her head as she delights in my culinary creation, and when her lids flutter open again, that same look is there. Needy and desirous. My eyes drop to her lips where the sage butter left behind a sheen reflecting in the light of the kitchen.

I resist the urge to lean forward and take her mouth with mine. Instead, I shove that thought aside and cut another piece, take a bite, then lift the other half for her again.

I repeat this several times until we've finished the dish, nothing but a layer of butter and seeds left on the plate.

"That was incredible," she tells me. "You sure do know what you're doing."

"Yes, I do," I say, the thickness in my voice betraying the alternate meaning. I may know my way around the kitchen, but I know my way around a woman's body just as well. Maybe better.

I let my mind wander, imagining her legs wrapped around me, her hands lifting my shirt, my fingers slipping under the little sweater that she put on and cupping her breast.

My eyes drop down when I feel something against where I'm braced on the counter, then widen in surprise to discover Murphy's little finger is tucked against the side of my hand.

Without thinking, I shift my hand slightly, my fingers tracing gently around her wrist. I hear her breath catch in her throat, and when I look up into her eyes, that needy look is still there.

"This okay?" I trail a path up her calf and past her knee, my hand coming to a rest on her bare thigh.

Her head bobs, but she doesn't say anything.

And I get it.

There's something delicate here, something fragile that could snap and break at any moment.

I feel just boozy enough on the wine and far too drunk on her to pay my own internal warning system any further notice. I can smell the subtle notes of her perfume over the diminishing scent of dinner, and it's intoxicating.

I slide my hand upward, rubbing in gentle circles, my eyes never leaving hers. Her pupils begin to dilate and her breathing picks up pace the farther up my hand travels.

I move so my body is directly in front of her, her legs hanging off the edge of the counter on either side of me.

I'm playing with fire. I can feel it in my skin, in my bones, in the tiny cells pumping their way through my veins.

But I can't stop.

Part of me wants to believe that if we're barely touching, it doesn't count. That just this tiny little movement isn't anything to be truly worried about.

I have both hands on her now, one on each thigh, my thumbs stroking and massaging, then slipping just barely under the hem of her shorts. The skin there is just slightly warmer, and it's suddenly driving me crazy that I can't feel the rest of her. All of her.

"This okay?" I ask again.

She nods this time with her lips parted, her chest rising and falling in labored breaths that pick up pace as I reach the crease of her thigh.

"How about . . . this?" I whisper, one thumb stroking gently down the seam pressed against her core.

She gasps audibly, her eyes growing hooded. Her tongue pressing against the ridge of her front two teeth.

Her hips shift minutely under my hands, so I stroke her again, my dick growing firmer with each second of contact between us.

When she whimpers, I bite the inside of my cheek and try not to come just from that little noise alone.

"Wes," she whispers.

I shake my head, not wanting her to say anything else.

There's too much risk of either of us realizing the mistake we're making, and I feel too far gone to let my conscience get any louder than it is.

Murphy raises her hands and rests them gently on my shoulders. I take that as encouragement to continue and move my fingers again.

I stroke against the material of her shorts, reveling in the dampness I can feel beginning to soak through the fabric.

"Are you wet for me?" The question comes out practically a growl.

"Yes, Chef," she says, her words a breathy moan that hit me square in the chest.

Fuck.

Murphy closes her eyes, digging her fingers into my shoulders as her hips begin to shift and search for what she wants.

But I grip her firmly, slowing her movement until her eyes fly open and connect with mine.

"Don't move."

Murphy stills, but desperation lingers in her eyes.

I continue stroking her, lightly at first, a gentle pressure that's meant to tease her, before pressing more firmly to get a deeper reaction, then lightly again.

Minutes go by, and I can only imagine the torture building up inside of her, because it's certainly growing inside of me. A deep, pulsing throb that reverberates through my entire body.

She digs her fingers into my shoulders, her head falling back. Her eyes close and her mouth opens with a thready cry. She tremors under my hands as a climax works its way through her body. As she comes down from the high, I watch her in awe. The sight of her falling apart is the most erotic thing I've seen in my entire life.

She pants, attempting to catch her breath, as her gaze returns to mine, a lazy smile on her face.

I smile back at her, but it slips away as she reaches for my belt.

Her body freezes as I grip her hands, halting her movements.

And in that moment, I know any of the endorphins that were racing through Murphy's body have very suddenly and dramatically disappeared.

"Wha—" she starts but abruptly cuts off whatever she was about to say.

Then she's pushing me out of the way and hopping down off the counter.

"Are you kidding me?" She rounds the counter in the center of the kitchen and stands on the other side.

Something slices through my chest when I realize she's actively seeking physical distance from me.

"Look, Murphy—"

"Don't fucking *look, Murphy* me. You just made me come."

I wince, feeling the fire I allowed myself to play with burn and singe.

"And I'm glad I could do that for you," I say, the sound of my own words making me sick to my stomach. "But that's really as far as this can go."

She watches me, an incredulous look on her face.

"You're *glad* you could *do that for me?*" she echoes, her voice coming out high-pitched and awkward. "What the fuck was this?"

She looks . . . mortified. Regret slams into me, but not fast enough to right the wrong.

Murphy huffs out a laugh and then she's gone, out of the kitchen, her little Keds stomping against the smoothed concrete in the dining room before I hear the front door of the restaurant open and then close.

All the different things I should have said come to mind in that moment.

It's not a good idea.

I made a mistake.
I'm your boss.
But the truth is, all those are excuses.
And not a single one feels like a good enough reason to have ended things the way I did.

Chapter Eleven

MURPHY

Instead of returning to the house, I stomp angrily through the vineyard and over to the wine cellar. I punch in the code Micah used the other day and yank the door open.

I deflate almost instantly. The woody smell of the oak barrels mixing with the different fragrances of wine is somehow like a balm to my injured spirit.

Whenever I was upset when I was younger, I'd go into the wine cellar and hide in the back behind all the barrels, almost like I needed the lower temperatures to cool me off. That old building is gone, replaced by this new one that is taller and filled with more than three hundred barrels, according to Micah. But the feeling is the same, as if the scent does enough on its own to soothe me.

I wander between rows of different vintages, and I can't help the way my mind replays what just happened with Wes.

The way he watched me.

The way he touched me.

The way I fell apart in his hands.

And how quickly those incredible feelings and emotions turned sour when he shut me down seconds later.

I don't understand what the hell happened. How we could have been enjoying a moment like that, how he could make me come like that, only to deny moving things further? Was it some weird power trip? Play around with me and then pull away? Keep me wanting more?

I can't be sure, so I do what any girl would do in similar circumstances.

I grab a bottle of wine and a glass from the display that's kept stocked for winery tours, and I call my best friend.

"Hello?" she says, her voice groggy.

"I need to talk to you," I tell her as I drop cross-legged on the ground in the back of the cellar, the cool cement floor quickly seeping through my shorts and chilling my skin.

"Why are you calling me so late?"

I uncork the wine bottle and pour an oversize glass as I talk. "What if I told you that my boss just fingered me to an orgasm in the kitchen of our new restaurant and then refused to let me touch him afterward."

A beat passes, then I hear Vivian's voice again, sounding much more awake than she did a few seconds ago. "Girl, tell me *everything*."

After I take a long, healthy sip of my cabernet, I do. But I start at the beginning. What happened at the gas station, finding out he was my boss, and the way he's continued to lure me in only to shut me out. Then the nights at the bench . . . and the dirty talk outside his cabin yesterday.

When I'm finished, I'm worried she's hung up until she clears her throat.

"Say something," I beg, once I've gotten it all out. "I feel like I'm going crazy."

"I mean . . . What is there to say other than 'Come-gratulations'?"

"Be serious," I reply, half laughing.

"I *am* serious. He gave you one of the best orgasms of your life and barely touched you? Asked for nothing in return? Do you know how rare that is? That hasn't happened to me in weeks." There's a slight pause, and then her voice comes through the speaker much louder as she shouts out, "It must be very nice that your guy is so good at making you come!"

I tug my phone against my chest, giggling. "I hope your neighbors weren't woken up by your loud ass."

She laughs. "It would make me feel better knowing I'm not the *only* one being awoken in the middle of the night."

I scoff. "V, it is not even midnight."

"So? I went to bed two hours ago. I'm getting some beauty sleep. I have a meeting with a producer from Humble Roads in the morning."

"What's Humble Roads?"

"It's an indie label," she tells me, excitement thrumming through her voice. "Apparently they're very selective, but they're specifically looking for strong female recording artists. Joanie told me they're amazing at launching unknowns, so . . . we'll see what happens."

"God, that's so amazing. I'm so excited for you!" I hope my smile and happiness for her translates through the phone.

I made her promise me before I moved away that she'd update me on her success. The last thing I'd want is for her to keep things from me because she doesn't want to hurt me or something stupid like that.

I can be pissed for me and excited for her in the same breath.

"I know you are. And I hope you know that if they sign me, they'll also be signing all of our amazing cowrites."

I sigh and lean my head back against the wall, staring up at the wine barrels stacked high and looming above me on racks, my mind flitting over that idea before dismissing it outright.

"Well, don't be too attached if they tell you to scrap those songs, okay? You don't owe me anything."

"Enough about the stupid meeting tomorrow." Her tone brooks no argument. "I want to get back to this Wes guy."

I take an unladylike gulp of my wine at her return to our earlier topic.

"What do you think it all means?" I ask her. "There's something about it that makes me feel slutty."

"Okay, first of all, we both know you're not slutty or you'd still be here in LA, *amiright?*" her words coming out rapid fire. "And second, we also know you're not slutty because we denounce the existence and use of that word, *amialsoright?*"

My lips turn up at her sass. "Yeah, I know, but it just—"

"No buts," she interrupts. "You know the kind of woman you are. You know that you can do anything, or be anybody, or do anybody or be anything, and your worth is not impacted. Am. I. Right?"

I smile, my love for Vivian Walsh growing ever larger.

"I wish you had someone there to remind you of these things on a regular basis," she continues. "Like a me, but not as awesome as me, you know? Because clearly your family aren't going to be the ones to do it."

I snort, but the humor isn't really there, and I take another large sip of my wine.

"Have you hung out with anyone other than your hot boss?"

"Does sitting at a table with vineyard employees and my family count?" I ask, feeling a little embarrassed.

"No, it does *not*." Her voice rises slightly. "You need friends, lady. Real friends. People who are going to be in your corner and tell you what a baddie you are."

I contemplate her words. Do I need a friend? Do I need someone here to remind me of all the things Vivian has been saying?

Maybe.

"Official task for the to-do list!" she enthuses, and I groan.

This is a thing Vivian does all the time. She says it's how she keeps herself on track for her career, but it always seems like the *official tasks* she gives to *me* are never career related.

Typically they revolve around men. And self-care. And *being a baddie*, which makes me want to laugh just thinking about it.

"Finding a girlfriend that you can invite over for a slumber party."

I huff a laugh. "I'm twenty-seven, Vivian."

"So the fuck what?" she replies, and I giggle again. "We spent the night together constantly."

"That's because I hated my roommate and you wanted some-one who would keep you from eating family-size portions of frozen macaroni."

Vivian scoffs. "Don't act like our slumber parties weren't the *literal* joy of your life, Miss Hawthorne. I don't associate with liars."

I roll my eyes, but a smile is stretched wide on my face.

"I miss you," I tell her. "A lot."

"I miss you too, cutie-pie. It's why I'm getting the girls together to come visit you soon, okay? Don't think I didn't notice you've been a ghost in that conversation, either."

My nose wrinkles. "I know, I just don't know if it's a good idea to have everyone up here. You know? My life in LA was so different than my life here, and I feel like I need to sort things out with my family before I invite anything from that life to mix and mingle with this one."

"It better not be because you're embarrassed of me, Murph. Just because I speak loudly about the fact my boyfriend doesn't give me orgasms anymore," she says, yelling the latter part of her sentence loudly again, "doesn't mean I would do anything to embarrass you in front of your family."

I cover my face with a hand, trying to control my laughter. I know she's yelling at her boyfriend somewhere in her apartment, but I can only imagine what her neighbors must think.

"I know, V. I know."

"Listen, I really do need to get this good sleep, all right? But I'm not kidding about finding a friend, okay? Everyone needs friends."

I nod, but she can't see me so I just hum my agreement.

"And keep me posted on the chef. He sounds like fun."

I laugh, then tell her I love her and say goodbye.

I never had girlfriends like Vivian when I was younger. I was involved in choir and hung out pretty regularly with Quinn and her group of friends, but nothing like this. I've never laughed like I do with Vivian. Hell, I didn't even realize how much I enjoyed laughing until I met her.

It's hard to realize how much you love someone, and how import-ant they are to you, right before you leave them behind.

I read through the advertisement for what feels like the fifth time, double-checking that I've caught any grammatical errors. Once I feel satisfied, I send off the information in a mass email to the list of con-nections who will help get the word out. From larger, more legitimate sources, like the city's online employment listings and the high school career counselor, to more personal ones, like some of Dad's friends who still live around town.

My hope is that we get enough interest to be able to select from the most qualified applicants rather than just hire whoever applies.

But in this economy, you never know.

Clicking off the internet browser, I shift the mouse to the top cor-ner, preparing to set Memphis's computer to sleep mode when the name of a file on the desktop catches my eye.

Financials.

There's no real reason for me to go snooping through the vineyard's finances. Not really.

Except . . .

With his comment the other day about keeping the vineyard from bankruptcy, there's been a little voice in the back of my mind whisper-ing that things might be a lot more serious than I realize.

So.

I click on it.

It feels like another language. I've never been great at math or num-bers. Not like Memphis. He took a bunch of classes at the community college to help him manage the business side of things, and I remember my senior year hearing him brag about getting the top grade in his accounting class.

Yuck.

But some sort of understanding of finances would come in handy right now as I peruse a massive spreadsheet that looks to be tracking several years' worth of finances. The tabs on the bottom go back five years, and if I remember what Micah said correctly, that's about the time they built up the new cellar and upgraded the warehouse.

When I scroll all the way to the bottom of this year's page, though, it's easier to see what the problem is.

Every column has a negative number in bold red.

Even an idiot can deduce that's probably not a good thing.

And when I look at each of the other pages for the previous years, it's the same.

But before I can snoop any further, Memphis walks through the door.

"What are you doing?"

I click out of the spreadsheet and put the computer to sleep.

"Just finishing up sending out the hiring ads," I reply, shocked at how level and cool I sound considering I feel like a spy.

Memphis nods, seemingly appeased, and then we swap spots as I slip out to the other side of the table and he takes a seat.

I eye the door, thinking I got away with my snooping and should bolt. But if something's wrong with the vineyard . . .

Spinning to look back at Memphis, I decide to take the risky route instead.

"Hey, Memphis."

"Hmm," he replies, staring at his computer screen.

"How are things going? With the vineyard."

At that, he looks back to me, his expression serious, then leans back in his chair and crosses his arms.

"What do you mean?"

I sort of regret asking now that I have his full attention, but I push on anyway.

"I mean . . . Is everything going okay? You mentioned something about keeping the vineyard out of bankruptcy the other day and I was just"—I shrug a shoulder—"wondering."

There's a tic in his jaw, and that's when I realize his entire body looks tense and uncomfortable.

"Things are fine."

That's all he says, and I've never been less convinced.

But I decide not to push. I mean, if something was seriously wrong, there's no way Memphis would keep it a secret. There has to be some kind of explanation—a wrong formula or something—in the spreadsheet.

I'm sure that's it.

Or at least, I'm hoping that's it.

My brother has already turned his attention back to his computer, so I turn to walk out the door.

"Hey, Murphy," Memphis calls after me.

I spin, hope and worry both fluttering in my heart. Maybe he'll actually talk to me. Share what's really going on.

There's a risk that comes along with that, though. If he tells me something is seriously wrong, it's time to roll up my sleeves and help. Whatever it is. And part of me worries I'm still feeling too bitter. I came here because I need a soft-ish place to land, not because I wanted to invest myself fully into the family business again.

"Wes is heading to the Trager farm tomorrow to look at their supply and put in a recurring order for delivery. He needs some extra hands, but I can't spare anyone from the vines. I need you to go with him."

Whatever I was hoping Memphis would share isn't the direction he goes at all. I let out a long sigh, my emotions pinging all over the map.

Of course that's what Memphis would need me to do. Spend almost an entire day in the car with Wes—the man who is infuriatingly attractive and frustratingly closed off.

"Will that be a problem?"

I sigh again at the sound of Memphis's brick-wall voice returning. "No, it won't be a problem."

When I wake up in the morning, I text Memphis to ask him when I'm supposed to be meeting Wes. Instead of responding with a time, he just sends me Wes's number.

Which would have been fine had we just been a boss and employee, or whatever we are. But of course, now it looks like I've snooped around trying to get his phone number.

Though I can't deny the fact that a tiny part of me is glad to have it. Should I ever need it. Or something.

So I text Wes to let him know Memphis is sending me along, and we agree to meet up at the restaurant at ten o'clock, since that's where the vineyard truck is parked.

He gives me a friendly smile when I arrive, and the butterflies in my stomach take flight.

I still feel confused by what happened between us in the kitchen two nights ago. I'd been planning to spend my Sunday evening doing a little self-care and giving myself a pedicure. But instead, I'd sat on a kitchen counter and let Wes stroke me between my legs until I came.

And then he refused to move forward? Like, what hot-blooded man doesn't want to get laid? Or at least get a blow job?

Part of me wants to demand an explanation. What possible reason could there be for him touching *me* but refusing to let me touch *him*?

Instead, I return his smile, hop into the truck, and stare blindly out the window as Wes removes tools from the truck bed and places them in the bin on the back of an ATV parked a few feet away.

Then he loads up next to me.

"Mind if I turn on some music?" he asks, and when I shake my head, he reaches over and adjusts the radio. "All right, let's go."

The drive out to the Trager farm takes about thirty minutes, and we spend most of it in silence, each of us just staring ahead as some early 2000s punk band plays through the shitty speakers.

The nice thing about the relative silence is that it gives me a chance to just sit and stare out the window, watching plot after plot of farmland pass by as we drive farther into Rosewood.

Even though I never wanted to live here growing up, it wasn't ever about the area. Not really. I've never taken issue with the rolling hills, the quaint but bustling towns, and long rows of grapes that stretched on for what feels like forever. The weather's decent, if not a little dry, and the sunsets are beautiful.

It's the reason we came here in the first place that set me and Rosewood at odds. My mother's death, and my father's fear of handling two children and a newborn all on his own.

During a time of grief and pain, my brother and I had to also mourn the loss of our house and our friends and the life we had before. Unfortunately, I was just old enough for it to be the most horrible thing in the world, which also meant I was predisposed to hate Rosewood, regardless of how terrible or wonderful it really was when we arrived.

Part of me feels like I'm stuck in that same cycle now that I've been forced to return. But this time, I'm not so sure if I'll ever be able to leave again or if I'll be destined to stick around, which makes the emotional upheaval feel all the more dramatic.

As a child, this was the place I was forced to come after my mom died.

Now, it's the place I was forced to come after having someone intentionally ruin any chance I have at following my dreams.

Anybody would hate this town if they were in my shoes.

"I'm sorry about the other night."

I startle at the sound of Wes's voice, having been lost in my thoughts for who knows how long. He looks straight ahead, one arm forward, his wrist resting easily on the steering wheel.

"What?"

"I said, I'm sorry about the other night. In the kitchen," he continues, glancing at me briefly before returning his eyes to the road.

"What *was* that?" I prod, wanting answers if he's willing to share. "Because it feels like . . . I mean, were you grossed out by something or not . . . turned on or . . . ?"

I wrinkle my nose at how insecure that makes me sound, but I don't try to backtrack. Even though I'm not insecure about most things, I *am* in this moment.

Wes sighs and flicks his blinker, turning us down the dirt lane that leads into the Trager farm. We both jostle at the uneven ground, the wheels bouncing us lightly.

"Part of me feels like I *should* tell you that I wasn't turned on. That might make everything easier. At least for you." He glances at me again. "But it couldn't be further from the truth. I can't remember being so turned on in my entire life."

I give him a look that says *I call bullshit.* "And that made you . . . *not* want anything to move further?" Confusion lingers heavy in my voice and heart. "Because that makes absolutely zero sense to me."

He's quiet for a while, but I get the feeling he's trying to sort something in his mind. Wes seems similar to Micah in that way, like he wants to fully think something through before he says or does it.

"The only thing I can tell you, Murphy, is that I *really* need this job."

Something inside my mind clicks, and my shoulders ease. But I prod him a bit more, just to make sure I'm understanding him correctly.

"You're pushing me away because you're worried about Memphis?"

"You can probably get away with doing whatever—or whoever—you want," Wes replies, and I can't help the small smile that blooms at what he says. "But I'm disposable. I'm not family. I'm not a close friend or someone who has been working for your family for years. And I can't . . ."

He trails off, his voice growing tight.

"I can't take that kind of risk, Murphy. I'm sorry."

I stare out the window as we pull up to the massive barn at the end of the lane. Wes brings the truck to a halt and turns off the engine.

"So if we weren't a boss and employee, and if you weren't working for my brother . . ."

I glance down when I feel something touch my pinkie where my hands are slightly tucked under my thighs. Wes's hand is right there on the seat, his own finger pressed lightly against mine.

It's a repeat of how I touched him in the kitchen, and it blends this moment with that one.

"It took *everything* inside me to stop," he whispers.

His eyes seem to search mine. It sends a surge of need racing through me, and my heart picks up speed.

I'm not sure whether knowing his true thoughts and feelings makes everything better or worse. It feels good to know I wasn't being rejected. But it also feels like the absolute worst torture to know we both want something to happen that won't because circumstances are in the way.

I want so desperately to lean in and kiss him. To taste his lips and give us both what we've been craving since that night we first met.

My face must give away the fact I have a lot going on inside my head, because Wes's gaze is just as hungry. He opens his mouth like he wants to say something else. But a tap on the truck jerks us both out of the moment.

Keith Trager is standing by the front bumper, grinning at us. I wave hello, a tight smile on my face, and he waves in return.

Then I take a deep breath and let it out.

"Let's get to work," I tell Wes.

He nods, and we push our doors open and hop out of the truck.

"Well, look at you, Miss Murphy!" Keith says, his smile growing as I round the front to give him a hug. "I didn't know you were home."

"Just got back to town," I reply. "Gonna be helping with the new restaurant."

"That's just great. I bet your pops is really glad to have you around, helping out."

I smile, but don't address what he said. If only he knew how my dad has been ignoring me since I've gotten back.

"How's Quinn doing?" I ask.

At the mention of his daughter, Keith beams at me. "Ah, she's doing great. She's pregnant, you know. Seven months."

"I saw something about that online. Congratulations." I'm tugging some hair that has blown into my face back behind my ear when a thought occurs to me: "Hey, does she still have the same number?"

He nods. "Sure does."

I grin. "I've been thinking I might give her a call."

Keith gives me a fatherly look at that. "Aw, you know I bet she'd love that. You two were thick as thieves growing up. I'm sure it'll be fun shootin' the shit and catching up on old times."

I'm not so sure about the whole *thick as thieves* thing, but he's right that it will be nice to catch up. And who knows? Maybe I'll be able to tick *making a friend* off the official task list.

Keith turns to look at Wes, who's just joined us at the front of the truck. "And you must be the new chef. Keith Trager, nice to meet you."

"Wesley Hart. Nice to meet you as well." Wes shakes the man's hand. "I believe Memphis spoke with you about giving me a tour of the farm and the produce you harvest. I have a menu I'm finalizing for the restaurant, using almost exclusively local produce and protein. Sourcing as many of those items from you as possible would be wonderful."

Something softens in Keith's grin. "Isn't that nice," he says. "You're doing that farm-to-table stuff we always hear about on HGTV."

Wes chuckles. "You're absolutely right."

"I've got lots for you to look at," Keith says, turning to walk toward the barn and waving at us to follow. "We sell about eighty percent of our harvests to grocery stores, since they generally order large quantities. But we have a handful of restaurants and other businesses that put in regular orders as well, so we're definitely familiar with the distribution lines. There's a local guy who handles the deliveries, and I can get you in contact with him if you end up wanting to put in an order."

Keith motions for us to join him on a golf cart parked next to the barn, and then we're riding along a dirt path that splits the farm.

I've been to the Trager farm plenty of times growing up to hang out with Quinn. Plus, Dad and Keith have known each other since *they* were in primary school, and both grew up in families that tended to land. But it's been a while since I've been here, and I love getting a chance to drive around and see everything again.

I listen quietly as Keith points out the different crops to Wes, and the two discuss the restaurant menu and what the Trager farm might be able to provide during different times of the year.

I didn't realize that Wes was doing a farm-to-table menu. Most of the places I've waitressed at have been highly processed chains, though the Italian place I worked at most recently was a lot pricier and had better ingredients.

"Why farm to table?" I ask him a little while later as we walk behind Keith toward a row of harvest trailers. "Seems a lot more complicated."

"It is," Wes says, "but my mentor was always preaching about it. It's not only better ingredients, it also serves the community where the restaurant is located in a more direct way. Plenty of farms are now completely reliant upon major corporations that undercut them on pricing, and sourcing local means I get to give our dollars directly to my neighbor instead of a big-box store."

I'm surprised at his answer, but not because I doubt him. Everything he says makes sense and meshes with the things I heard growing up about not only our vineyard but also the local farms and crops. I'm surprised because I pegged Wes as a kind of bad-boy-chef type. Someone who might do well on those cooking shows on TV. A little rugged, a little charming, good with a knife, and hot as hell.

But really, it sounds like he's a softy at heart. Someone who cares about small business and the environment. The type of person who wants to care for his neighbor over self-profit.

The more I get to know him, the more he shows me who he is. And the more he gives me, the closer I want to get.

Shit.

Chapter Twelve

Wes

After we look through the harvest trailers, Keith puts together a couple of boxes of produce for me to take back to the vineyard.

"This will give you a pretty good idea of our crops and the quality we yield," he says as I look through everything. "Just give me a call if you want to do a single order or if you want to set up something recurring. Jack and I go way back, and I'd love to be able to support this new venture."

I reach out and shake Keith's hand, then stack up two of the boxes to carry them out to the truck. Murphy grabs the other two. And then we're loading up and giving Keith a wave goodbye before pulling back onto the long dirt road heading out to the highway.

"He seems like a nice guy," I say to Murphy, both of us jostling again over the uneven dirt road.

"Keith's great," she says, her gaze wandering out the window.

"You're friends with his daughter? The pregnant one?"

"Yeah. Quinn and I were in choir together."

"That's right . . . You can sing."

She shakes her head, a barely perceptible movement, though her gaze stays fixed on the passing fields. "I *used* to sing."

I want to pry, but something tells me now isn't the time.

We pull out onto the highway heading back to Rosewood, and get about ten minutes away from the Trager farm before I start to notice a little wobble to the ride.

"Shit." I pull off to the dirt embankment on the side.

"What's wrong?"

"I think we have a flat."

Murphy groans. "Seriously?"

I get out and, sure enough, the back right tire is flat.

"Must have popped on that dirt road," I say as I step back up into the cab. "Looks like you are officially the bringer of flat tires."

Murphy laughs and pulls her phone out, glancing at it before showing me her home screen. It's a picture of the beach at sunset, and the time says 1:45 p.m.

I must look at her for too long because she points to the top corner. "No service," she says. "We can either try and flag someone down who will drive us to the vineyard, we can walk back to the Trager farm, or we can walk home. We're kind of at the halfway point, so"—she shrugs—"it's up to you."

Chuckling, I step back out of the truck. "Looks like we have a bit of a walk ahead of us, then, don't we?"

"Looks like it," she echoes, hopping out and eyeing me across the bench seat. "Too bad there isn't some heroic Good Samaritan ready and willing to help this time around."

"Oh, I'm willing. I just gave you my spare already."

We laugh and round to the back, tugging out the boxes of produce and moving them to the cab before I lock up and we begin our walk west. Thankfully the spring weather is still just cool enough that nothing will go bad before we get back.

"You said your mentor was into farm to table," Murphy says after we've been walking for a few minutes. "Have you been cooking that way your whole career?"

I kick the dirt slightly. The question stings a little bit. "I wish. It's hard to put those kinds of boundaries on a job search when you're in desperate need of one that pays well. There are plenty of times people are forced to sell their soul in the restaurant industry."

And that's not nearly the whole story. Just about everyone I know has been through it. Half make it out alive, the other half get burned.

I'm in the latter group, unfortunately.

"What do you mean?"

I tuck my hands in my pockets, the direction of Murphy's questions making my palms more sweaty than the sunny walk is.

"Oh, you know. Everyone has their own idea about how things should be run, that's all. And if you really need a job, you just have to follow orders and bank the experience so you can do it your own way one day."

Murphy hums, but it sounds like she doesn't exactly agree with me.

Instead of prodding, I decide to turn the spotlight back on her. We'll see how she likes all the invasive questioning.

"You were a waitress back in LA, right? You know how toxic restaurant culture can be."

"I do. It's rife with big egos and alcoholism, and it's incredibly incestuous."

"Incestuous?" I repeat, laughing.

Murphy laughs, too. "Oh, you know what I mean. Everyone sleeps with everyone." Then she pins me with a look. "And don't try to deny it."

I give her a tight grin. "I wouldn't dare."

"I wasn't really that person, though. At my first job, almost the entire restaurant got gonorrhea from one guy, and that was enough of a warning for me to keep my lure out of the company pond." Then she looks at me again. "For the most part."

At that, my smile comes a lot easier and something inside me becomes lighter.

I don't know what it is, but talking with Murphy just makes me want to smile. When her brother isn't talking down to her, and when I'm not being an asshole pushing her away, she's a pleasure to be with.

Our conversations are relaxed, and I can't remember the last time I had something like that. Something that felt equal parts fun and good and easy.

That's what it is. Talking with Murphy is *easy*.

Hell, everything with her is easy. The laughter, the conversation, the way she turns me on.

I'd tried to be as honest as I could with her earlier without intentionally making things more difficult. For me or for her. Just talking about the other night in the kitchen sends little sparks of need flickering through me. Remembering the way she fell apart under my touch is indelible in my mind. Of course I replayed it at least a dozen times when I was back in my cabin later that night, desperate to relieve the tension.

But Murphy doesn't need to know those things. If she really knew exactly how interesting I find her, how much she turns me on, how amazing I feel when I'm near her, I'm not sure if she'd let me pull away so easy.

And part of me thinks she feels the same.

She has her own walls up, whether from her family's issues or whatever she left in LA. I can sense it, and I can't help wanting to know why.

"What was it like balancing being a waitress with the singing stuff?" I ask casually, hoping she'll want to open up to me about it.

"Not too terrible. After nine years of trying to get my name out there and trying to make connections, I was starting to feel a little exhausted, to be honest." She pauses. "I've never actually admitted that before. Not even to myself." She is studiously focused on the dirt and gravel along the side of the road where we're walking. "It makes me wonder if I wasn't really cut out for it all."

When she finally looks over at me, she must not like something in my expression.

"It's okay, you can tell me you think I was stupid to try to be a singer. Everyone else did."

My brow crinkles. "What? I don't think it's stupid."

"You don't?"

I shake my head. "No. I think it's incredibly brave."

She looks surprised at my answer. "Well, you're the only one."

"Really?"

Murphy nods. "My family thought I was crazy for moving so far away. That I was too young and went too far for a dream that was out of reach." This time, she's the one who kicks at the dirt, her foot connecting with a small rock that shoots forward and rolls to a stop about ten feet in front of us.

"Well, they're wrong. And unless they're the ones who picked up and moved away, who took on all of the uncertainties and risks that come with striking out on your own, they don't get to judge your choices like that."

Her eyes are still on the dirt road, and she kicks the rock again once we reach it, but I can tell she's listening intently.

"They should have told you what they really thought, which is probably that they were sad you left, and they missed you while you were gone, or that things were more difficult for them while you were away. But most people don't like to get vulnerable that way because it makes them sound selfish. And it *is* selfish. It's selfish to make someone else carry your emotions because they're a burden you don't know how to carry yourself."

Murphy stops suddenly. I come to a halt and face her.

"You know, I've never had anyone explain things to me like that before. Are you sure you want to be a chef and not a therapist?"

I laugh, and she does too, before we start walking again.

"God, I wish I had my shit together enough to be a therapist." This time I kick the rock Murphy has been nudging along. "But alas, I'm just as fucked up as you are."

"Oh, thanks a lot." She laughs.

"Everyone's fucked up, though. We all have trauma and emotional baggage from our past that we wouldn't wish on our worst enemy."

At that, I kick the rock a little too hard and it shoots way out in front of us.

"Just because you were starting to feel exhausted in the end doesn't mean anything except that you were on a hard road. Going after your dreams isn't supposed to be easy. There are supposed to be challenges and things that knock you off-balance. It's that line from Tom Hanks in *A League of Their Own*, you know? 'If it wasn't hard, everyone would do it. It's the hard that makes it great.'"

"Yeah," she says, her voice suddenly much more quiet and melancholy.

I can feel her wanting to say something else, so I keep my mouth shut, hoping that she'll get whatever it is off her chest. That she'll share whatever this thing is that she's carrying around inside her.

We approach the rock again, but Murphy passes it by without even looking at it.

And the longer we walk without saying anything else, the less likely I think it is that she'll end up sharing whatever is swirling around in her mind.

We're both exhausted and sweaty when we finally make it back to the Hawthorne property about an hour after we left our truck on the highway. The back half of our journey was a lot quieter than how it started.

I think Murphy was lost in her thoughts about LA, and I was wrapped up in thinking about the reasons I left Chicago.

"I'd like to go take a shower," Murphy says as we reach the end of the long drive that leads to their house from the road. "But I can drive you back out to the truck to change the tire if you give me about a half hour?"

I shake my head. "Don't worry about it, Murphy. I can get one of the grounds crew to help me out. Or your brothers."

She considers me for a moment. "Are you sure?"

"Yeah."

"Okay, well . . . Thanks for the chat." Her eyes glimmer in the sunlight, and she seems to have a little more spirit than she did on the last part of the walk. "You're really easy to talk to."

I grin at her. "Make sure you call your insurance and see if I'm in your network. These therapy sessions aren't free, you know."

She laughs, and I relish the sound. But I can see the cloud of whatever is on her mind still lingering, and I wish there was something I could do to help.

"Have a good afternoon, Wes," she says with a little wave.

"Later, Murph."

I watch her as she heads through her front door, wishing there was something I could do to pull her out of the weird headspace.

But with nothing immediate and curative coming to mind, I turn to head on up the path, hoping to bump into someone who can help me load a spare tire and take me back to the truck.

Eventually, I find Naomi jumping onto the ATV at the end of one of the vines, and she gives me and a new tire a lift. But the tire replacement takes longer than I expect, and by the time I've returned to the property and get the produce put away, I've missed dinner. So I trudge out to my cabin and take a shower, eager to rinse off the sweat and grime from the day.

As I stand under the water, letting the heat pound down on my body, I think back to everything that happened, starting with our conversation in the car.

It didn't surprise me that Murphy asked about where my head was after we fooled around in the kitchen on Sunday evening. But it *was* surprising how talking to her about it made it seem more manageable. Like having her know that I'm concerned about my job has now released me from solving the *problem* of my attraction to her on my own.

And maybe *that's* why I love talking to Murphy so damn much.

I thought it was easy earlier, as if having simple conversation and some good laughs were the highlights.

But that's not it at all.

I love talking to Murphy because it feels like we're both coming to the table with heavy burdens, excess baggage on our shoulders, and sharing some of that with each other takes away some of the stress, even a little bit of the pain.

It's not that things with Murphy are easy. It's that simply being around Murphy makes things easier.

I've heard it said before, but trauma bonds people. I've always assumed it needed to be a shared trauma. But really, it's just the ability to look at the other person and acknowledge that you've both been through some really hard times.

Because you can look at the other person and know you're not alone.

◆ ◆ ◆

That night, I get a text from Murphy. Her name popping up on my screen sends a surprising shot of excitement through me.

Murphy: Any chance you're heading to the bench tonight?

I'd been planning to go for a walk, absolutely. I don't think I've gone a single night here when I haven't taken advantage of the wide-open space to clear my head, but the added appeal of getting to bump into Murphy has definitely changed the way I anticipate that time.

I try not to reprimand myself for how quickly I respond. My desire to see her and spend more moments together isn't something I'm willing to address just yet.

Me: Yeah. I'll be leaving in a few minutes.

A thumbs-up bubble shows up in the corner of my message, and I set my phone down to search my cabin for a clean pair of socks.

Ten minutes later, I've got my shoes on, a bottle of wine in one hand and two glasses in the other. For the first time, Murphy is already there when I arrive, and I can't help the way my chest swells when I see her eyes brighten at my approach.

"Hey."

She smiles. "Hey."

I take a seat next to her and hand her a glass, before making quick work of pouring each of us a glass of Syrah.

"Cheers," Murphy says, clinking hers against mine before taking a long sip.

I follow, placing my nose to the edge and inhaling first, then tilting the glass back and enjoying the way the tannins burst across my tongue.

"Thanks for coming out tonight," she says, after we've been sitting silently together for a few minutes. "I'm sorry for being such a downer earlier. We were having a fun conversation, and I just got kind of lost in my head."

I reach out and place my hand on hers, squeezing gently.

"You don't have to apologize. Life is hard and sometimes reflecting on it is even harder."

She nods, and again, like earlier, I get the sense that she wants to keep talking, that she has something important to say.

"And if you want to talk about it, I'm happy to listen," I add.

Murphy looks at me, and something softens in her face for just a brief moment, before a glimmer of sadness begins to creep back into her expression.

"I went to LA to become a singer, right?" she starts, her voice quiet.

She shifts where she's sitting, so her body is angled facing forward, and I get the feeling she's putting a barrier in place. As if it's safer to tell me her secrets without looking me in the eye.

"For years I worked every shift I could, lived in shitty roommate situations, and dealt with asshole coworkers and nightmare customers. For nine years, I sacrificed. And then, right when I was this close to my dream"—she lifts her fingers up and pinches them together—"it got snatched away by this fucking . . . misogynistic *creep*."

She sets her glass on the bench next to her and shakes out her hands, like even thinking about it is too much to handle.

"I was signed to an agent. Paul was a real, honest-to-goodness agent with a really great record label. It was literally the dream. There was another girl . . . Dierdre. We'd crossed paths at various gigs around Hollywood, and we got along okay. So when Paul called us in together to talk about 'our futures,' we went together and sat in the waiting room and talked about what this could all mean for us and . . ." She takes a deep breath and lets it out long and slow.

"He called us in together and the conversation started simple enough. Expectations. Attitude. *Performance*."

I wince when she says the last word like that, something icky creeping into the back of my mind at where this is going.

"And I guess I was a little more naive than I thought because he literally took his dick out and started stroking it while he was talking, and when I looked over at Dierdre, absolutely horrified, she looked like nothing was wrong. You know? Just a penis out, no big deal."

She growls then, her anger and frustration and whatever happened coming out in a guttural noise.

"And then he let us know that if we expected to get anywhere in the music world, we'd need to get used to knowing how to *get ahead*. The unspoken part of that sentence was 'by giving head.'"

My nostrils flare, my own anger beginning to course through my body at the idea of some gross prick talking to her like that.

"Dierdre walked up to his desk and dropped to her knees, right there, with me in the room," she continues. "I nearly vomited on the floor, and I told Paul he was a disgusting asshole and didn't he know that men like him couldn't get away with shit like this anymore."

Her voice hitches, and that's when I realize she's crying.

"And then he looked me in the eyes with this . . . glint, this smug fucking glint, and said, 'Watch me,' and then tilted his head back as Dierdre . . ."

She stands then, walks a few feet away, and kicks at a stick on the edge of the grassy hill where we are, sending it flying into the vineyard stretched before us. Her hands are balled into tight fists, her eyes closed. Her posture feels like a contained scream, and I swear it echoes in the open space around us.

I want to hug her or something. Pull her into me and take her pain away. But I know I can't fix something like this. This kind of manipulation and abuse of power is . . . so wrong.

Murphy stares out into the distance and wipes at her face before she turns to sit next to me again.

"He called me the following day," she continues, her voice returning to that quiet, melancholy state. "Told me the label had decided they were going to pass, and that I was a cunt who would never have a singing career." She turns and looks at me. "He blacklisted me, so I came home."

I run a hand through my hair, my anger at the injustice she faced melding with my frustration at the fact I can't do anything to fix this.

What I'd like to do is find this Paul guy and wring his neck.

I shift over, bringing my body up next to hers, and wrap my arm around her shoulders. It's the only thing to do right now, and the idea that I shouldn't be this close to her because of work is like a puff of smoke disappearing in the breeze.

"I did the right thing," she says, her voice choking slightly. "I refused to do something that felt so . . . wrong. All I feel is this sickness in my stomach, like he didn't just steal my dream, you know?"

I rub her back, trying to be here for her in any way I can. She leans her head on my shoulder, a sob racking her body.

"I thought he signed me because he thought I was talented," she continues. "He was the first person to make me feel like I could be something, and it was all a lie because he wanted something else."

"I'm so sorry, Murphy."

But my words feel hollow and unhelpful, and Murphy continues to cry.

I hold her close and wish there was anything else I could do. Anything else I could say.

Instead, I'm overwhelmed by the feelings coursing through me.

Because listening to Murphy's story reminds me a little bit of my own. Of a chance I had to get ahead by selling a chunk of my soul.

Murphy looked the devil in the face and told him she wasn't for sale.

And there isn't a day that goes by that I don't look back and wish I'd done the same.

Chapter Thirteen

MURPHY

Wes and I reach a level of friendship after that night at the bench that I wasn't anticipating. I guess sharing horribly embarrassing stories with someone bonds you.

All I know is, after that, it feels like I'm not so alone.

I spend the next few days helping wherever I can with getting things ready for the opening. If we're planning to get staff in here and trained soon, we need things to be set up.

Long hours go by in the dining room setting up tables and chairs, unloading and unpacking all the plates and bowls and cutlery, and organizing things in a way that makes sense behind the bar until the sommelier comes in and sets it up better.

And through all those hours over those several days, I can't help but notice how often Wes pops his head out of the kitchen, or comes over to help me move something heavy, or asks me to taste something he's working on.

He's started training two line cooks on his tentative menu, and we spend time in the evening, on our bench, talking about how green they are and how dire the résumé situation is for the server and host positions I advertised at the start of the week.

There's a kind of camaraderie between us. A *we're in it together* feeling that I'm really enjoying.

And in the same breath, I can't help but acknowledge how quickly I'm beginning to fall for him.

Wes isn't the charming guy I first met at the gas station, and he's not the playboy I thought he was when his attitude soured, or the jerk who kept me at arm's length. Those were masks he put on, at first to entice me and then to push me away.

No. He's so much more than any of those small, insignificant labels.

Wes is . . . Well, he's kind, for one thing. He's also a man who legitimately cares about the people around him. And after years and years of being surrounded by self-centered, egotistical fame-seekers, I can't help but admire almost everything about him.

I don't know his backstory, or how he maneuvered his way through the culinary industry, but I get the feeling he's been through something difficult. He's mentioned his younger brother a few times and hinted that he might have taken care of him when their parents weren't around.

That kind of heart, that dedication to family, is something I so admire.

It makes me feel a little ashamed of how quickly I turned tail and scurried off to LA. How little effort I made to stay connected to my family.

That fight with Memphis? It's true . . . He *could* have called me. He *could* have come to visit me. But he's not the only one. And I can either shove all the blame onto him or Dad, and stay mad at them for all the ways they failed, or I can acknowledge that all of us were hurting, for whatever reason, and try to repair the relationships that have fallen into disrepair because we were each too stubborn to extend a hand.

◆　◆　◆

I knock on the door to Memphis's office, poking my head in when I hear his brisk "Come in."

I cross over to take a seat opposite him at the desk.

"What do you need, Murphy?"

I shake off the clipped way he speaks to me, reminding myself that I'm here to bridge the gap, not critique my brother when he's under a lot of stress.

"I don't need anything. I was just coming to see how you're doing."

His gaze disconnects from the computer screen, and he turns his body toward me, a single eyebrow rising infinitesimally higher than the other.

"What do you *need*, Murphy?" His voice is a little softer this time, as if I'm a child coming to ask Dad for fifty bucks.

I roll my eyes.

"I'm telling you, I just came to see how you're doing. I don't *need* anything."

He assesses me for a minute before turning to focus on his computer screen again.

"How's the dining room coming along?"

"Tucked the last of the extra chairs into the storage closet and put the decor along the mantel. It looks really good."

"Mm-hmm, and how's the hiring going?"

I cross one leg over the other and settle back in my chair, realizing that trying to "check in" with my brother means he's going to go over all the work stuff. Because the man doesn't know how to have a life outside of this vineyard.

"I have a handful of applications, but I need to look into more creative ways to advertise because I am *not* impressed."

He clicks his mouse a few times, his eyes narrowing at whatever he's looking at.

"You should talk to Ryan, see if he can help."

My brow furrows. "Who's Ryan?"

"A friend of mine from high school. He works for the radio station. Maybe you could do an advertisement or something." He looks to me briefly. "I've been prepping text for a spot that's scheduled for this week, but maybe two birds with one stone? I know you were hoping to interview in a few days, so this could be perfect timing to grab some last-minute résumés."

I purse my lips, surprised at my brother's creativity. "Great idea, Memphis. Email me the text you prepped and I'll merge them together."

He nods, then returns his focus to the computer.

"All right, now that work stuff is handled, how are *you* doing?"

Memphis sighs. "And I'll ask again, what do you—"

"Jesus Christ, Memphis. I don't *need* anything." I clench my hands into fists. "I'm literally just asking how you're doing. Is that so hard to believe? That a sister would care about how her brother is doing?"

He turns his chair so he's facing me dead-on, then leans forward so his arms are resting on the desk, his hands steepled together.

"Murphy—"

"Memphis, I'm sorry I heaped all the blame on you, okay?" I decide to get straight into the nitty-gritty instead of trying to chat first. "I could have called. I could have visited, too. But sometimes it feels like you see me as an employee instead of a sister. Like the only times you care about me are when I'm giving you *extra hands* for the vineyard. It felt that way before I moved away, and it feels that way now."

I cross my arms, but then uncross them, leaning forward and resting my own arms on the table and placing my hands on my brother's.

"Right now, I'm trying to find my way back to a place where you're my brother, not my boss. And the only way I can think to do that is to try to talk to you about *you*. Not the vineyard. Not the restaurant. Not Dad or Micah or anybody else. So I'll ask you again. How are *you* doing?"

Concern flickers behind Memphis's eyes. It reminds me of how he looked that first day at the restaurant, when I stormed out and he told me I had no idea how much he needed things with the new restaurant to be successful. Now that I've seen the spreadsheet on his computer—the one bleeding red with debt—his intensity makes a lot more sense.

He looks tense and agitated, and I'm preparing for him to shut me down and get back to work when he sinks down into his chair. The mask falls away, revealing to me just how exhausted he really is.

"I don't know how I'm doing, Murph," he finally says, his voice tired.

He runs his hand across his face before digging it into his hair.

"I appreciate the sentiment. I do. But right now, there is no delineation between me and this vineyard, or me and this restaurant, okay? I live, sleep, and breathe this place, every day. So I can't separate for you. I don't have anything personal going on in my life to talk to you about, Murphy. I just have work."

I know how that feels. I did it for nine years while I was in LA, only rarely getting the chance to visit the beach or go on a hike or take advantage of being in one of the most exciting cities in the world. Instead, I worked constantly. And in the free moments I had, I was either writing music, performing at open mic nights, or trying to set up more gigs.

It was exhausting.

And the only thing that helped was having people to talk to about it. People who understood. Like Vivian, who was also working her ass off and trying to climb the ladder of success.

Maybe I can be that person for Memphis.

"Okay, then tell me about work. And I don't mean ask me questions about how I'm pulling my weight. I mean talk to me about work. If you're sleeping, eating, breathing it, you must have a lot on your mind."

He lets out a long sigh and rubs a hand against the stubble on his jaw, glancing back at his computer before returning his attention to me.

"You want to know what's really going on?"

I nod, giving him a soft smile of encouragement, thankful that he's finally going to share whatever is burdening him.

"We've got one year to figure things out, or Dad's selling the vineyard," he says.

My smile falls, shock coursing through my body.

"What?"

Memphis nods, his expression solemn. "He's a hard worker, our dad, but he had no idea what he was doing when Grandpa handed over the reins. We've been in the red for far longer than is sustainable, and a couple months ago, Dad said he was considering selling to some rich couple who offered him way more than the vineyard was worth."

"What? Why would he do that?"

"It's happening a lot more now. People with money buy up vineyards as pet projects, something to show off to their other rich friends." He rolls his eyes. "The Sheltons did it a few years ago, and the people who bought it ran that place into the ground within two years."

My nose wrinkles, trying to even picture that happening.

"And he seriously considered it?"

Memphis nods. "More than considered. He invited the couple to stay at the vineyard for a week. They walked around and talked about everything. I thought it was a done deal."

My mouth parts at the knowledge that my father was contemplating the idea of getting rid of this place.

"But . . . our whole lives he's been talking about how Hawthorne Vines is our legacy. *Your* legacy," I say, repeating something my father has said to us literally for as long as I can remember. "How can he just—"

I'm not even sure how to finish my sentence.

"Give up?" Memphis finishes for me. "Easy. He convinced himself he was doing me a favor."

"But, I mean obviously he didn't do it. Right?"

"I convinced him to give me time to try to salvage things."

My shoulders fall.

"That's why you're doing the restaurant."

Memphis nods.

"Now you understand why I need it to go well. Why I hired someone like Chef Hart to oversee everything. I figured a name like his could draw people in, people who are really into food and wine in a way we haven't been able to reach yet."

My head tilts to the side as I try to understand what he means.

"Why would Wes draw people in?"

"Wes is like . . . an internationally recognized chef," Memphis says, his brow furrowed like he can't believe I didn't know. "He's won a ton of awards and has opened up like five restaurants. He's one of the youngest James Beard winners ever." Then my brother chuckles. "Seriously, Murphy, do you not google people when you meet them?"

I blink a few times, trying to catalog what he's just told me against what I know about Wes so far.

Wes . . . the soft heart. Wes . . . the guy who cares about everyone. Wes . . . who puts family first . . . is a celebrity chef?

"So when I say I'm betting the farm on this restaurant," Memphis continues, leaning back in his chair, looking deflated and more exhausted than I've ever seen him, "I really mean it."

It makes sense now, why he was so intense the other day as we were starting to talk about servers and staffing. He wants Wes to be in charge of everything because he's hoping this renowned chef will be his star quarterback and lead him—and everyone—to victory.

But even if Wes *is* as talented as Memphis claims, that seems like way too much pressure to put on the shoulders of a single person when there are a lot of factors that go into a successful restaurant.

"How can I help?" I realize this is why my brother was so enthused about me coming home to help when we first talked. "What can I do?"

He lets out another long sigh and scratches the back of his neck. "Honestly? I've been really impressed with everything you've done so far, Murph. Just keep doing what you're doing."

I try not to let his compliment puff me up so visibly, but I can't help it when I sit taller at his words.

"I'm serious, Memphis. Tell me what else to do. There has to be something more. You said you needed extra hands. I have extra hands."

He runs his hand through his hair again, seeming to think it over. "I'll think about it," he finally says. "And I'll let you know."

I nod. "No problem. And I'll keep you posted on staffing, okay?"

He gives me this look—one that's slightly pleased but also tired and spent, both mentally and physically—before he returns his attention to his computer.

Taking that as my cue, I push out of my chair and head for the office door.

"Hey, Murphy?"

I turn back, and he's smiling at me. And I feel like it's the first time since I've been home that I've actually made him happy.

"Thanks. I really appreciate it."

I give him a wave and then head through the house and down the hall to my bedroom. Leaning back against the closed door, I let the severity of what Memphis just shared with me truly sink in.

Selling the vineyard.

I can't even . . .

My brain doesn't know where to go with that information. It's so contrary to everything Dad has ever said about this property that it feels false. Incredibly false. But it's not like I'd really know or anything, considering the fact we've exchanged only a handful of words in the few weeks I've been home.

And while I might have felt strong enough to face my brother and try to patch things up, it feels like my wounds with Dad are a lot deeper. I'm not ready to throw myself on the grenade to repair things there just yet.

So instead of focusing on what we discussed, I start trying to figure out my own ways of helping. Any little thing I can do that might help alleviate some of the stress on Memphis's shoulders, and help my father realize what he's considering is a grave mistake.

"Thanks so much for taking the time to come in and interview."

Harper, a sweet high school senior, gives me a grin and shakes my hand.

"I'll be in touch later this week."

"Thanks, Miss Hawthorne. I'll look forward to it."

She tugs her purse strap over her shoulder and gives me one more smile and then heads out, leaving me mercifully alone for the first time in what feels like two entire days.

When I launched the advertisements about the server and hostess positions, there were only a trickle of legitimate responses over the first few days. The rest were spam messages or people with no experience.

But after I got connected with Memphis's friend Ryan at KWNE, and he did a spot on the new restaurant and the open positions, I received dozens of inquiries from people with *real* hosting and serving experience.

I also received a bunch of unsolicited résumés from people looking for sous chef and prep chef positions, and I think some of that was due to Ryan mentioning Wes's name as the new head chef. It wasn't something I'd included in my notes, but I'm assuming Memphis had spoken with him about it.

It feels wild to me that people would want to work here because of Wes. But apparently in the culinary industry, Wes's name means a lot.

I let out an exhausted sigh and stretch my arms high above my head. Then I begin sorting through the stack of résumés in front of me, weeding out the few that I *know* are not getting hired. That would include the college freshman who stared at my chest for the entire interview, the woman who scrolled on her phone while she was answering my questions, and the middle-aged guy who said he couldn't provide a reference because he got fired from his last job for punching his manager.

Those are no-brainers.

Then I split the remaining dozen résumés into piles based on what job they were interviewing for and stack them in order of preference.

It takes me about an hour to read through them all again and look back at my notes. The two days of interviews are all blurring together and making a lot of the candidates merge into one.

After I make my decisions, the only thing left is to run everything by Memphis to make sure we're on the same page. But when I pop into his office, it's my father sitting in his chair.

He looks over when he sees me, then returns his focus to whatever paperwork he's going through.

"What do you need, Murphy?"

I roll my eyes. It's clear where my brother got it from.

"Just looking for Memphis. Do you know where he is?"

"I do not."

He doesn't say anything after that, and I bristle on the inside.

Before I can think better of it, I cross the threshold and approach where he sits at the desk.

"I can't believe you would ever think about selling the vineyard."

He doesn't even look up at me, just continues staring at the paper-work in front of him. "I'm surprised you even care, considering how you couldn't get away from here fast enough."

Gritting my teeth, I try to remember what Wes said on our walk along the highway. About people not liking to feel vulnerable, and how they act selfish and insecure instead. And what Memphis said to me that first day home, about Dad not knowing how to talk when he's deep in his feelings.

"Of course I care. Working the vineyard might not be what *I* want to do, but Memphis has spent his entire life dedicated to this place."

"Memphis will be fine."

"He won't be fine. Why do you think he's so desperately trying to get you to change your mind?"

"This isn't your concern, Murphy."

"Yes, it is. This vineyard means everything to Memphis. And Micah loves it, too. You can't just throw that all away."

It's the longest conversation I've had with my father since returning home, and he's barely looked at me since I walked into the room.

When he doesn't say anything else, something inside me breaks.

"Look at me!" I slap my hands on the desk.

He startles, then looks up at where I loom over him.

"You have been preaching the importance of this vineyard to our family since the day we arrived. And now you want to just . . . sell it off? Like it means nothing? I don't know what you think about me, or why I left or why I'm back, but honestly it doesn't matter. You have two sons who have been working this land since they were old enough to hold a fucking shovel, and they deserve more from you than this."

Then I storm from the room, just before the first tears begin to fall.

Chapter Fourteen

WES

The phone rings for so long, I'm almost positive it's going to go to voice mail, but just before it does, someone answers.

"Yeah."

I clear my throat. "I'm looking for Sonia?"

"Oh, you are, huh? And why the fuck should I let you talk to her?"

Licking my lips, I rest my palm against my forehead and close my eyes.

"I'm her son." I try to keep my voice calm.

There's a pause, and the guy grunts before I hear footsteps and shuffling. Then my mother's voice comes across the line.

"What."

I instantly know she's sober. She's only angry when she's sober.

"Hi, Mom."

"Look, I don't have a lot of time. Troy and I have things to do."

"I just wanted to check in."

She snorts. "I don't need you to check in. *I'm* the mother here."

Sighing, I squeeze my cell phone in irritation.

"All right. I was thinking about heading into the city to see you." My stomach roils with every word. "Maybe I could take you to lunch."

I know exactly what's going to happen if I meet up with my mother in San Francisco and *take her to lunch*. She's going to end up having me meet her at some roach-infested corner store and try to hustle me out of money instead of eating with me. Because this is what happened the three times I met up with her before I moved to Chicago, and my mother is nothing if not predictable.

"I don't know if I'll have the time," she finally tells me. "But if you let me know when, and I'm free, I'll meet you somewhere close to me."

"Where are you now?" I ask. "Still near Union Square?"

She's roamed around quite a bit over the years, but she's most consistent about staying within certain neighborhoods with a larger homeless community. Even when she finds ways to put a roof over her head, she tries to stick in the same area. It really just depends on how dark things have gone in her mind.

"I'll let you know where I'm at when I want to," she answers, her voice suspicious. "I don't need you and your lazy-ass brother getting into my business."

"'Course not, Mom."

She makes a noise like she doesn't believe me, and then I hear her talking to someone else. Maybe the guy who answered the phone . . . Troy? He yells something and then she yells something.

I wince, feeling helpless. I truly wish there was something I could do for her that could change this devastating recurring pattern of her life.

But addiction is complicated. I'd like to get her into rehab. I'd like to be able to set her up with an apartment. I'd like to get her away from whoever this guy is that sounds like an asshole.

Hell, I'd like to believe anything she says to me, ever.

But Ash and I have tried the rehab road. We've tried the apartment thing. We've tracked her down in cities and offered to help, tried to get her out of whatever toxic relationship or environment she's settled into.

We've tried countless times to reach into the drunken hole she likes to bury herself in and support her as she climbs her way out.

None of it has worked.

I don't know if it ever will.

"Mom." I try to get her attention again. "Mom."

I hear her mumble something, and then the line goes dead. I pull the phone away from my ear on a pained sigh.

I can't call anyone to go check on her because I don't know where she is. The only person who might is my brother, but when I call him, it goes straight to voice mail. I leave a message letting him know about the chat with Mom and then send him a text to call me.

Instead of heading to the shower and bed, I sit for hours on the porch in the cooling night breeze, worrying about my mother.

Like I've done on so many other nights throughout my life.

"Thank you everyone for joining us this evening," Memphis says to the crowd of people seated in the restaurant's dining room on Sunday evening. "Chef Hart has been hard at work perfecting his menu for our opening, which is happening this coming Friday!"

My stomach dips as the room breaks into applause. I put on a smile as I stand at his side.

He has no idea how close I was to ripping my entire menu apart yesterday, but thankfully I was able to calm down long enough to realize how foolish that would be.

I'm still waffling over a few things, but the way I plan to organize the menu allows for those little last-minute adjustments.

That's what I'm hoping, at least.

"Tonight, we'll be getting a sneak preview of what we can expect from Chef Hart and this season's menu. Chef, is there anything you'd like to add?"

I lick my lips and clear my throat.

"Everything you'll be served tonight is farm to table, with the majority of the produce coming from the Trager farm." I give Keith Trager a nod where he sits at a table with his family—his wife, Brooke, and who I'm assuming is his daughter, Quinn, if the very pregnant belly is a giveaway.

I'd been surprised to receive Memphis's final number of attendees two days ago, as it was nearly twice the size of what I'd been assuming.

The dinner had originally been just for the Hawthorne Vines restaurant and vineyard staff. That's twenty people. When Memphis let me know I'd be serving dinner for over forty guests, my entire plan for the evening had to be rethought, not to mention the fact I needed to make sure I had all the supplies necessary.

We might have a fully functioning kitchen right now, but it's far from fully stocked, and it will stay that way until we get our first major delivery on Wednesday.

Thankfully, everything fell together without too much fuss, but Memphis and I had exchanged some terse words.

"When I was coming up in the food industry," I continue to our guests, "I was lucky enough to have a mentor who preached the values of fresh ingredients and supporting local food producers. It was a principle he tried to uphold in any restaurant he was involved in, and I have vowed to do the same. Not only will our patrons get the best of our local farms' organic produce and other offerings, I get the joy of designing our rotating menu around seasonal ingredients. I have done so this evening, and will continue to with pleasure, because restaurants who source locally cause less harm to the environment and play an important role in supporting the local economy—the very neighbors and community who are likely to frequent the establishment."

I glance to Memphis and give him a smile. "Memphis and I were fortunate enough to share the same vision, and I'm thrilled to have been able to execute a portion of that for you this evening. If you take a look over to the windows, you'll see tables of food set up for you. While the restaurant will be sit-down service, tonight we've opted for buffet style so that you can test and try the entirety of the menu. Bon appétit."

At my final words, everyone begins chitchatting and rising from their seats to explore the long line of tables Murphy, Memphis, and I set up earlier today.

I'm not nervous that they'll like the food. I know I'm a good chef. An amazing one, actually. I didn't win a James Beard Award by being average.

But the feedback tonight is important. There's a level of pressure that comes along with the start of a new restaurant. I never know what people are going to prefer, what they're going to critique, what might go wrong. There's constant scrambling to keep operations afloat, even in the most successful establishments, and it's difficult to keep all the pieces straight and organized.

In the past, though, someone else was always making the major decisions, either a manager or a restaurateur who oversaw the nitty-gritty of things.

Here, I'm acting as both head chef and manager. There's a lot more than just the menu to oversee, and it has been quite a challenge learning how to navigate it without asking constant questions.

The last thing I want is for Memphis to lose confidence in me, especially because I'm sure that I'm capable of handling it all. There's just a learning curve when taking on more responsibility than I was expecting.

Like tonight. I was expecting a dinner that I could cook entirely on my own. Sit-down service. But timing is everything. Once I realized how many people would be here, I knew it was unrealistic and I had to pivot to the buffet.

I also assumed I would just be in the back, cooking and bringing out food the entire time, that all the speaking would fall on Memphis. Then he let me know this morning that he'd like me to make a speech to welcome everyone and talk more about my plans for the restaurant.

And then there's Murphy.

God, I'm starting to forget all the reasons why staying away from her was supposed to be the smarter choice.

We were setting up the tables and serving station earlier, and she was telling me this story about a night when a reality TV star rented out her restaurant for a private party and informed the staff that a group would be hounding the front door trying to get in, but that the staff shouldn't worry because they're paid fans.

It was a weird story, and every time she stopped to imitate this pseudo-celebrity, she tried to do an accent. I think it was supposed to be a New Jersey accent or New York or something, but she'd scrunch up her face to try to pull it off, and I just couldn't stop laughing.

It's been so long since I've been able to laugh like that. So freely.

Seeing her laugh is just as satisfying, too. It makes me want to reach out and take her face in my hands and kiss her until she's not laughing anymore.

"Grab a plate, Wes," Memphis says, nudging me slightly with his elbow as he passes by me with his own plate full of food. "There's a spot for you next to me."

I make quick work of loading up with pesto pasta, a chicken slider, mashed potatoes, and the vinaigrette salad I was struggling with a few weeks back. I finally perfected the dressing yesterday. The missing ingredient turned out to be mint.

"This salad is wild," Naomi says as I take a seat between her and Memphis. "Who knew that peaches would taste good in a salad?"

I spear my fork into my pasta. "I'm glad you like it."

The sound of the restaurant door opening has the entire room turning to look, and my stomach flips when I see Murphy walking in.

My throat goes dry.

She looks . . . incredible.

She always does, whether she's wearing little sleep shorts or sweaty from an hour-long walk in the blazing-hot sun. But tonight she's wearing a gauzy summer dress that makes her look . . .

Wow.

When Murphy finishes grabbing her plate, she takes the empty seat across from me, and I can't help but watch her. Her smile is wide, and her eyes are bright.

"This really is incredible, Wes," Jack says, snagging my attention away from Murphy and over to where he sits at the head of the long table. "I can't remember the last time I had such a delicious meal."

Then he raises his glass.

"To the chef," he says, and then everyone is lifting their glasses and echoing him.

I lock eyes with Murphy as her glass is in the air, and she gives me a soft smile I'm not expecting. "To the chef," she says, her voice low and raspy.

I smile back because looking at her means I can't not.

"You know what this calls for." At the other end of the table, Keith Trager is setting down his wineglass. "A little music. What do you say, Murphy?"

"Oh yes, please," Brooke says, her face lighting up. "Murphy, you've always played so beautifully. Especially that one song you wrote. Something about mistakes or—" She snaps a few times. "You know the one. You played it at The Standard when they first started doing those open mic nights."

When I look to Murphy, there's a panicked look in her eyes. But then she blinks a few times and it's gone.

"'Sacrifice,'" she says with a tight smile. "But I don't have my guitar with me."

"Why don't you go grab it from the house, Murphy."

Her head whips to the side at the sound of her father's voice.

"It'll only take a couple minutes. And"—he looks around, then back at his daughter—"I think everyone would like to hear you play."

Something passes between the two of them—a tense, uncomfortable look, like Jack doesn't really want to ask her but is doing it anyway—and a few seconds later she stands, crosses the room, and exits out the front door.

"That's why she moved to LA, wasn't it?" Brooke asks Jack. "To play music?"

There's a pause before he replies, "Yeah. She wanted to be a singer."

"She had the best voice in choir," Quinn announces, one hand resting on her stomach and a big smile on her face. "And it wasn't just me who thought so. Everybody did."

"She really was something," Brooke adds. "And it's just the neatest thing that she tried to make it big. You know, so many of us have these huge dreams, and we're never brave enough or lucky enough to go after them. And she did it. I bet she has a million stories."

Jack doesn't say anything else, and everyone goes back to their meals and conversations.

Soon enough, Murphy's back, holding a black guitar case and setting up a chair in the corner. She tugs a beautiful old guitar out and slings the strap around her shoulders. She plucks at the strings for a few seconds while she tunes it up.

"Sorry, it's been a little while," she says, her voice breathy.

But then she clears her throat and begins to strum the keys more intentionally.

"How about a little Mumford & Sons?" Without waiting for an answer, she begins to strum a slowed-down version of a familiar song.

It's clear she's incredibly talented, her fingers moving adeptly over the strings.

Then she starts singing, and I'm stunned. The raspy quality to her voice settles over the room, like rough velvet, burrowing its way under my skin.

The words go in one ear and out the other, but the sound of it vibrates through me.

As she gets further into the song, the bit of shakiness she began with starts to flake off, revealing the true confidence of who she is as a performer. Her smile begins to emerge, and she makes these little faces when she hits certain notes.

I don't think I've ever felt so captivated by a performance.

Of course it feels like it's over before it even really started, and we all burst into a round of applause.

I search the table, gauging the reactions from my fellow listeners, and I'm unsurprised to see everyone looking at her in awe.

Except her father.

He glares at her for too long, and when Murphy looks to him and sees his expression, her gaze dims.

Jack turns toward the table, giving his back to his daughter, then digs almost angrily into his dinner.

"Great job, Murph," Memphis says as she lifts the guitar strap from around her shoulders. Then he bumps his father, and I watch a stare down between the two of them.

Something is happening, but I don't fully understand what.

The only thing I know for sure is that the woman who stood up there singing was incredible. An absolute showstopper. And her father didn't offer a single note of praise.

I'm grateful that the other dinner guests don't seem to notice the unease in the family. I'm flooded with relief, for Murphy's sake and mine, when the evening's agenda comes to an end.

"That was really something, sweetheart," Brooke says to Murphy as the Trager family rises from the table, all of them exchanging hugs as they prepare to go. "Next time you come by the farm, make sure you give me a hello. I'd love to hear about LA."

I wince. It's doubtful Mrs. Trager will get the same story I did.

It makes me wonder if Murphy has shared how things ended in LA with any of her family. I can't imagine she's told her father. He'd probably say *I told you so*, if I had to guess.

There's a small possibility that she'd talked to Memphis about it. My money's on Micah, though. She's said she's much closer with her younger brother, and that he was the only one to visit her when she lived in Venice Beach.

"I didn't know she could sing like that," I say to Memphis a little while later as we're reclined in Adirondack chairs on the patio, looking over the vineyard.

He takes a swig from his beer. "She's always had that killer voice. She'd never admit it, but she really was the star of her high school choir. People might have shown up for their own kids, but it was Murphy they wanted to hear."

I chuckle, then take a sip from my own bottle. "Why'd she go to LA?" I already know the answer, but I'm curious to hear her brother's thoughts on it.

It takes him a while to respond, and when he does, I'm surprised at his answer.

"She wasn't happy here. Never was, and I don't know if she ever will be." He stares out over the vines. "Besides, she's got way too much talent to be stuck here. She's just gotta figure it all out."

I ruminate over his answer long after he's left the restaurant for home.

Murphy seems like a generally happy person, but there's definitely a side of her that seems a little lost as she tries to navigate whatever life will look like for her now that, according to her, the dream she's always had is no longer an option.

Feels like just another reason that I'm so drawn to her.

There's something inside of Murphy's soul that mirrors my own.

That sense of loss.

Of all that hard work, gone.

This restaurant, being here and working as the head chef, creating the menu and building myself back up . . . that's my redemption for everything I went through. Everything I did.

Murphy just needs to find hers.

When I finally push out of the kitchen, I'm surprised to see Murphy standing just outside the front door, peering in through the glass.

I cross the room and unlock it, opening it wide so she can come in.

"Sorry," she says, giving me an embarrassed smile. "I forgot my phone."

She scans the room, locating the phone sitting on the chair she'd sat on when she performed. She glances at the screen and then closes it out, her attention turning to me.

"You were incredible tonight," I tell her, unable to keep how I really feel about it to myself.

Murphy gives me a shy smile. "Thanks."

"No, I mean"—I walk toward her, wanting so badly to communicate to her the way hearing her sing impacted me—"*really* incredible." I shake my head, coming to a stop a few feet away. "I mean, no wonder you went for it in LA."

At that, her smile turns slightly sad, and I want to kick myself for bringing up that lost dream.

"Clearly it wasn't enough." She shakes her head slightly, and some of her hair falls forward from where it was tucked behind her ear. Like she's trying to hide behind it.

"That's not who you are." I take another step closer and push her hair back so it doesn't cover her face. "You're not the one who doesn't believe you're enough."

She looks at me, so much emotion swirling behind those beautiful golden eyes.

"You're that brave girl who went after her dreams, remember?"

"It doesn't feel very brave when you flee back to your hometown with your tail tucked between your legs. I don't feel strong or brave or anything like that. I feel like a failure. Like I had to come back home because I couldn't hack it on my own. Now I have to face the family that never believed in me and show them—" Her voice cuts off and her eyes pinch shut, a single tear finally breaking free. "Show them that they were right all along."

I reach forward and take her face in both my hands, wishing with everything inside me that I could make her understand exactly how amazing she is.

"You wanna know why you're wrong about everything you just said?" I swipe my thumb over the wet streak trailing down her face. "Because you *were* brave. And you *are* strong. You took on the world, you faced down someone who held your future in their hands, and you refused to cower. *That* is bravery. *That* is strength," I say, wishing she had any idea just how deeply I know that truth.

Murphy doesn't say anything, she just looks up at me. I lean in, still holding her face, and brush my lips against one cheek, and then the other, erasing the trail left by her self-doubt and turmoil.

When I pull back to look at her, I find her gaze locked on my lips.

It's the final straw, the last movement to communicate to me that she wants to be kissed again just as much as I want to be the one kissing her.

So I lean down and press my lips against hers.

It's somehow bigger than the kiss we shared on the tailgate of my truck weeks ago. It tastes like magic, and it feels like all the breath has been stolen from my lungs. I'd been captivated by Murphy that first night, but this is something else entirely. I don't remember kissing ever being like this before. Or ever *feeling* anything like this before.

I dip my tongue into her mouth and twist with hers. I want to melt into the floor when I hear her quiet moan.

Her hands move, resting lightly at my waist as the two of us continue a slow, lazy, sensual kiss unlike anything I've ever experienced. And then she nibbles on my bottom lip and I nearly come unglued.

We separate, our heads pulling back, and I revel in the way her cheeks are flushed and her eyes are glazed.

She smiles.

Even though I know we've broken some rules and probably made a mistake to give in to our desires, I can't seem to muster up an ounce of me that cares.

Chapter Fifteen

MURPHY

"They signed me!"

It's the first thing Viv says when I answer her FaceTime. I squeal and start doing a happy dance. I experience a brief pang of envy, though it takes a firm back seat to the excitement I feel for my friend.

"Are you fucking kidding?" I shout.

"No! I'm not fucking kidding!"

"Oh my god, when did this happen? When I didn't hear from you after your meeting, I figured you were licking your wounds."

Her smile looks like it hurts her face with how wide she's grinning, the joy radiating off her.

"They said they loved me at the meeting, and they had me do some studio time this week. They've been drafting up paperwork, and I just signed it all today!"

"Holy shit!"

"I know, holy shit!"

We both squeal, and I dance around my room as Vivian does the same.

"I'm so proud of you, V. Seriously. You've worked so hard for this."

"There's more."

"How much is your signing bonus?" I ask, not even sure that's a thing.

She rolls her eyes. "No, stupid. I'm talking about you."

My smile freezes, not sure what she means.

"I told them that I have an amazing friend who is an *incredibly* talented songwriter, and after they heard 'Sweet Shame' and 'Lonely Girl,' they said they wanted to meet you."

I blink a few times, feeling . . . Honestly, I don't know what I'm feeling.

"Viv . . . ," I start, my voice trailing off.

"Look, I know you always wanted to perform. But maybe this is a way for you to stay connected to your music without having to cross paths with that sicko again, you know?"

Her voice sounds so hopeful and the expression on her face confirms it.

"I've always told you that you're one of the most incredible song-writers I've ever known."

"Like you know so many."

"I'm serious, M!"

I scratch at my cheek, my body suddenly vibrating with an energy that feels unfamiliar.

"Look, I'm not sure. Can I think about it?"

Vivian sighs, her disappointment clear. "Of course you can, but I don't know how long Todd is going to wait around on you, so don't take your sweet time, okay?"

I try to give her an encouraging smile. "I won't. Promise."

I keep what happened with Wes tonight to myself, wanting to just focus on my friend and her excitement. She tells me all about her week with Humble Roads and her thoughts about the contract and the plans moving forward.

Eventually she says she needs to call her mom and we say our good-byes, but not before one more demand that I'll seriously consider coming back to LA to meet with this Todd guy.

I lay on my bed and stare up at the ceiling again, but this time the presence of the glowing stars irritates me, so I get up and start cleaning my room and sorting laundry. I make my bed even though I'm going to get in and go to sleep soon.

And then, I do something that feels surprisingly natural.

I text Wes.

◆　◆　◆

"You got here fast."

"I was already here when you texted me," Wes answers, but the smile on his face begins to fade when he sees me. "Everything okay?"

I shake my head and drop down onto the bench next to him. "No. It's not."

He leans forward, resting his arms on his knees and clasping his hands together.

"I'm sorry. You know, I made that whole ordeal about how important this job is to me, and then *I'm* the one who crosses the line."

"Wes, I'm not talking about the kiss," I say.

He sits back up. "You're not?"

I can't help but smile, touched by his concern. "No."

He smiles back at me. "Oh."

"No, the kiss was . . ." My smile grows, and part of me is just a tiny bit embarrassed at how my entire body feels like it's blushing at the memory. "It was perfect. This is something else."

Wes turns so one knee comes to rest on the bench.

"My friend Vivian is a singer, and she was signed to an indie label last weekend, which is a huge deal. And before your mind even goes there, I'm not jealous, okay? There's a part of me that wishes it had happened for me, but I'm *thrilled* for her. Really."

I pause, trying to figure out the best way to explain this to him without sounding ungrateful.

"Some of the songs that she's going to record for the label are songs that I wrote, and when this Todd guy found out, he said he wanted to meet me."

"Holy shit, that's amazing!" Wes says, the excitement clear in his voice. "I haven't heard anything negative yet, so . . . what's the problem?"

I tuck my hands into the pockets of my hoodie. I'm sure to Wes it doesn't sound like a problem. Viv doesn't think it is either, and I bet there are thousands of people who would love an opportunity like this.

But I'm not sure *I* want it.

"I don't know what the problem is," I answer him, as honestly as I can. "I'm just not sure I want to meet anyone."

Wes is quiet for a long moment. It makes me wonder if he's trying to figure out what to say, or if he knows what to say but doesn't know how to say it.

"I don't want to seem ungrateful for the opportunity," I add. "But when I left my apartment in Venice for the last time, I had an eight-hour drive ahead of me. And I spent the *entire* drive convincing myself that I would never go back." Letting out a humorless laugh, I tilt my head back and stare up into the night sky. "I realize it sounds dramatic. And with how exhausted I was and overworked and broke, you'd think I might be able to see all the reasons that leaving was the best choice."

Then I look at Wes.

"But I worked so hard to create a life for myself, so I could pursue my dream. And to have all of it gone in a blink has been a lot to deal with." I puff out a long, irritated breath. "So the idea of dipping my toe back into the entertainment industry feels like a horrible kind of torture. Like, we're gonna let you get as close as possible to your dream, but just far enough away that you have to watch everyone else as they step past you across the finish line. Does that make any sense?"

He nods. "It does. It's not easy watching everyone around you succeed. I haven't been through exactly what you have, but I get what you mean."

"So I don't know what to do. Help me out, therapist."

Wes laughs, and the sound of it helps loosen up some of the tightness in my chest.

It really is mind-blowing how quickly this man has become not just someone I'm attracted to, but a confidant. A refuge.

I can't remember ever having that before. And now I wonder how I might ever be able to live without it.

"I can't tell you what to do, Murphy. You went through a lot, and it doesn't surprise me that this would make you emotional. I mean, part of me thinks it's probably highlighting the fact that you still have a lot to process."

"Don't say that. It's nice to pretend that I'm totally healed and everything's fine."

He gives me a sad smile.

"But you're not totally healed, and everything *isn't* fine."

"Ugh, why do you have to be such a good therapist?" I tug my hoodie over my head and yank on the cords so that the opening closes around my face, blocking my view so I can no longer see him and—hopefully—he can no longer see me. "It would be great if you could just tell me that I should turn Vivian down and continue about in my new life."

I feel Wes shift closer, and then he wraps his arm around my shoulders. Then he begins loosening the scrunched-up hoodie from around my face.

"I think," he tells me, his voice low, the sound of it sending little tremors running through my body, "that you should sit down and really think about what you want next."

He pushes the hood back, pinning me with his thoughtful gaze. "I had a rough time in Chicago, and when everything fell apart, I had to make a choice. Was I going to give up on everything I had worked for? Was I going to try to repair the pieces of the life I'd been working toward?"

He reaches his fingers out to tuck some of my flyaway hairs behind my ear.

"*Or*, maybe instead, I could find a way to create a new dream out of the scraps of what was left behind."

He makes a good point. Really, he does.

But with how close he is, and how gentle he's being, my mind can't seem to focus any longer on my conversation with Vivian or the idea of going back to LA to meet with the people from Humble Roads.

Instead, all I can think about is how it feels to have his arm around me, and how much better I would feel if we were kissing again.

So I lean in and press my lips to his.

He opens immediately, and the taste of him explodes on my tongue, like a drug I doubt I'll ever stop craving.

There are so many things to worry about right now. Too many things.

Whatever the future holds for me. What's going on with the vineyard. The opening of the restaurant. My argument with Dad. Training that starts tomorrow.

But for now, I can ignore it all and just think about this.

When I walk into The Standard and scan the room, I can't help the smile that crosses my face.

It's the kind of bar that isn't supposed to allow anyone under twenty-one but turns a blind eye to locals and regulars. My father used to bring Memphis and me when he wanted to grab a drink with a buddy. The two of us would run off to the pinball machine, playing with the little baggie of quarters that my dad gave us until they inevitably ran out. Then we'd head to the pool table.

There's something sexy about the game that I can't pinpoint exactly—maybe somewhere among the sticks and balls and getting it in the pocket.

I glance over to where the pool table still sits. It's been re-covered, the tarnished old green felt I remember replaced with blue. I wrinkle my nose at it, then continue on to the bar.

It gives me an unexpected thrill to hop up on a stool at the bar itself. My prior visits here only happened when I was too young to drink. Well . . . too young to be served anyway, even in a place like this.

"What can I get you?"

The bartender, an older gentleman I've never seen before, sets a coaster down in front of me and gives a kind smile.

"Can I see the wine list?"

He nods, dipping a little to grab a menu from under the bar and then passing it to me.

"Take your time, and just give a little wave when you're ready," he tells me, smiling again before moving to the other end to continue his conversation with another patron.

My eyes scan the menu but focus on the options from our vineyard.

I may not want to tie my future to the family business, but even I can't deny that the wines our grapes produce are top shelf. You can't grow up in wine country without becoming a bit of a wine snob, something my friends in LA always rolled their eyes at when I turned my nose up at their bottles of Two Buck Chuck from the local Trader Joe's.

I know enough to appreciate that wine doesn't have to be expensive to taste good. But if refusing to drink something that tastes like vinegar just because it's cheap makes me a snob, so be it.

I flag down the bartender and order one of our cabernet francs from last year. I haven't forgotten how much I enjoyed the bottle Micah sent to me. I brought it to a Friendsgiving in West Hollywood, and after one taste, immediately regretted that I couldn't keep it all for myself.

In LA, I rarely had extra money to spend on things like nice wine, so I always savored the bottles from the family vineyard. Thankfully, just a few miles from my house, I don't have to pay an arm and a leg to get a glass.

When a generously poured glass is set in front of me, I reach out to take it just as I hear my name.

"Hey, Murphy!"

I spin, grinning at my old friend as she hoists her very pregnant self up onto the stool next to me. She reaches out for a hug, which surprises me at first, but I almost instantly lean into it, reminded of the fact that Quinn was always a hugger.

"I'm so glad we're finally getting together."

"I'm sorry I didn't reach out sooner after I moved back," I say, feeling a little embarrassed about it. "I've been wanting to catch up, but everything's just been . . . so crazy."

Quinn shakes her head. "Don't even worry about it. I could have called, too."

I wave my hand at her massive belly. "It's not like you don't have other, far more important things on your mind."

"Oh, trust me, I'm always looking for something that takes my mind *off* this pregnancy," she says, just as the bartender stops in front of us.

"Miss Trager," he says, grinning at her with almost fatherly affection. "Shirley Temple?"

"With lime, please."

He nods and gets to work, and Quinn blushes. "I might not be handling the no-drinking part of growing a human very well. So Gabe makes me a Shirley Temple that almost keeps me sane."

"Can I?" I ask, my hand hovering between us.

"Oh, sure!" she exclaims, her smile growing as she practically shoves her rounding belly into my hand.

"I mean, logically I know it's been almost a decade but . . . I can't believe you're having a baby." I feel a slight movement under my palm and I gasp. "It moved."

Quinn smiles. "She's very active. I think she's going to salsa dance her way out of my vagina."

I bark out a laugh, then laugh harder when I realize the bartender is standing across from us with Quinn's drink and an uncomfortable expression.

"Thanks, Gabe." She grins and takes a big sip. Then she looks back at me. "Mind if we go grab a table? These stools are murder on my back."

"Oh, absolutely."

We grab our drinks and find a booth. Quinn slides in and leans against the wall, her legs up on the bench.

"That's better," she says, letting out a big sigh. "All right, now tell me everything about LA! I've been following you on Instagram and things looked like so much fun."

I lick my lips, gearing up to give her the watered-down, *it was great but wasn't for me* speech that I'd prepared in my head on the way over here as a means of deflecting. The perspective she got from my social media accounts—the ones I'd curated as part of my hopes to catch the eye of a talent manager—definitely communicated that my life in LA was fun and wild and everything most people think of when they imagine pursuing a career in entertainment.

But as I take in Quinn, sitting across from me with that wide-open, caring expression, I know that if I'm going to really take Vivian's advice and find someone to talk to, someone to truly call a friend, I can't have the first thing I say be a lie.

"You know, some of it was good. But a lot of it was shit."

She gasps and rests her chin in her hand. "Tell me everything."

It reminds me so much of Vivian even though the two of them are completely different people. Vivian is loud and brash and sassy with zero filter. Quinn is one of those relentlessly positive, eternal-optimist types who smiles through everything and always knows how to say just the right thing.

But what they both have in common is they are great listeners.

4

So I spill the tea. All the dirty bits. About my shitty apartments and horrible roommates and barely scraping by and everything that happened with Paul.

And she listens, gasping at all the right moments and reaffirming me when we get to the hardest parts.

Vivian was right.

I *do* need someone here to talk to. As incredible as it is to have Wes, there's something really important about having a girlfriend. And while I'm sure Quinn has plenty of friends around town, I am all too happy to have her take pity on me and lend an ear.

"Jeez Louise, girl. I'm so sorry you had to deal with all that. That Paul guy sounds like a real piece of work."

Downing the last of my wine, I set my now-empty glass on the table with a clink. "Oh, he was."

"Well, at least you're back here now."

I snort. "Because this is exactly where I want to be."

The words fall flat as soon as I say them, and I briefly catch a look on Quinn's face that she's heard them the same way. Like an insult.

But before I can say anything, her smile is back.

"I'm sure our small town can at least serve as a temporary reprieve from the insanity before you figure out what your next big dream is, right?"

There isn't anything unkind about her words. In fact, I imagine she's being incredibly gracious. I can't help wondering if what I said is boiling beneath her skin.

Because the residual feeling of having said it is still boiling beneath mine.

"Absolutely." I glance down and see that her drink is empty, too. "Do you want me to grab you another Shirley?"

Quinn shakes her head. "Nah, I think it's time for me to head out." She rubs the top of her belly. "This little goober makes me a whole lot more exhausted than I ever plan to be, and the idea of splaying out on the couch to watch TV sounds like exactly what I need tonight."

I feel bad. We spent the entire time we've been here talking about me.

"How about we make a date soon for you to come ride around the vineyard with me? I wanna hear all about the baby and how *your* life has been."

I don't imagine it when I see a tiny wrinkle between Quinn's brows smooth out.

"I'd love that."

We crawl out of the booth and embrace, then she gives me a wave and leaves.

I thought I'd have more mixed feelings about spending time with Quinn. When I look back on our friendship, it always seemed like she was friends with everyone and I only had her. But tonight felt good. Like slipping on an old sweater that I used to love and realizing it still fits and still makes me smile.

Maybe I really *can* mark *find a friend* off the official task list.

I roll my eyes. Vivian has me brainwashed.

A familiar face catches my eye, and my stomach twists, a giddy feeling beginning to thrum through my veins at the sight of Wes. He strides toward the bar, where he leans up against the counter next to a half-empty beer, a coaster resting on the top.

He must have arrived earlier, while I was talking with Quinn. I can't believe I didn't notice him, especially because I can't seem to pull my eyes away from where he stands, enjoying the view that his long, lean frame and killer ass provides.

Quinn's departure had me thinking I was ready to leave, but I feel my interest in sticking around rejuvenated.

And with that thought, I head his way.

Chapter Sixteen

WES

"Mind if I sit here?"

I turn at the sound of Murphy's voice, surprise ricocheting through me as she plops down next to me with a smile on her face.

I blink a few times, my mind freezing up because I don't know how to feel about seeing her.

Obviously I'm always glad to see her. But this really isn't a good time.

And clearly my thoughts are written all over my face because the smile on hers disappears quickly.

I glance past her briefly, then shift in my seat when Gabriel approaches with a new coaster and a fresh beer, setting them both down in front of me.

"Here you are," he says before turning to look at Murphy. "Another glass?"

"No, I'm actually—" She glances at me. "I'm good for now, thanks."

He nods, then moves down the bar to help another gentleman, and the tension in my shoulders eases.

Tonight is the first time I've actually spoken with my father since the time I came to The Standard a few days after I moved to Rosewood.

I haven't told him who I am—haven't even given him my name—but we struck up a conversation about the recent Giants game.

In my previous visits, I was always looking at his face and his body, trying to find the similarities. But tonight, when he started talking to me, I finally saw the connection between us. His voice is like a deeper, raspier version of my own, and the way he moves his hands when he talks feels like I'm looking in a mirror that shows the future.

I'm not ready to share this with Murphy. I'm not ready to share it with anybody. Not even Ash.

"I'm actually . . . kind of busy," I finally tell her, the words coming out stiff and uncomfortable.

The last thing I want to do is hurt her feelings or make her think that I don't want her around. Any other day, any other place, sitting on the stool next to me would have been a perfect move. Another opportunity for us to talk, for me to learn more about the little quirks that make up Murphy Hawthorne.

But tonight is not that night. My head is not in the right place to manage what might come from her sitting here, next to me, as I try to get to know a father who has no idea who I am.

"Sorry for bothering you," she says, then moves to walk past me.

"Murphy," I say, grabbing her hand and halting her in her tracks. "I'll explain later, okay?"

She seems to assess me, as if she wants to be sure I really mean it, before nodding and walking off. I watch her go, her petite figure crossing the room and pushing out through the front door and into the warm air of another early-summer night.

I sigh and turn back to my beer, knowing that when Murphy and I talk later, she's going to want to understand why I brushed her off tonight. And I'll need to come up with a reason, whether that's the truth or something else.

"She's a pretty thing." Gabriel steps in front of me with a smirk. "I'm surprised you turned her down. Got someone at home?"

Shaking my head, I rotate the beer between my hands. "No, nobody at home."

"A good-looking guy like you should have somebody. Or maybe quite a few somebodies."

I shrug, not really wanting to talk to him about Murphy. "You from around here?" I ask, trying to divert the conversation.

"That I am. I grew up in St. Helena, then moved to San Francisco for a few years before coming to Rosewood."

I bob my head. "And do *you* have anybody at home?"

He grins at that, tugs his phone from his back pocket, and lights it up so I can see the home screen. "My wife, Gigi, and my son. Preston." He pulls the phone back and looks down at it, affection clear in his eyes. "He just turned twelve."

I don't hear a lot of what he says after that, just a rushing sound filling my ears. I'm thankful when he steps away to help someone else.

I tug my wallet out of my pocket, blindly grab a few bills, and place them next to my beer. Then I'm out of my seat and crossing the room, shoving the door open as I gasp. I try desperately to breathe, but it feels like my body is screaming, like the walls are caving in.

It takes everything inside me to stumble down the street and get into my car, but I don't turn it on. Instead I sit there, gripping the steering wheel, trying to get back in control of myself. Trying to overcome the anxiety attack that feels like it's crippling me.

It still doesn't feel like I've taken a full breath, and I try to focus on that. On the sounds of my breath coming in and out, on the feel of it entering my lungs and exhaling through my mouth.

What I want to do is scream. What I want to do is crawl into the ground and never come out.

Leaning forward, I rest my head against the steering wheel, trying to focus on feeling calm even though I'm anything but.

The passenger door opens and then I feel a hand pressed against my back, then smooth circles there. When I turn, my eyes focus on Murphy.

"You're going to be okay," she tells me, her voice soothing and warm.

I close my eyes and lean my forehead against the wheel again, my hands still gripping it for dear life.

"Deep breaths, okay?"

"Distract me," I tell her. "Please. Talk about anything."

It's something I read online, that giving the brain something else to focus on can divert some of the energy being used to focus on whatever caused the anxiety attack in the first place. But I've always been alone in the past. Holed up in my studio apartment in Chicago, which is when they first started. So it's not something I've ever tried.

"Anything?"

I nod, though the movement is so small, I'm not sure she sees it.

A few seconds later, she starts to sing. It's not a song I'm familiar with, the melody slow and soothing. If I'm honest, I don't even really hear the words.

But just the sound of her, and the way her hand moves in careful swaths across my back, begins to ease the tightness in my chest and arms.

When I *do* finally hear the words, something inside me knows instinctively.

This is one of Murphy's songs.

> You want to take the parts of me
> That do not serve you best
> You want to take the heart of me
> And then what will be left
> But skin and bones
> Your sticks and stones
> Have left a tragic mess

She sings for a while, and most of it blurs together as I try to calm myself and climb out of the emotional hole I've fallen in.

But I'm so thankful that she's here, and that I'm not alone.

Eventually, my heart begins to slow and my breathing evens out.

I close my eyes, the acute stress fading and the beginning of a post-anxiety slump creeping in to weigh me down.

"It started in Chicago," I say, my eyes still closed, not ready to look at her just yet. "I got fired from my job, and one night I just felt like I couldn't exist in my skin anymore." I finally look at Murphy. "It's the only way to describe it. I thought I was dying."

She reaches her hand out and rests it on mine, giving a gentle squeeze.

"I'm so sorry. It sounds horrible."

"It *feels* horrible. And it's embarrassing. Because literally *nothing* is wrong."

"That's not true. It's just not something you can see," she replies, squeezing again. She pauses, her thumb stroking along the back of my hand. "Do you know what caused it?"

I sigh, deciding in that moment that I should tell Murphy about Gabriel.

"The bartender," I say, glancing at her briefly. "He's my father."

Murphy's silence is enough for me to know I've shocked her.

"Since when?"

At that, a laugh bursts from my chest, and Murphy giggles too, the simplicity of it slicing a sharp blade through the thick tension filling the car.

"You know what I mean," she corrects, still smiling. "When did you find out?"

"I knew before I moved here, actually. My brother and I never knew our father growing up, always heard these really weird stories from our mom that just seemed . . ." I shake my head. "My mom is an addict, and it's hard to believe anything she says, but when we were kids we just assumed she was telling the truth. That he abandoned us right after my brother was born."

"I'm assuming that's not true?"

"We don't really know what's true. Ash took one of those DNA tests during college and it connected him with a guy who lives in New York. And everything we'd heard my mom say made it seem like our father lived in California. So I took the test too, and we found out we're actually half brothers."

Murphy's eyes widen. "Oh my gosh."

"Yeah. Different fathers. And mine is here. In that bar. And I don't think he even knows I exist."

She turns so she's facing me and leans to the side against the headrest, then adjusts her hand in mine so our fingers are linked together.

"He has a family," I continue. "A wife and a son named Preston. I guess he just turned twelve, which means I have another brother."

We sit in silence for a long moment, the weight of what I've just said resting heavy on my shoulders.

"What can I do?" Her sweet voice is so earnest and caring.

I squeeze her hand in mine, wanting her to know just how glad I am that she came to find me.

"Just be here with me."

Murphy nods. "I can do that."

Then she lifts my hand to her mouth and kisses the back of my palm.

And even though I've just had this terrible anxiety attack, and I feel shattered and broken and exhausted in so many ways, I'm still able to pinpoint it.

This is the moment I begin to fall in love with Murphy Hawthorne.

The next two days fly by way faster than I would like them to, considering how much there still is to do if we want to be ready for the opening. But that's how it always is, so it's actually a comforting kind of chaos.

I lose myself in prepping the galley with everything we might possibly need, refining the menu and setting up orders for ingredients, and teaching the two young part-time line cooks who are going to be helping me in the kitchen.

Kellan and Mark aren't that much younger than me, but they both have limited experience, so we spend a lot of time reviewing standards for certain menu items and expectations for plating.

Memphis asked me why I hired two green twentysomethings without culinary degrees instead of chefs like me, and I told him the truth: these kids will bust their asses to learn, and sometimes that's what you need in a kitchen to make it a success.

I'm not entirely sure that I sold him on it, but he didn't question me any further.

It really is nice having someone trust me with the decisions. It always felt like someone was critiquing my every move in my previous positions. It was understandable—if someone invests millions in opening a restaurant, they're going to have opinions and concerns.

Thankfully, Memphis's investment into this place wasn't quite in seven-figures territory, and it seems like his concern is on par with the dollar amount.

"Do you have a second?"

The sound of Murphy's voice in the kitchen sends something light rippling through my chest. I glance back at her from where I'm stirring a nearly finished leek and potato soup.

"Hey. What's up?"

She steps forward, the kitchen door swinging closed behind her, and extends a piece of paper my way.

"I was hoping you could review this before your training with the front-of-house staff later today."

I take the sheet and glance it over, my lips kicking up when I see what she has.

"Training objectives?" I look up at her with an amused expression.

Murphy tilts her head. "I've been working them through a series of steps, and if you can make sure to cover these specific items, I'd appreciate it. Obviously, you're welcome to cover whatever else you think is relevant for them to know about this space and your work. But these are the things I think are going to be the most beneficial."

I look at the sheet again, reading over her list. Menu specifics, safety protocols, kitchen layout, tool and resource organization, expectations regarding cooking staff.

"This is great," I tell her. "In my past kitchens, it was always menu conversations and the rest was just learned on the fly. I like this."

I can't help the easy smile that mirrors hers.

"How's the training going so far?"

"Really well, actually. Everyone seems excited to learn, and we have a good mix of personalities." She shrugs. "I don't want to say I did an amazing job before I've seen them handle opening, but I'm feeling pretty good about it so far."

"Good. I'm glad to hear that."

Both of us stand there for a while, just looking at each other.

"Hey, listen—"

"About the other night—"

We laugh, and Murphy twists her hands together in front of her.

"Go ahead."

I drop the burner lower and set a lid on the soup, then turn around and face her, leaning back against the counter and crossing my arms.

We haven't really talked since my breakdown outside The Standard two days ago. The reality of opening week has finally settled in, and there has been a lot on my plate. A lot on Murphy's too, if the way she's been running around is an indicator. And even though we'd been making a habit of meeting up at the bench, for the past couple of days I've been trying to recover from my anxiety attack with some alone time.

"I just wanted to say thank you again for the other night. For helping me through that."

She shakes her head. "Don't thank me. I was glad to be there so I *could* help."

"I was also wondering if you wanted to come over tonight. Hang out for a bit. Maybe I could make you something again."

A smile stretches across her face. "That sounds fun."

"Good."

God, I could look at her forever. Every little thing about her, even the things that plenty of people would consider imperfections—the way her lips tick up to the side when she smiles and those little freckles on the bridge of her nose—are absolutely perfect.

"How're things coming?"

The sound of Memphis's voice is like nails on a chalkboard, and I don't miss the way Murphy sidesteps around me and grabs something off the counter—a whisk—and holds it up like something she was looking for.

"Found it. Thanks, Wes!"

And then she's smiling at her brother and walking past him, pushing through the swinging door back out to the dining room.

Something uneasy slithers through my stomach. Her quick actions are a reminder of my original thoughts about Murphy and this job. My fears about something going wrong.

I tried to keep things between us as clinical and work-appropriate as I could, but it's time for me to accept that my feelings for her aren't going away any time soon. And now that it feels like we're moving in a direction that's a little more serious than *fooling around*, it occurs to me that maybe there needs to be a conversation at some point. With Memphis or Jack.

Not right now, obviously. I couldn't do something like that without talking to Murphy about it first.

But the realization that I feel so seriously about her that I'd want to make sure things are aboveboard with her father and brother alleviates something in my chest.

The idea of hooking up with Murphy always had a rule-breaking edge to it because that's what it was. Hooking up. But now it doesn't feel that way. Now it feels like I would be able to look her father or brother in the face without feeling like I'm doing something wrong.

And that knowledge puts a smile on my face for the rest of the day.

Chapter Seventeen

MURPHY

When I get to Wes's cabin later that evening, I stand outside his door for a few minutes before knocking.

My nerves are shot. I've been distracted all day, trying to keep my mind off what tonight might bring. The two of us alone and tucked away in his cabin. Possibly finishing what we started in the kitchen several weeks ago.

Letting out a long breath to calm my nerves, I finally knock. I hear movement inside, a thump, and then footsteps.

When Wes answers, he gives me that smile—the one that's charming as hell, that about knocked me off my feet the first time I saw it at the gas station—before inviting me inside. I'm instantly hit with the delicious aroma of something warm and rich.

"Hey," he says, closing the door and then tugging me in for a kiss. One that's somehow both chaste and sensual at the same time.

I grin at him once he pulls away. "Hi."

He leans in and kisses me one more time, then turns and heads into the little kitchenette in the corner.

"I don't have the same supplies here as I do in the restaurant kitchen." He tugs something out of the tiny microwave oven on his countertop. "But all good chefs know how to use a microwave."

I cross the room, grinning when I see the little mugs with brownies inside. Wes then pulls a small container of vanilla ice cream from the freezer and scoops some into each of the mugs.

"This is perfect," I tell him. "Nothing sounds better right now than a warm brownie with some ice cream."

He grins, hands me a mug, and then clinks his against mine.

"Bon appétit."

We lean against the counters as we enjoy our treat, making small talk about how training went in the afternoon, when Wes went over everything the new servers and hosts need to know.

"I can't believe we're opening in two days." I shake my head. "It feels so fast."

"It always feels fast," he tells me, finishing off his last bite and then putting his mug and spoon in the sink. "I've never opened a restaurant and felt ready on the first day. You just have to jump in and make it work, or it'll never happen."

I nod. "I guess that makes sense. How many restaurants have you opened?"

"Five."

My eyebrows rise. "Wow. That's a lot."

"It is. And it's always exhausting, but it's also incredibly gratifying."

"Really?"

He shrugs a shoulder. "Just all the work that goes into it. You know, chefs are inherently people who find pleasure in feeding others. There's a kind of satisfaction that comes along with preparing a meal and knowing that someone who was hungry has now been fed. Most chefs aren't a part of a restaurant's opening, so they don't get to see all the nitty-gritty and hours of prep and planning that go into the months and years before that first service."

Wes takes my mug once I've finished my last bite and places it next to his in the sink.

"And there is *nothing* like putting in all that work, plating the first meal, and looking out into the dining room to see someone smile as they eat what you've made."

"I don't think I've ever thought about any of that before. Or how much joy might come from watching someone eat what you cook. Is that—"

My words choke off, and I can feel the blood rushing to my cheeks when I realize what I was about to ask him.

A curious look comes over Wes's face. "Is that what?"

I nibble on my lip for a second, considering, before I decide to just ask.

"Is that how you felt when you made me the butternut squash ravioli?"

Wes's voice dips low. "You mean, did I get pleasure out of feeding you?" A mischievous grin lifts the edges of his lips. "Of course I did." Then he takes a step forward, his body coming close to mine. "It's why I made you brownies tonight, too."

"It is?"

He braces his arms on either side of me against the counter, caging me in. "You make these little sounds when you like the way something tastes," he continues, his mouth dropping so it's close to my ear. "Little moans that turn me on."

I close my eyes.

Any other time, I'd be curious what he means, the idea that a small sound could turn someone on a new concept to me.

But having his voice rumbling low and sensual in my ear is sending little threads of lust to every corner of my body, and his words make perfect sense.

"You closed your eyes," he continues, pressing his lips, light and soft, against the curve of my neck. "Moaned around your spoon." He kisses the underside of my jaw. "And it made me wonder what other things I could do to make you moan."

He kisses my mouth then, and the taste of him is mixed with the hint of chocolate and vanilla, the sweetest treat I can ever remember on my tongue.

Wes moves his hands to my waist, grips my ass and squeezes, then trails up the back of my shirt. His fingers trace lightly against my bare back, sending shivers racing through my body. I feel my nipples go hard when he unhooks my bra and slips his hands under the cups.

I whimper into his mouth when he pinches them, my own hands grabbing on to his biceps, partially to keep my balance and partially because I'm desperate to touch him any and everywhere I can.

My top is off seconds later, Wes pulling it over my head, and my bra immediately after that. And then he licks up the center of my breasts, his hands pressing them together before he turns his head slightly and strokes his tongue in circles around one taut bud.

I squirm, the sensation tugging at something in my core. My hands come up to the back of his head, my fingers stroking through his hair.

He groans, then switches to my other breast as his hands begin to work at the button on my jeans.

"I'm on the pill," I tell him, feeling out of breath even though I've barely moved.

Wes begins kissing down my stomach, then drops to his knees, tugging at my zipper and beginning to shimmy my pants down my legs.

"Good to know, but we're not having sex tonight."

My body freezes. "What?"

He continues working at my pants, but looks up at me with a mischievous grin. "We're going to open the restaurant this weekend, and then on our first day off, I'm taking you on a date."

Wes taps my right foot and I lift it off the ground. He tugs my pants off my right leg, then repeats on the left.

"So then what are we doing?" I ask, realizing that I'm standing in just my underwear in the middle of Wes's kitchen, while he's still fully dressed.

"Having a little . . . dessert," he replies, that mischief still present in every line of his smile.

His hands stroke up my legs, the gentle movements again sending shivers through my body. He traces along the backs of my knees and then the sides of my thighs before his fingers slip under the edges of my panties and tug them up just slightly.

I moan, the movement causing a tiny bit of pressure against my clit, and I shift my hips, wanting so desperately for things to continue.

"I'll make you a deal," I tell him as he slides my underwear to the side, exposing my lips to his gaze. "I won't be mad at you for keeping sex off the table tonight if you promise to let me give you a blow job."

He pauses, looking up at me with an arched brow. "Is this a trick?"

I laugh, but it turns to a moan as Wes presses his lips against me, and I feel his tongue stroke through my center. "Oh fuck."

Watching him is incredibly erotic, the visual mixing with the physical pleasure, and then he grips one of my thighs and lifts to the side, opening me up so his tongue is able to stroke along every ridge and valley.

My head falls back as he slips one finger and then two inside of me, the pressure ratcheting up my response. I grab my breasts and begin tugging on the tips, and it's only a few seconds later that I feel the warmth pooling below my belly button, letting me know I'm heading toward the peak.

"Wes, I'm almost there," I tell him, looking back to where he's still kneeling before me.

"What do you need?" His fingers still pulse gently inside me, and his tongue flutters against my clit.

Instead of answering, I pull away from him, then tug him up off his knees and wrap my arms around his neck, pressing my mouth to his. Then I'm pushing him backward as we kiss, my fingers making quick work of his fly.

"Last time, you made me come alone," I tell him as I reach for his belt. "What I need is for us to come together."

He tugs his shirt over his head as I push his pants to the floor, but I pause when I see the extensive tattoos covering his skin.

"How did I not know about these?" I ask, roaming my hands along his chest and shoulders, then down his arms.

It's my first time seeing him shirtless, and I'm almost irritated that I didn't get to see him like this sooner.

"Long sleeves and chef coats," he tells me, and then I feel his body shiver at the way I'm lightly tracing my hands over his skin. "Besides, I didn't want you objectifying me."

I pin him with an amused look, enjoying the way his smile stretches across his face.

"Okay, I'm joking. Can you please objectify me as often as possible?"

I laugh, but Wes cuts me off by pressing his lips to mine again, and then we're falling into his bed, our kissing a much more languid affair, our hands moving and touching and stroking anywhere we can.

When Wes's hands travel between my legs again, I follow, letting my hand reach between his legs and grip on to the thick length of him. He moans into my mouth, then bites my lip just a pinch too hard, the move sending a shot of pleasure through me.

He feels large in my hand, warm, and I can feel the throb of his pulse as I stroke him up and down.

"God, you drive me crazy," he says, shifting his hips and thrusting into my palm. "Why is everything with you so damn good?"

I twist my hand and his head falls back. His hand stills where he'd been drawing infuriatingly slow circles around my clit.

"I want to taste you when you come," he tells me, his voice raspy and strained. "Sit on my face."

I smile, maneuvering my body so I'm straddling him backward. His hands come between my thighs and tug me backward, and his mouth is back on me, his arms wrapping around my hips and holding me there.

I cry out and begin shifting my hips against him, before dropping down and taking his dick deep into my mouth until I feel the tip of him against the back of my throat.

Wes shouts, the wet heat of my mouth surprising him, and then he dives back into my pussy. We're both ravenous, the joy of giving and receiving pleasure driving each of us forward, our movements beginning to mirror each other.

The warmth at my core begins to build again, and I grip his thighs, moaning as I suck, desperate for him to come when I do.

And when I feel my body tip over the edge, white heat races through me, constricting each muscle in my body. Wes follows seconds later, and I pull off to stroke him through it.

I roll off Wes and collapse on the bed beside him, trying to catch my breath as little tremors still flicker their way through me.

"When we actually have sex, you're going to kill me," he says, his words coming out between pants.

I giggle, trying to imagine how anything could possibly be better than what just happened between us.

Wes shifts his body and crawls around so that he's now sprawled next to me, slipping his arm under my head and tugging me close.

Eventually, we fall asleep like that. Our arms wrapped around each other.

Naked.

Sated.

Warm.

Together.

◆ ◆ ◆

I'm wrapping up the second day of training for the waitstaff when Micah steps through the doors. I can see two of my new part-time hostesses visibly swoon at the sight of him, and I know anything else I say is going to be in one ear and out the other.

"I'll see you all here tomorrow at three," I say. "Good job, everyone."

As the staff shuffles around, grabbing their things, I head over to Micah.

"Hey, what's up?"

"Just swinging through to see how things are going," he says, but it feels like there's more on his mind.

Part of me wants to find out what Wes is up to. I haven't seen him much all day. I've been too focused on training and getting the final details wrapped for all the visuals through the restaurant. It's wild how much time can fly by when you're setting up table centerpieces and rolling napkins, even when several people are helping.

But I haven't seen my baby brother nearly enough since I moved home, so I'm thrilled that he's stopped by unexpectedly. And I know I should take advantage of this opportunity to spend some time with him.

"I have to slip the final menus into their covers. Wanna help?"

He grins. "Sure."

We make quick work of setting up a station where my brother slips the left page in and then passes it to me to add the right. And as we work, Micah talks about one of the vines on the west side of the property that has contracted red blotch, a new virus that has been identified only in the past few years that impacts the flavor of the grape.

"The plan is to tug up the current roots and plant new sav ones. Red blotch doesn't really affect the whites as much, so we'll test that for a little while to see if that's a long-term solution."

Micah is smart. *Really* smart.

Sometimes I wonder if my dad and brother give him the credit he deserves for the incredible way his mind works.

"Do you think . . ."

My voice trails off when I spot Wes emerging from the kitchen, his chef coat slung over his shoulder. He slows briefly when he sees Micah and gives us both a wave before crossing through the restaurant and heading out the door.

"Still wanna pretend like nothing's going on?" Micah's voice drags my attention away from Wes's retreating form and back to where we're seated. "Because the way you're looking at him with hearts in your eyes says otherwise."

I return my focus to the menus, not answering Micah right away, uncertain about what I really want to share.

We've always been close, the two of us. Much closer than either of us ever were with Memphis, especially as we got older. And because he has a much higher emotional IQ than my father or older brother, I've always tended to be a lot more vulnerable around him. More transparent about the inner workings of my mind.

I'm not entirely sure I want to share what's been going on between me and Wes with Micah, though. Mostly because it's so new and still feels fragile.

And partly because sharing kissing stories with my brother doesn't sound like the most comfortable conversation.

"At least tell me this," Micah says, tapping my hand lightly to get my attention. "Are you doing this to fuck with Dad or Memphis?"

My eyebrows twist violently. "What are you talking about?" The insinuation lands like a stone in my gut.

He assesses me for a moment before he answers. "I know there's a lot riding on the restaurant. I'm just making sure you're not trying to rock the boat."

I shake my head. "I can't imagine a world where I would even *consider*—" I shake my head again. "I would never do anything to intentionally jeopardize the vineyard or the family or the restaurant, okay?"

Micah shrugs. "I know you wouldn't, but I had to ask."

Irritation bristles inside me. The entire time I've known Wes, it has seemed like the concern has always been how Dad or Memphis might react to us crossing this invisible boundary. He made it clear that this job was the utmost priority.

It never occurred to me that anyone in my family would assume I'm doing something nefarious. Like some kind of sabotage. That is just . . . wild. And hurtful.

"Look, I'm not trying to hurt your feelings," Micah says, his voice soft. He reaches out and places a hand on mine. "I've just been really concerned about things with the vineyard. I shouldn't have jumped to conclusions."

It doesn't surprise me that my brother instantly catches on to how hurt I am. He's sensitive like that. Knows how to pay attention to the small things.

And knowing that there really *are* some serious problems going on at the vineyard, I can't be too mad at him for picking up on the fact things are in a precarious spot.

So I place my other hand on top of his and give it a squeeze.

"Love you," I whisper.

"Love you," he whispers back.

We continue working on the menus, leaving the conversation of Wes behind and instead returning to the vines.

It's the topic my brother loves the most, so it isn't surprising that he slips right back into it.

Something warms in my heart, sitting here, setting up menus with my baby brother. Knowing that I get these moments with him now that I'm back home makes a rickety part of my heart click into place.

I think it's the first time I've truly felt thankful to be back.

The very next day, we're opening the doors for our first dinner when Memphis drops a bomb on me.

"I need you to go get your guitar."

I look at my brother, confusion surely covering every square inch of my face.

"We're ten minutes into our first service," I tell him, plucking a few menus from the basket at the host stand. "I'm not going to get my guitar."

"You have everyone working tonight, and I know they know what they're doing because I watched you train them. They're good without you. But the guy who was supposed to be playing live music called and said he had a family emergency and wouldn't be coming, so . . ." He points to the spot in the corner where I performed for the family dinner, where there's now a stool and microphone set up. "I need you to do it."

I roll my eyes. "The guests will be fine without music, Memphis."

"Murphy, you asked me what you could do to help," he says. "You said you have extra hands. This is what I need."

I pin him with a glare and purse my lips. "You don't get to just pull that out every time you want me to do something. And there's no way that me singing tonight is going to help save the vineyard, or whatever."

"Murphy, please?"

I grit my teeth, my eyes tracking around the room. But as hard as I try to find something I desperately need to be doing right now, it's very clear that Harper and Enid are fine at the host stand without me, and that the servers on the floor are in control and doing their jobs.

So I let out a loud, grating sigh and untie my apron from around my waist. "Fine." I chuck the black fabric at his chest. "But don't ever spring something like this on me again."

He beams at me. "You won't regret it."

I ask Enid to keep an eye on things for me before heading out the front door and finding the little golf cart that Dad likes to drive around the property. I ride it through the vineyard and over to the house. It takes me only a few minutes each way, and before I know it, I'm unbuckling my case and throwing the guitar strap around my shoulders.

The conversation across the room quiets just slightly, and I see people glancing at me with interest as I twist the pegs and pluck at the strings.

Something thick coats my throat, and I clear it a few times before feeling fully ready to go. I lift onto the stool and place one heel on a footrest, leaving the other on the floor. I scan the room and remind myself that I've done this before. That this is just for tonight . . . just for Memphis and to help out.

I strum lightly against the strings, playing a melody as I try to decide what song to start with.

"Play *your* stuff, Murphy," Memphis says as he walks past me with menus in hand and a group following behind him. "No covers."

I actually smile at that and begin to strum the notes to "Tragic Mess," the song I sang to Wes in the car when he was having his anxiety attack. Closing my eyes, I begin to sing, staying far enough away from the mic that I'm giving our patrons some light background music instead of a full-fledged performance.

This was a song I wrote in high school, surprisingly. It perfectly encapsulates my hormonal teenage years—all the times I felt like I wasn't enough coming together in a single song.

As I'm singing the last chorus, I glance to the side and see Wes standing just outside the kitchen, his gaze thoughtful on me.

He's seen me perform before, though the first time it wasn't my own music and the second time it was a quiet solo performance in his car. So something proud and beautiful blooms in my chest at the way he's watching me. At the way he's nodding his head along with the beat of it.

There's a pride there. A happiness for me that has nothing to do with him.

I'm starting to learn that Wes is selfless like that.

And it makes me love him even more than I already do.

Chapter Eighteen

Wes

It's after eleven when we finally get the kitchen cleaned up, and even though I'm exhausted, I'm also rejuvenated in a way I wasn't expecting. In every instance of opening a restaurant in the past, I crawled home afterward and curled into the fetal position on my couch completely depleted.

Tonight, there's a sense of being tired, absolutely. But I also feel like I could work another opening night straight through if I needed to.

Not only was the response from customers better than I could have imagined, everyone was on point. Kellan and Mark were focused; there were no major mistakes; the front of house didn't send anything crazy our way that might have bumped us off our game. Memphis kept popping in to let me know about the compliments he was receiving from guests, too.

Then there was Murphy.

I don't think I've ever been so determined to poke my head out of the kitchen as I was tonight, and I had to remind myself a few times that my priority was cooking. Not watching Murphy like a lovesick puppy.

She was incredible, though. Tonight only further highlighted to me how talented she is. Which makes me think she would be a fool not to at least *meet* with those people from her friend's new label.

But she has to decide that for herself.

I pick up my phone where it's been sitting in the little office off the kitchen and prepare to send Murphy a text to let her know I'm wrapping things up.

My heart shoots into my throat when I see the twelve missed calls from Ash.

Clicking on his name, I bring the phone to my ear, waiting with bated breath as it rings. And rings. And . . .

"Mom's in the hospital."

He says it the second he answers the phone, and my throat tightens.

"Mira and I went to fucking Vegas, and I can't get a flight home until tomorrow morning. Can you go?"

I sigh. Part of me wants to say no, as horrible as it sounds. When you have an addict as a parent, you can only repeat the same actions over and over again so many times before it feels useless.

But I won't say no. Not just because I love my mother and want to make sure she's okay and not alone. Because I love my brother. He's a lot more emotionally connected to her than I am, and if this is something I can do to help ease his stress and worry, I'll do it.

"Text me the details. I need to go change, but I'll get on the road in the next half hour, okay?"

I hear Ash exhale on the other end of the line, and I know I've alleviated at least a little bit of the stress.

"Thank you, Wes."

"Don't worry about it. Just text me, okay?"

We get off the phone, and I drop into the desk chair, giving myself a moment before I soldier on.

My mother has been in the hospital, on average, every few years for as long as I can remember. The first time, I was seven and Ash was two, and she got in a car accident because she was drinking and driving. We were at home for four days without any adults when she finally came home.

The most recent time was because she was drunk and passed out at a bus stop, and a Good Samaritan called an ambulance for her. I was in Chicago for that one, but I remember the way Ash sounded when he called me. She was supposed to be in rehab, and he'd been so hopeful for something good to come from it.

Everything about my mother is a mess, and I've tried to be there for her as often as I can. But it's hard sometimes to go see her when it's like that.

When she's lying in a hospital bed with a broken wrist because she fell off a slide at a playground in the middle of the night. Or picking her up from jail because she was taken in for a drunk and disorderly.

My brother continues to believe she can change, but I gave up on that possibility years ago.

Eventually I push myself out of the chair and through the kitchen, flipping off the lights as I go. When I emerge into the dining room, my gaze strays to the patio, where the fairy lights are still illuminated.

That's when I see Murphy sitting on the short stone wall that divides the sitting area from a large grassy knoll, her guitar propped on her knee, her fingers plucking at the strings.

She smiles when I step outside, her frame rocking slowly from side to side as she strums an unfamiliar melody. But the smile dips when she sees me, and her hands stop moving.

"Everything okay?"

I shake my head. "My mom's in the hospital," I tell her, crossing the patio and dropping down on the wall next to her. "I need to head into San Francisco."

There's a pause, and then her hand rests on my knee.

"Do you want some company?"

My immediate reaction is to tell her no. The last thing I want is for her to have to deal with the bullshit I've been handling since I was a kid. Nothing prepares you for seeing someone in the hospital, and I don't even know the reality of what I'll be walking into because Ash didn't give any details.

But when I turn to look at her, to tell her I appreciate it, but no thanks, something inside me says I should take this gesture.

I've thought several times to myself that some of what connects Murphy and me is our mirrored history of facing really difficult things. We've both been through a lot, and each of us have had to handle those things alone.

Maybe this time, it's okay to lean on someone, just a little bit.

So instead of turning her down, I rest my hand on top of hers and give it a squeeze, thankful for her willingness to be there with me.

"That would actually be amazing."

"It's really not a big deal," Murphy tells me as we trudge down the hall-way. "I've been in a hospital before. I knew about visiting hours, and I didn't think about it, either."

I know she's right, but that doesn't change the fact I feel like an idiot for driving ninety minutes only to arrive at the hospital and find out I have to wait until eight in the morning to see my mother.

"The good news is that, whatever it is, it's not critical, right? It's *better* that they won't let you see her. It means she's stable."

I come to a stop next to where Murphy stands in front of room 304, setting the key card against the door handle. It beeps, a little light turns green, and then we're pushing into the tiny room at the chain hotel across the street from the hospital.

The thing I'm the most irritated about is that I didn't even need to come. Maybe that makes me selfish. Maybe that makes me a shitty son. But the truth is that if I'd thought about the visiting hours, I would have let Ash come in the morning once he got back from Vegas.

Instead, I've had to text my boss in the middle of the night to let him know I'll be late to my second fucking service at my brand-new job that I've been preparing for months for. I've needed to call my line cooks and make sure they know they're on their own for the very first lunch service of the restaurant's existence.

I'm not an angry person, but there is nothing that lights me on fire and makes me want to chuck things across the room like the ways in which my mother's addiction fucks with my life.

"Why don't you take a shower," Murphy suggests.

I sigh and drop my jacket on the edge of the bed, then kick off my shoes before pushing into the bathroom. Once I've closed the door, I brace my hands on the counter and look at myself for a long moment in the mirror.

As frustrated as I am about tonight's events, I'm actually pleased with what I see in the mirror. When I left Chicago, I was a little gaunt looking, and my normally muscular frame was on the leaner side. In the two months I've lived in Rosewood, I've put on a few pounds of toned muscle, and I'm looking a lot like my normal self.

Rolling my eyes at my own vanity, I turn and swat at the shower handle, turning the water on and then beginning to strip.

Nothing sounds better than scrubbing off the grit and grime from my first full service. It's like a reward for all the hard work I put in, and that first blast of the hot water against my tired muscles feels incredible.

I grab the little bottle of body wash and give myself a rubdown, then tackle my hair and face, before just standing under the hot water and enjoying the heat.

A noise behind me draws my attention, and when I turn my head, I see Murphy pulling the shower curtain to the side. My eyes travel down her naked frame with admiration.

"I thought I might be able to help with a little stress relief," she says, a playful smile on her lips.

I give her a mischievous grin, and she steps into the tub behind me.

Her arms wrap around my middle, and I sigh at the feeling of her body pressing up against mine from behind. Murphy's lips touch gently against the center of my back, leaving a trail of kisses. But it's hard to focus on that when her hands are lightly tracing along my pelvic muscles.

My cock throbs between my legs, growing harder as she continues teasing me. I let my head fall back slightly, my eyes closed, just mentally focusing on her.

Nothing feels as incredible as having Murphy's hands on my body. Her hands, her mouth, her gorgeous tits pressed against me . . . I'll take any part of Murphy snuggled up against any part of me whenever I can.

I hiss in pleasure when her hands grip my length and begin to stroke, and with her petite frame pressed against me from behind, my movements are restricted, leaving me with no choice but to just stand there even though I feel desperate to thrust into her hand.

But eventually, it becomes too much, and I spin around and yank her in for a kiss. Our mouths open instantly, this kiss so much more erotic than any that has come before it.

I crowd her against the shower wall, then lick into her mouth with desperation, my tongue tangling with hers as my hands grip at her bare flesh. First her hips, then her ass, and I groan as my dick presses against her warm body.

"I want you inside me," she whispers, her hands gripping my back and her hips undulating against me.

I drop a hand and touch between her legs, groaning when I feel the slickness between her lower lips that is *definitely* not from the shower.

"I'm clean," I tell her as I tug her leg to the side so she can set her foot on the edge of the tub. "Haven't been with anyone in over a year."

She nods, then reaches between us and grabs me, lining me up so the head of my dick is pressed against her tight opening.

"How do you want it?" I ask her, then begin to suck on her neck as my hips pulse lightly, teasing us both.

Murphy moans, her hips shifting, her fingernails beginning to press into my back.

"Fuck me, Wes."

I smile against her wet skin, then raise my head so I can look into her eyes.

"Good answer," I tell her, and then I watch as I slide into her pussy in one long, slow movement.

The tight, wet heat of her is almost too much. I grit my teeth at how good it feels.

"Oh my god," she whispers, and then I feel her inner walls squeeze me.

"Yes," I tell her, drawing back before thrusting in again, this time with more force. "Do that again."

Her pussy clamps down on me again, and I groan, wanting to both stay right where I am and continue to move at the same time.

"It's so good." I draw back out and spear forward again. "So fucking good."

Murphy's fingernails dig in deeper, then scratch down my back with enough force that I don't doubt she's leaving marks.

I grip beneath her knee, lifting her leg off the edge of the tub and raising it higher, opening her wider so I can fuck into her harder.

"Fuck, Wes. Fuck," she moans, moving to place her hands on my shoulders.

And then I begin thrusting at a steady pace, the slap of our bodies colliding echoing around us in the tiny space.

I drop my face to her neck and suck at her damp skin, losing myself in the sensation of being inside her.

"I'm gonna come," she tells me, and the knowledge that I've gotten her near the peak so quickly has my own orgasm stirring, the pleasure coiling inside me tighter and tighter.

I feel her clamp down on me a moment later, a cry falling from her lips.

And I'm tumbling behind her, lost in a sea of bliss.

◆ ◆ ◆

"I didn't mean to seduce you into shower sex," she tells me later as we're lying in bed together, my fingers twirling in her damp hair. "My plan was just a shower BJ."

"Well, I'll definitely take one of those next time."

She tucks her body into mine and kisses my chest, and I wrap my arms around her. It isn't long before I hear her breathing begin to slow, soft snores coming from her that make me smile.

God, I don't know what I was expecting with Murphy Hawthorne, but it sure as hell wasn't this. And the deeper we fall, the more pressure I feel to tell her about what happened in Chicago.

I don't want to.

Fuck, I really don't want to.

But I feel like I need to.

And if I'm honest, she deserves the truth. Not only about what happened, but about who I am and what I've done.

I lie in bed for a long while, thinking about everything, and when I open my eyes in the morning, I know I probably only got a few hours of sleep, if that.

I gently wake Murphy, and she gives me a groggy smile. I drop a kiss to her forehead, wishing that after our first time together, we had the ability to laze around in bed and enjoy each other some more.

Instead, we both tug on our clothes, check out of the hotel, and walk across the street to the hospital.

Last night, the woman at the desk provided me with a room number but said I'd need to come back in the morning. So when we walk through the front doors, Murphy and I are able to just head straight to the elevators and up to the seventh floor.

"How can I help you?" a nurse asks as we exit, a flat expression on her face.

"My mom is in 705. Sonia Hart."

"Bed 705 is empty."

I blink a few times, then change my question, figuring I must have just been given wrong information.

"Can you let me know where I can find her then?"

The nurse sighs and rolls her chair to a computer. "What was the name again?"

"Sonia Hart."

She clicks around for a minute or two. "She was discharged this morning at 6:00 a.m."

My entire body bristles in frustration. "What? Why? When I came last night they said I could see her if I came back during visiting hours. They didn't say anything about her leaving before then."

"You family?" She eyes me with a level of passivity that has me gritting my teeth.

"Yes, I'm her son," I tell her again.

"All I can tell you is that she was unconscious when she arrived yesterday, and this morning she left against medical advice. We did a blood panel overnight and it came back with a BAC of 0.31."

I feel a hand on my back and I startle, having forgotten for a moment that Murphy is here, but almost immediately, something inside me settles just a little bit at her touch.

"Did she say anything? About where she was going, or . . . ?"

"I'm not her babysitter," she says. "Sorry."

Sighing, I turn away from the nurse, frustrated at not only her lack of compassion, but at the situation in general.

How can they just let her leave? Clearly something was bad enough that she was brought unconscious to the hospital.

Murphy slips her hand in mine and gives it a gentle squeeze as we wait for the elevator.

I hate that she's here, seeing this. That she has any idea about this part of my life.

And at the same time, I've never felt so thankful to have someone at my side.

No, not just someone.

Her.

I wrap my arm around Murphy's shoulders once we're in the elevator, and slowly we descend to the parking garage.

Pressing my nose into her hair, I breathe in deeply, the now-familiar scent of her weaving its way around the tightness in my chest and settling there like a balm over a sore wound.

If there was any doubt how I felt about Murphy Hawthorne left inside my mind, it is most assuredly gone, replaced with overwhelming feelings of love and gratitude.

"I'm here if you want to talk," she tells me as we buckle our seat belts.

I rest my hand on her knee as I pull out of the parking spot. "I know you are."

She lifts my hand to her mouth and kisses my knuckles before returning it to her knee, the gesture soft and sweet and exactly what I need.

Then we pull out into traffic and begin the drive back to the vineyard, her hand on mine the entire way.

Chapter Nineteen

Murphy

We're mostly silent on the drive home, each of us lost in our thoughts. Other than pulling over and getting out of the car to have a conversation with his younger brother, Wes doesn't say much. The only real thing he mentions to me as we're getting off the highway is that he's glad we'll be back in time for him to be able to help with the lunch service.

I know he has a lot on his mind, and I'm sure the past twelve hours have been hard on him. So I just keep holding his hand, singing quietly along with the radio that's playing country music on low in the background.

Eventually, we pull into the gravel parking lot outside the restaurant, and when Wes shuts off the car, I turn in my seat to look at him.

I wish there was something I could say. I racked my mind for so much of the drive trying to come up with anything that might make him feel better. But nothing seemed right, so I just stayed silent.

This moment is the same. Because there *isn't* anything that can make things like this better.

"Thank you again for coming with me," he says, staring straight ahead. "You didn't have to go, but you made a really shitty trip so much better just by being there."

"Don't forget the shower sex," I joke, hoping to alleviate some of his serious attitude so that he doesn't go into work feeling so down.

He shakes his head, a soft smile on his face, then finally turns to look at me.

"You're a nut."

"Yeah. Just a little bit."

His eyes search mine for a beat, then he kisses the back of my hand and we both unbuckle and climb out of the car.

"I've gotta head in," he tells me, rounding the front and coming to a stop just a few inches away. "Make sure these kids are doing all right."

"I won't be that far behind you, but I'm going to run back to the house and change first. You might be able to get away with your outfit if you put on a chef's coat. My pink leggings aren't gonna fly."

He smiles, then reaches out and takes my hand. "I'll see you in a little bit."

I pop up on my toes and press my lips to his, giggling at the bit of stubble that's grown in on his face scratching lightly against the skin around my mouth.

"Murphy?"

I freeze, blinking in surprise when I turn and see Memphis standing at the front door of the restaurant, a kind of bewildered look on his face. But that look is only there for a second before it's replaced by anger, and I drop back down on my heels as he storms toward us in a fury.

"What the fuck is going on?"

"Memphis—"

"Are you screwing my sister?" He cuts me off and glares at Wes, his hands on his hips.

"That is none of your business," I tell him. "And also why would you ever want to know if that was true?"

"I can understand why you might be upset," Wes begins, "but if—"

"No. This is not happening," Memphis says, interrupting him and then pointing a finger at me. "You do not get to fuck with my head chef and cause problems for this restaurant."

My head jerks back. "What?"

"And you do not get to screw around with staff, okay?" he continues, returning his attention to Wes.

I sigh, clenching and unclenching my hands in little fists. "Memphis, you're being ridiculous."

"Wes, go to work," my brother demands, moving to the side and pointing at the front door.

"He's not a *dog*."

"Memphis, I know this might—"

"I don't want to hear it."

Wes looks like he's ready to stand here and have a face-off with my brother, but I'm one of the few people who knows how stubborn Memphis can be, and there's no way he will hear anything Wes has to say right now.

The best thing for everyone is for Wes to just go to work, and we can all talk about this later. "Just go. I'll see you in a bit."

He looks back and forth between the two of us a few times, then turns to walk up the sidewalk, giving one last glance before heading inside.

"I cannot fucking believe you."

"I can't fucking believe *you*!" I reply, poking my brother in the chest. "In what world is it okay for you to shout at someone because I kissed them?"

"It was more than just a kiss and we both know it, Murphy." He glares down at me. "I saw you pull in together. Did you go with him to San Francisco?"

"How the hell is that relevant?"

"Answer me."

"I am twenty-fucking-seven years old, Memphis, and you're not my parent, so you don't get to demand anything from me."

"That's bullshit."

"How the hell is it bullshit?"

"Because I thought we were on the same team!"

I take a step back in surprise when his growled words become a shout.

Memphis spins around and stares at the trees along the edge of the parking lot that line the eastern perimeter of our property, his hands clasped behind his neck.

"I told you what was going on with the vineyard, and how this restaurant was my Hail Mary," he says, his voice so low I can barely hear him.

Then he spins around, and I'm pained at the way he looks at me.

Like I've hurt him.

Deeply.

"How could you be willing to jeopardize everything?"

I shake my head.

"I'm not jeopardizing *anything*," I reply.

Even though I mean it, there's something hollow about my words.

Because they imply that I don't see any problems with my relationship with Wes, and that's not true.

Wes knows as well as I do that something happening between us could create plenty of complications. It was a smarter choice to avoid each other and try to keep things platonic.

But that time has come and gone.

Now, we're in too deep. We've fallen too far.

Or at least, I have.

"Memphis, I'm in love with him."

My brother scoffs and shakes his head. "You're not in love, you're in lust. It's fun sneaking around and breaking the rules. That's all this is."

"It's not."

Crossing his arms, Memphis just looks at me, then shakes his head again. "Go change for work. We can discuss this later."

Then he turns and heads in the direction he just sent Wes.

Something behind my eyes pinches tight, and I can feel tears building up inside me, so I take the path away from the restaurant and through the vineyard back to the house.

I change quickly, then get back to the restaurant about fifteen minutes before we open for lunch. Memphis is nowhere to be seen, and even though it's easier to not think about him when he's not around, the look on his face is hard to get out of my head.

Thankfully, the opening night numbers translate into a large crowd for lunch as well, and I'm able to somewhat distract myself from thinking about my brother or the things he said for most of the afternoon.

Eventually, though, the rush dies down. I send the other server home, and then it's just me and my thoughts.

And the longer I think, the angrier I get.

So after I say goodbye to the last lunch table, I hastily begin clearing away their dishes, desperate to get out of here, track down my brother, and give him a piece of my mind.

"Hey."

The sound of Wes's voice startles me out of my thoughts, and I look up from where I'm stacking empty plates on my serving tray.

Just the sight of him lifts some of the weight off my shoulders.

"How did the service go out here?"

I put the last of the dishes on my tray and hoist it onto my shoulder. "Good. Everyone *loved* the pesto today."

Wes bobs his head, but his smile is pinched, so I set the tray back on the table and walk the few feet to where he's standing.

"Hey, everything's going to be okay," I tell him, taking his hand in mine and giving it a gentle squeeze. "I'm going to finish up and then go talk to Memphis. He doesn't get to have a say in who either of us . . ."

I trail off, realizing Wes and I haven't officially established anything yet.

We aren't dating. He's not my boyfriend, I don't think. And we aren't just hooking up.

"If we want to be together, he'll have to get over it," I finally say, happy with how I've phrased it.

His eyes flick across my face for a second before he steps into me, bringing his free hand to the back of my neck and pulling me in for a kiss.

I sink against him, my mouth opening and my tongue lightly grazing his.

Wes pulls back just a little bit, his eyes on my mouth, before pressing another kiss against my lips as his thumb strokes along my jaw.

"Don't talk to Memphis yet," he says, and that's when I realize he looks far more serious in this moment than I do, a deep crease forming between his brows. "Just wait. I want us to talk first."

I can feel my heart skip a beat at his words, something foreboding sinking low and hard to the bottom of my stomach.

"Is everything okay?"

He nods. "Yeah."

But nothing about the way he looks inspires confidence that he's being honest, and I can't help but wonder what's really going on in his mind.

This time, when he leans in and presses his lips against mine, I realize it tastes an awful lot like goodbye.

The dinner service goes by at a glacial pace, made even slower by the guitarist who seems dead set on playing incredibly slow, drawn-out covers of pop songs all night.

And even though I'm able to keep a smile on my face and do a decent job of handling guests and taking orders, I'm surprised I make it all the way through dinner without giving in to the desire to find Wes in the kitchen and demand we start speaking. Because part of my brain keeps reminding me how often I get so close to the things I want and how rarely they work out.

Memphis barely speaks to me and instead just kind of hovers all evening long, and honestly, I'm thankful I don't really have to talk to him. I barely register his presence, the things he said earlier falling by the wayside as I try to deduce what Wes might want to talk to me about tonight.

I mean, the easy answer is that he's calling things off. Right?

He's made it clear to me that this job is incredibly important. We even talked about why we *shouldn't* get involved, because he believed he'd be considered disposable if something went wrong.

My brain talks in circles all evening long as I try to convince myself that he cares about me too much to end things, and battle the fears I have that he might take the easy road and call things off to protect his job.

I'm a mess of uncertainty as we close the restaurant at the end of the night, and instead of lurking around the patio and waiting for Wes to finish in the kitchen, I return to the house for a long, hot shower to wash away not only the workday, but also my nerves.

It works for the former, but not the latter.

Once I've changed, I stand in front of my mirror, twisting my long, thick hair into a braid that hangs over my left shoulder. My mother used to braid my hair when I was a kid. It's one of my few memories of her. I'd sit in the chair in front of her bathroom vanity and she'd do a long braid that hung perfectly down the center of my back.

After she died, I tried to teach myself how to do it. But when doing it on my own, it has always fallen off center because I pull all the hair to the left side to braid it.

I was always mad at her for that, even though it wasn't her fault.

As I'm tying a rubber band around the end, I notice someone standing in the doorway.

"You doing okay?"

I can tell by the pitch of Aunt Sarah's voice that she knows about my confrontation with Memphis.

"Memphis tell you?"

She shakes her head and crosses her arms, then leans against the doorjamb.

"Naomi and I were delivering a few boxes of wine to the restaurant when you and Wes pulled up."

Of course that's what happened.

"Honey, I didn't realize anything was going on with you and Wes."

I turn around, lean back against my dresser, and tuck my hands into the pockets of my sweater.

"Is it serious?"

"Yeah. I think it is."

Aunt Sarah watches me for a minute before pushing off the frame and entering my room. She crosses over to my bed and takes a seat on the edge, facing me.

"I couldn't hear the argument from inside the restaurant, but it looked like Memphis was pretty upset."

At that, I laugh. "That's an understatement. He's just . . ." I shake my head.

If I get into the nitty-gritty about Memphis and why he's so mad at me, I'd have to tell Aunt Sarah about what's going on with the vineyard, and how Dad's thinking about selling it. That's just not something I want to get into tonight. Not when I have so much else on my mind.

"He's just worried," I end up saying. "He really wants the restaurant to be a success, and I think he's stressed that something could happen if Wes and I are seeing each other."

"Do you think he'd be so upset if he wasn't worried about the finances?"

My back straightens then as surprise tumbles through me.

It must show on my face because Aunt Sarah gives me a knowing smile.

"I know the vineyard's struggling, Murphy. Have for a long time. You don't have to hide things from me."

I blink a few times, not really sure what to say.

"I've known about the problems for years," she continues, "and I've been begging your father to either hire someone to help sort things, or at the very least let me try to help."

211

"And he wouldn't?"

She sighs. "Your father is stubborn. I don't have to tell you that. He's never been good with numbers or finances. But he refuses to ask for help, and the vineyard is suffering now because of it."

"Unfortunately Memphis has inherited Dad's stubborn streak."

"Oh, Memphis doesn't hold a candle to your father," Aunt Sarah says with a laugh that tells me she's seen a thing or two. "The fact your brother talked to you about what's going on instead of living in denial means he's willing to accept suggestions or ideas. But your dad grew up listening to *our* dad talk about responsibility and the job of *the men of the house.*" She rolls her eyes. "With the way that man talked, you'd think my mom and I never did anything around the vineyard."

Something occurs to me then. Something I hadn't ever thought of before because it just wasn't on my radar.

But now, talking to Aunt Sarah, it just makes me wonder.

"Did you ever hope Grandpa would leave the business to you instead?"

Something sad flashes across her face, but only for a second. "Oh, that just wasn't their time, you know?" She waves her hand in the air. "Women didn't run businesses when he was learning everything from *our* grandfather, so it's only natural he'd pass it on to your dad."

"But did you ever *want* him to?"

There's a long pause where I think she's deciding how best to answer. And when she does, it breaks my heart a little bit.

"Murphy, as you get older, you start to realize that a lot of things in life are out of your control. And you can either lay in bed at night and think about all that's gone wrong, or you can choose to focus on what has gone right." She shrugs. "It's no use thinking about whether or not I wish my father had given the vineyard to me. Besides, I love my brother too much to resent him for something that wasn't his choice in the first place."

There's truth to what she's saying, absolutely. But there's also a heartbreaking element as well.

My father left the vineyard when he graduated high school, much like I did. He proposed to my mom—his high school sweetheart—moved to San Jose, got a job working in sales, and had two babies. And then my mother died giving birth to Micah, and my dad moved back here to work on the vineyard and get help from my grandparents and aunt in taking care of us.

In all the years my dad was gone, Aunt Sarah was still here, working the fields and handling things that would have been Dad's responsibility. Yet my grandfather still gave the vineyard to my father.

And she's still here, working hard and demanding nothing.

I hate that for her.

"Can I give you a suggestion? Don't let Memphis make decisions for you," she says. "If there's something special between you and Wes, fight for it."

"I was planning to. I love Memphis, but I'm *in love* with Wes." I puff out a breath. "I guess I just have to see if he feels the same."

Aunt Sarah gives me an empathetic smile. "I know you two will figure it out, sweetie." She pauses for a moment. "And keep it logical when you talk to your brother, not emotional. He responds better that way."

I laugh, realizing the truth of what she's said.

"I love you, sweetheart. And I'm so proud of you."

My chest constricts at her words, and I feel the pressure of distant tears building behind my eyes.

"Thanks, Aunt Sarah. I love you, too."

She says good night and gives me a hug before leaving my room.

I feel a little bolstered by our conversation, knowing I have the support of at least *somebody* in our family. But by the time I make it out to the bench closer to midnight, my nerves are rattling me again. When Wes takes a seat instead of giving me a kiss, it makes me even more concerned.

"Everything go okay with locking up?"

Wes nods, but his eyes are cast downward, his hands fiddling with one of the buttons on his chef coat. He looks . . . not upset, exactly, but apprehensive.

"I'm sorry about this morning." He clears his throat. "I wanted to stay and talk things out with your brother, and it was shitty of me to leave you on your own to deal with it."

I shake my head. "I knew that you sticking around wouldn't resolve anything. That's why I told you to go inside, too. He's *incredibly* stubborn."

"Yeah." Wes pauses for a second. "But he's also not wrong to be worried about his chef getting involved with his staff, not to mention his sister. It can make things really complicated."

As much as I want to avoid whatever this conversation will bring, I decide it's better to just get down to business. Because tiptoeing around will only make me more and more uncomfortable.

"Is that why you wanted to talk tonight?" I ask. "Because you think things are getting too complicated?"

Wes's head falls forward, and he runs a hand through his hair.

My heart takes off at a sprint. My stomach tightens.

I hate the way this feels.

"No," he finally says, surprising me. "I think you and I can handle Memphis, regardless of what he throws our way."

Blinking a few times, I replay what he just said over again in my mind, making sure I'm not misunderstanding him.

The tight band around my shoulders loosens, and I feel the weight in my stomach begin to dissolve.

What he just said has a future implication. There's a belief there that he and I will be fine moving forward. That he sees things between us not just continuing, but thriving even through a potential disruption from my brother.

"So what did you want to talk about?" I ask, not wanting to give myself too much permission to exhale in relief until I know why we're here right now. "You made it sound really serious."

He licks his lips and looks at me. "Because it is serious. But it has nothing to do with Memphis."

I try to think back over anything we've talked about that might lend itself to such an intense conversation, but I can't seem to pinpoint an event or topic or person that fits the bill.

I scoot toward him and slip my hand in his. "I'm sure whatever it is, we can handle that, too."

He looks at my hand in his, and his thumb strokes gently along the back of my palm, the movement sending little goose bumps skittering up my arm.

"First, I want you to know how crazy I am about you." His eyes are still focused on my hand. "I can't remember ever feeling like this about someone."

My heart warms, the statement a much-needed confirmation that Wes and I are on the same page when it comes to how we feel about each other.

"But I'm not going to ask you to tell me how you feel about me," he continues. "Not until after you've had a chance to hear what I have to say."

The pit in my stomach is back, though it feels more like acid as it stirs up a kind of nausea I haven't felt in a really long time.

"Because what I tell you might change how you feel about me, and I don't want to trick you into saying anything you might regret later."

I take a deep breath as quietly and as slowly as I can, then let it out just as quiet, and just as slow.

"I've told you a few times that I left Chicago, but I've never told you why." He pauses, and I get the feeling he's trying to muster up the courage to tell me.

But when he finally speaks again, I'm not ready for what he says.

"I left Chicago because I got fired," he tells me, stopping again and taking a breath. "I got fired for sleeping with my boss's wife."

Chapter Twenty

WES

The shock of what I've just told her ripples through her body.

Eyes wide, she seems to be trying to process what I've said.

I just hope she'll give me a chance to explain. To give her a true picture of what happened. But I also understand if what I've said is enough. If she doesn't need to hear anything else from me.

Because something like what I've done can be a deal-breaker. Even though I technically wasn't a cheater, I still did something with serious moral implications. And with the things Murphy has shared with me about her time in LA, it makes me think she might not be able to brush this off.

Which is why I'm talking to her about it now.

"Can I tell you what happened?" I ask after a bit of time has passed and she still hasn't responded.

I can understand why she might say no. I doubt she wants to hear about an affair I had with someone else, let alone a *married* someone else.

So when she takes a deep breath and gives me a quiet, "Okay," I feel grateful. What I don't expect is for her to reach over and put a hand on my forearm.

"Whatever it is, I'm sure that you'll feel better once you talk about it."

Her words are so kind, but I can't help the humorless laugh that bubbles up from my chest. Because the truth is that I'm not so sure I agree. It's very possible that sharing this with Murphy will ruin that wide-eyed way she looks at me, and in that case, I will definitely *not* feel better.

I clear my throat, and then jump in, knowing that if I don't just rip off the Band-Aid, I might never get it out.

"I spent years working for my mentor at an incredible restaurant in San Francisco," I tell her, wanting to make sure she understands where I was coming from. "All the things that Chef Hines preached about food are the things I'm bringing to my chef work here. The farm-to-table, community-oriented cooking."

Chef Hines was a wonderful mentor during the most important and formative time of my career, and he is a huge factor in the kind of chef I aspire to be. I only wish that I hadn't let him down in such a major way.

"But the beginning years in a culinary career are not incredibly lucrative. It's generally accepted that you'll be broke for years before you really feel comfortable, unless you make smart choices early on. So when I garnered some interest from a couple who were restaurateurs, I jumped at the chance to work for them. The salary was something I'd only ever dreamed of, and it was the kind of thing where I thought I could have the job, live comfortably, and pay for my brother to go to college so he didn't have to struggle like I did. So I picked up my meager little life and moved to Chicago."

I run a hand through my hair, sure that I've mussed it enough to leave things looking messy and neglected. It's an accurate representation for how things feel inside my chest as well.

"I was the head chef for a restaurant they'd just opened. But after the first year, they offered me a chance to partner with them on other projects, so before long I was helping them open several others. It was a fast-paced thing, and instead of being paid more, we discussed partnership opportunities for ownership, which felt like a huge move for me."

I pause, realizing this is where my story changes. That from here on out, there's no going back.

"We talked before about restaurant culture, how wild and toxic it can be and how everyone sleeps with everyone."

Murphy nods.

"Well, I guess it's not just restaurant staff, it's management, too. Everybody knew that the couple, the Santiagos, had an open marriage. Alejandro and Bridget *both* slept around—servers, staff, kitchen crew, guests, it didn't matter. Nobody was off-limits. And a guy from one of the spots I helped open told me that he hooked up with Bridget and got a bonus in his next paycheck. So when Bridget began flirting with me . . ."

I trail off, the shame I feel weighing heavy in my gut.

"It was only a few times, and it wasn't a hardship or anything. She was beautiful and funny and it felt like a normal interaction. A normal hookup."

I swallow thickly.

"Until I got that first paycheck," I continue, shaking my head at myself. "I've never felt so sick in my entire life, so . . . ashamed. I felt like I'd sold my soul. Or gave it away without realizing its worth. And that's not . . ."

I trail off again, and this time, Murphy surprises me when she reaches out and places her hand on mine where I'm gripping the seat of the bench.

"My brother is all I have, and I would do anything for him. But I realized as I was looking at that paycheck, there were other ways I could have tried to help him, you know?"

I squeeze the bench seat more firmly and continue to glare daggers at the ground. I'm not ready to look at Murphy. Not ready to see the look on her face.

"How did you end up getting fired? If they were in an open marriage, I mean, did he really fire you for that when he was doing it, too?"

At that, I actually laugh, because this is the part I can still barely believe myself.

"I went to work drunk the day after I got the paycheck," I tell her. "I didn't really know how to handle the whole thing and ended up making an ass of myself and talked about their marriage and sleeping with Bridget and getting paid for it. In front of them and their guests."

I still don't understand exactly how it all went down, the pieces of my actions only flittering in and out of my memory in drunken hazes.

"Alejandro walked me through the dining room, through the kitchen, out the back door. Gave me a black eye and shoved me to the ground. Told me I was done. That when he was through, I'd be lucky to work as a dishwasher. And he has the clout to make that happen."

I finally turn and look at Murphy.

"Almost a decade of work trying to build up my reputation, my skills, my salary. Gone. It took me weeks to find a new job, and it was literally as a dishwasher, and yes, I felt lucky as hell to finally find it because I couldn't seem to get anyone to call me about any chef positions, line cook work, nothing."

She looks surprised.

"Is that really a thing? One person can block you from work like that?"

I level her with a stare. "You tell me."

Murphy nods at the reference to her own story. To her own experience.

When Alejandro told me I was done, I knew he meant it. That he had that level of control and influence to ruin any kind of culinary connections I was trying to cultivate and keep me from forming new ones.

A chef further along in his career might have been able to weather this kind of situation. But I didn't have the connections to maneuver around Alejandro.

"What did your mentor say about it?" Murphy asks.

"I haven't talked to him since it happened."

She looks shocked. "What? Why?"

I shrug, because I know my answer isn't good enough. "He told me not to get involved with them and I did it anyway and look how things turned out. I ruined my career because I didn't listen to him, so I promised myself I would do everything I could to fix things before I reached out to him. Get back to my roots and what matters to me. Go back to the lessons I was taught in the beginning."

Then I chuckle, scrubbing my face with my hands.

"This is why I wanted to talk to you. Because my life is a mess, Murphy. And I feel like I need to be truthful about it, so you know what you're getting yourself into."

"Look," she starts, her eyes boring into my soul. "I can't even tell you how much I wish I'd had a mentor when I was in LA. Someone I could reach out to and share everything I'd been through, who might be able to provide suggestions on how to handle it. And you have that, Wes." She squeezes my hand. "You have someone who cares about you and wants to see you succeed waiting for you in your corner to patch you up and send you back out."

Then she moves to twist our fingers together.

"You have me in your corner, too," she adds, her voice gentle. "I might not have the ability to patch you up, but I can be here to listen. To make sure you feel heard. If I learned anything during my time in LA, it was how important it can be just to know that someone sees you. That they know you. Who you really are."

Murphy lifts my hand to her mouth and kisses the back, never taking her eyes off me.

"And I know who you are, Wesley Hart."

Her free hand rises and she places her palm against the center of my chest.

"I know how kind and thoughtful you are. How much you love your family, even when it hurts. How hard you work."

She pauses for just a breath, her eyes searching mine.

"And I know that I'm in love with you."

It takes a second for her words to sink in, and when they do, something heavy in my chest takes flight, leaving me feeling weightless.

"I'm in love with you, too," I tell her. "*So* in love with you."

At that, Murphy's leaning in and pressing her lips to mine, all thoughts of our earlier conversation taking a back seat to this moment.

It's not a kiss filled with lust or desire. It's a kiss filled with love. There's something special about it that I can't name. All I can do is feel it.

We pull back to look at each other, and I reach up and tuck some of her loose hairs behind her ear, then stroke my thumb down her jaw.

"I'm sorry about what you went through in Chicago," she tells me, sympathy written all over her face. "And how everything turned out."

I shake my head. "It was my own fault," I tell her. "Are you not at all upset with me?"

At that, her brows scrunch in confusion.

"Why would I be upset with *you*?"

"I mean, you had someone offer you your dream if you would compromise yourself, and you refused. I thought I saw a chance at something better, and I took it without a second thought."

She considers me for a moment, her eyes scanning my face.

"If you could go back to any point in time and talk to yourself about what happened in Chicago and give yourself advice, what would you say?"

Blinking a few times, I think it over, having never thought of this before.

"I'd probably go back to before I went to Chicago and tell myself that I should listen to Chef Hines. That I need to focus more on the things I value than the value of things."

Her lips tilt up at the sides.

"Wes, you talk about this mistake like it's one of the most horrible things a person can do." Her hand reaches out and twists into mine again. "But someone who has truly sold their soul wouldn't care this much about redemption."

I shake my head and just stare at Murphy.

"I can't even tell you how much I appreciate everything you've said."

She grins, something playful coming across her smile.

"Yeah, well . . . you'd better check if I'm in network," she teases. "This therapy session is gonna cost you big-time."

"Oh yeah?"

She nods.

"Do you take AmEx?"

Murphy giggles, her head falling back, the sound deflating the last bit of tension still lingering in the air around us.

"Hmm, that's a no. How about Discover?"

"Who even uses Discover?" she asks, still smiling wide.

"All right, not Discover. How about this?" I lean forward, so my lips are just a breath from hers.

I kiss her gently, and just for a heartbeat. When I pull back, she licks her lips.

"I might be able to accept those."

"Good to know."

We smile at each other, and then I pull her in for another kiss.

And if it was up to me, I'd never stop.

Murphy goes back to my cabin with me, where we strip each other of our clothes and fall into bed.

I kiss her for what feels like hours before finally trailing my way down her body, branding her with my lips in as many places as possible.

She watches me with wide eyes and open mouth as I pulse my tongue against her clit. Her hands grip the pillow behind her, soft whimpers falling from her mouth.

Only after I have her right on the crest of orgasm do I kiss my way back up her body and slip inside, groaning at how tight and wet she is.

"I love you," she whispers, her eyes piercing mine as she clamps down and then flies over the edge.

I moan, tumbling over as well, my forehead pressed to hers, my eyes never looking away.

They really do mean it when they say there's a difference between fucking and making love.

Before Murphy, I wouldn't have known.

I wouldn't have been able to explain how something that might look the same on the outside feels so different on the inside.

But now that I have her, I don't ever want to go back.

I don't ever want to be reminded of when sex was something other than the intimacy we just shared in this bed.

Because making love to Murphy might just be the most incredible, beautiful thing I've ever experienced.

And now that I know it exists, I don't want to settle for anything less.

Chapter Twenty-One

MURPHY

When I get a text from Memphis in the morning letting me know we need to talk before the Sunday lunch service begins, it drags me out of my love-induced sex haze and the cocoon that Wes's bed provides.

"I have to go talk to Memphis," I grumble, snuggling deeper into the crook of his arm and pressing my naked body flush against his.

"When? I'll go with you."

I look up into his eyes and shake my head. "I appreciate it, but this is a conversation between me and my brother. And even though it's about you, it's also not about you at all."

Wes looks confused, so I give him a quick rundown of what's going on with the vineyard without getting too into the nitty-gritty.

"Fuck," he whispers, rubbing a hand over the stubble along his jaw. "I could *feel* that something was up, but I figured it wasn't my place to ask. God, no pressure or anything."

I giggle and snuggle closer, lifting my face so I can press my lips to his. When I pull back, the concern that had crossed his face has eased.

"It's not your job to fix what's going on, Wes," I tell him. "And Memphis knows that. It's why he's scrambling to do anything and everything he can to salvage things before my dad throws in the towel."

He nods but doesn't look entirely convinced.

"Look at it this way," I continue. "You are a tool he's using to build something that might save the vineyard. But there are many tools he can use, and plenty of other possibilities for things he can build."

Wes grins. "Should I be concerned that you're calling me a tool?"

I poke his stomach, and he laughs.

"Does what I said make sense?"

"Yes," he tells me, turning on his side and pushing me onto my back. "It makes sense. But it's still a lot of pressure."

"Good thing you really know what you're doing, then, huh?"

He kisses me, his tongue slipping into my mouth, and I can feel his hand trailing downward.

Grabbing his hand, I pull back and pin him with a glare. "I need to go talk to Memphis."

"Five minutes."

I bite my lip and then nod. "Five minutes."

Twenty minutes later, I slip back into my bedroom through the veranda.

If I'm going to talk to my brother about Wes, I would feel a lot more comfortable doing it after I've taken a shower and swapped out my clothes.

I spend that time thinking about what I'll say to Memphis. Trying to figure out how this conversation will go. The main thing I want to make sure I remember is that it's fair for Memphis to be concerned. He *has* put a lot of time, energy, and money into getting this restaurant off the ground.

But being concerned doesn't mean he gets to dictate my life.

"Morning," I say, walking into the office after I've knocked. "You wanted to talk?"

Memphis spins in his chair, turning away from the computer and giving me all his attention.

Figures that he'd finally really focus on me when it's a fight.

"Murphy, I get that you think hooking up with Wes is fun," he says once I've taken a seat across from him. "But I am begging you to think this through, okay? Secret relationships never turn out to be anything other than disaster. For everyone involved. *Especially* when it's at work."

He leans forward, his elbows on the desk. I want so desperately to respond right now, to jump in and tell him he's wrong. That it's not about the secrecy—that literally *none* of our relationship has been about the secrecy.

If anything, that's why we avoided each other.

But instead of jumping down his throat, I stay silent, giving him a chance to share how he feels.

"I thought we were on the same side when it comes to this vineyard and trying to save it. And I'm sorry, but playing around with my head chef is a huge deal. Do you realize how catastrophic it could be if he just up and quit because things between the two of you go sour?"

He sits back in his chair and links his fingers together, resting them on his stomach.

"So, I'm sorry, but this isn't going to fly. You and Wes are not going to be able to . . . do . . . whatever it is you're doing."

I consider him for a minute. More than anything, I want to shoot out of my chair and give him a piece of my mind.

How *dare* he think he gets any say in my personal life.

But instead, I take a deep breath and try to remember what my aunt Sarah said.

My brother will shut down if I get heated about this. I can still tell him exactly how I feel, but storming around his office and yelling at him for being an idiot isn't going to accomplish anything.

"I just want to start by saying that we are absolutely on the same team. I want to help with any and every idea that you have to improve things and keep Dad from selling." I pause, knowing I'm about to stir the pot. "However, I'm not ending things with Wes. What we have is not about sneaking around, or rule-breaking lust. What we have is a lot deeper than that. It's a soulmate kind of love. So you can either stay mad, or you can let it go and move on. Either way it won't change us being in a relationship."

Memphis stares at me, and I can tell that he doesn't like what I said. Not surprising.

"I'm not going to go into detail about how things started, but you should know that both of us took the fact that we work together very seriously. This isn't a game. This is two adults who have fallen for each other deciding that they are willing to figure out how to make it work."

I can see the tic in his jaw, the way his nostrils flare slightly. Memphis is pissed.

"If you, as our boss, want to sit us down and put some boundaries in place, expectations for how we are to act when we're working, that is entirely fair. But you don't get to tell me who I can and cannot date. Ever. Boss or not."

He seems to think that point over for a beat, and I'm hoping that he'll see my position as fair and balanced.

"And what would you say if I said I'd fire Wes if you kept seeing him?"

Not fair and balanced, then.

Rubbing my lips together, I think over what he's just said. "I'd tell you that you aren't really concerned about the vineyard if you're willing to fire your most important employee because of something that has nothing to do with the reason you hired him in the first place."

"You don't think Wes will break up with *you* if I tell him his job is on the line?"

I sigh, then shrug my shoulders because it feels like the only thing I can do.

"You'll need to talk to him about it. I'm not his keeper. But I'll say this, Memphis. I'd reconsider your methods if your default way to solve problems is to get rid of the employees who are trying to help you."

Memphis exhales an irritated breath, and I can see him trying to figure out what to say or do to get this situation back under his control.

"I love you, Memphis," I tell him, deciding that maybe just a little bit of emotion is important to make him understand. "I do. I know this situation has been really hard, and that you're doing everything you can to try and fix things." I pause. "And I'm sorry Dad handed you something that was failing and then decided to take it away as if you're the one who broke it."

My brother's chin rises, and I know what I've said touches at his pride.

"But it isn't your fault," I continue. "You should be so proud of everything you've been doing. I know I'm proud of you. They might not say it often, but I don't doubt Aunt Sarah and Micah feel the same."

I can tell that Memphis has now shut me out, so I rise from my seat and come up behind him, wrapping my arms around his shoulders.

"I love you," I tell him again. "And I'll love you no matter what happens with the vineyard. Whether Dad sells it or not, whether the restaurant saves it or not."

I feel the tension leak out of my brother at my words, and then he raises a hand and squeezes one of mine where it rests on his chest.

"Love you too, Murph."

I stand there for a little bit longer, and only let go when my brother taps on my hands, the international sign for *Okay, let's wrap up this hug*.

When I get to the door, I turn back to look at him, finding his eyes on me.

"You can talk to Wes if you want," I tell him. "But I hope you'll try to think over what I've said before you do."

When he doesn't say anything else, I give him a little wave. "I'll see you over there in a bit."

Memphis nods, then returns his attention to the computer.

We still have a lot of problems, my brother and me. He's still stubborn and overbearing, and incredibly frustrating.

But I can tell with each one of these little conversations we're having, the times when we talk through something rather than let it go unaddressed, the brick wall that divides us is getting chipped away.

And maybe one day, it'll be gone altogether.

◆ ◆ ◆

"I think you should go."

I roll my eyes. "Of course you do."

Wes laughs. "I'm serious, Murphy," he says, shutting off the water at the sink and drying his hands on a dishcloth. "And that's me having only heard a few of your songs. I'm sure you have even more in your back pocket that would further blow my mind."

Pursing my lips, I pin him with a stare.

He crosses his arms, leans a hip up against the counter, and stares right back at me.

"What happened to the guy who said he can't tell me what decision to make, huh?" I keep my voice playful even though I'm only half joking.

"What happened to the girl who told me it was important to find your new dream?" he asks in return. "Have you taken the time to sit down and really think about what you want next? Because I suggested that, too."

Scoffing, I tuck my hands under my thighs, my palms flat against the stainless steel counter of the kitchen island.

I came in here after work to hang out with Wes while he closed down the kitchen after Sunday lunch. But I made the mistake of bringing up the fact Vivian texted me this morning, letting me know that the Humble Roads guy has been asking if I'm coming down to LA to talk to them.

"Not exactly."

Wes crosses over to where I'm sitting on the counter, steps in between my legs, and places his hands on my thighs.

"I know it's hard to figure out what comes next after you've had to let go of a dream," he tells me, his voice much more gentle now than it was just a moment ago. "I really do. So why don't you look at this as an opportunity to figure it out. You know? You're not committing to anything. You're just scoping it out. Seeing if it's right to you. If it *feels* right to you."

I lick my lips and let out a sigh.

I've been in a holding pattern ever since the day my future in the music industry took a nosedive. It's been three months since that horrible day, and even though it's easier to not think about the future outside of working at the restaurant and spending time with Wes, I know it's foolish.

"I'm not sure I'm ready to go," I say, trying to be honest. "I'm just barely starting to feel settled here. Shouldn't I let my wounds heal a little bit more first?"

Wes slips his arms around my waist and tugs me forward a little bit, and I wrap my arms around his shoulders.

"You *could* do that," he answers, his expression earnest. "You could wait until it doesn't hurt anymore. But the truth is that it will always hurt. There will always be a part of you that aches about letting go of that dream." He pauses. "*Or*, you can push through the pain and give yourself a chance to find something else that lights you up inside. And most likely, by doing that, you won't really notice that little pinch of pain anymore."

I consider that for a moment, my brain trying to sort through all the possibilities and fears and challenges that I could face by doing what Wes is suggesting.

"If I go, will you come with me?"

My shoulders sink when he shakes his head.

"Part of me would love to go," he says. "But going back to LA and talking with those people . . . That's a decision you need to make on your own. I wouldn't want my presence to distract from why you're there."

I lean forward and rest my forehead against his, closing my eyes.

This man is just . . . everything. I've never had something like this before, a relationship with someone who not only seems to understand me but also wants what's best for me.

When we first met at the gas station, there's no way I could have known all that he'd come to mean to me in such a short time. That the initial seed of attraction between us would grow into something so beautiful, with roots that are twisting ever deeper.

I bring my hand to the side of his face, look into his eyes.

"I love you," I whisper, then press my lips to his.

His mouth opens, his tongue tangling with mine as his hands grip my hips tightly.

"See, this is what I mean."

I pull back, turning my head to the side to where my brother is standing just inside the kitchen, the door still swinging slightly behind him.

"This is the stuff you can't be doing."

Pressing my lips tightly together, I give him a thin-lipped smile. I can feel the blood in my body rushing to my face.

"Sorry, Memphis," I say, nudging Wes out of the way and hopping down from the counter. "It won't happen again."

He stands there, staring at us for a minute, his gaze falling to where Wes is now holding my hand.

Memphis's expression barely changes, but I can see when something softens there. When some sort of decision has been made in his mind.

"Good job this weekend," my brother says to Wes, before his eyes flick to me. "Both of you. There was a lot going on, and you both handled it really well."

Wes nods. "Thank you."

There's another beat of silence before Memphis turns and walks into the little office connected to the kitchen.

I look up at Wes with raised eyebrows.

Didn't see that one coming, but I'll take it.

I will definitely take it.

Having already finished with the kitchen, Wes and I say goodbye to my brother and leave.

"Let's stop by your room first," Wes says as we emerge onto the patio, pausing for a second to lock the front door behind us.

"We're not having sex in my childhood room," I tell him.

Though the minute I say it, part of me thinks it might actually be a great idea.

"I want you to grab your guitar," he says, reaching out and taking my hand in his. "You don't have to play it for me. But in the few times you've talked about what your life used to be like, you've always made it seem like you never went anywhere without it. So . . ." He shrugs, leading me down the pathway toward the house. "Maybe carry it around for a few days and see if that helps you decide what to do about the Humble Roads thing."

Part of me wants to tell him no. That even though I've gotten it out a few times since being home, that I'm not ready.

But even as I think the words, I know they're not true.

More than a few times, I've found my fingers moving of their own volition, stroking invisible strings with my right hand or forming the finger placements for various chords on my left.

I've made a few notes in my phone for potential lyrics to songs that are beginning to float around in my head, these amorphous things that don't have any real focus yet but which are still very real to me.

So instead of saying what I want to, which is *absolutely not*, I let him lead me back to the house and watch as he lifts my guitar case in one hand, then retakes mine with his other.

It makes me think that maybe, sometimes, we need someone to lead us back to the things we love. To remind us of the joy we used to feel.

Because if we can remember that love, and feel that joy again, maybe we can eventually find our way back to what was lost.

◆ ◆ ◆

"I forgot how much I loved riding around on that thing."

"Oh, come on. You have to have cool ride-along equipment on the farm."

Quinn grins. "We do, but the golf cart reminds me of good times, you know? Sneaking off to the cabins with wine coolers and cigars."

I make a fake gagging noise. "Too bad we threw up after trying to inhale those things."

She giggles. "Remember that time junior year when your grandmother threw open the curtains in the living room just as we were sneaking back onto the porch after going to that party?"

My head falls back and I clutch my stomach on a silent laugh.

"She didn't have her glasses on and we just stood there, unmoving, until she closed the curtain again and went back to bed."

We keep laughing, both of us shaking in the front seat of the golf cart where it sits parked in front of the wine cellar. Quinn's belly is shaking almost violently, and I feel bad that our trip down memory lane is probably giving her little girl quite a ride.

It's been like this all afternoon as the two of us have slowly driven around the vineyard on the golf cart, reminiscing.

I used to claim I was a rule follower in my youth, but Quinn's iron-clad memory has proven me wrong. There were quite a few instances of rebellious behavior that I'd completely forgotten about, and each one of those stories resulted in me needing to bring the cart to a complete halt so we could break down with laughter.

This is what Vivian said I needed.

I can feel it in my soul that she was one hundred percent right.

And as it turns out, Quinn needs it, too.

In my head, my popular friend from high school stayed the belle of the ball after graduation. But it's amazing how differently life seems to turn out for people than what they'd originally planned.

Or what others assume.

And hearing about how rough the past year has been on her, how she's been facing this pregnancy alone . . . Well, I'm just really glad we're reconnecting.

"I'm so glad you came by today," I tell her a little while later as I come to a stop out near the shed where we park all our vehicles. "It was so good hearing about your life and the farm and everything that's been going on. Makes me wish I hadn't hated this place so much growing up."

I laugh, but I can tell instantly that Quinn has something on her mind that she wants to share. Because she *doesn't* laugh, and instead gives me a look I've only ever seen on her one time, back when she told Anthony Marley how unkind it was to call her fat because she'd gained weight over the summer.

So I know whatever she's going to say next is serious to her.

"I don't doubt you had big dreams of moving away from Rosewood," she begins, turning to face me. "But when you say how much you hate it here, and that this is the last place you want to be, I don't think you realize how that comes across."

Quinn shifts in her seat and rubs her hand over her stomach, almost like it calms her.

"I've lived here my entire life, Murphy. And *my* dreams *kept* me here. Because this is where I want to be. On the farm that has been in my family for over a hundred years. Near my parents, who are aging faster than I want them to. And in the town that might be imperfect, but has given me an incredible life."

"Quinn—"

But she shakes her head and keeps talking, determined to finish her point.

"When you talk about this place the way you do, you imply that a life lived here would be meaningless, or small. But that's *my* life you're talking about. I *did* stay here, and my life has been far from meaningless. And my daughter's life will be far from it, too."

A single tear tracks down my cheek, and I bat it away.

"I'm so sorry, Quinn. I *never* . . . I wouldn't ever say something that implied your life doesn't mean anything. You know I don't believe that, right? That I don't feel that way about you?"

"Maybe not me," she replies. "But I think you *do* think it about other people who live here."

I want to contradict her, but I know I'm guilty of what she's pointing out to me. That I've spent years wondering who the hell would want to be stuck in this small town for the rest of their life when there are so many other better, more interesting places to be.

Because in my mind, anywhere else would be better than being stuck here.

But even now, with those thoughts in my mind, I hate how they sound. Not just because it rings so much with bitterness, but also because it just feels less true.

The sour way I always felt about this town hasn't felt as sharp over the past few weeks. Spending time with my brother and Wes and Quinn has helped me find my own meaning in the home that never truly felt like home to me.

"I'm working on it," is what I eventually tell her.

I know it falls short. I know it's too revealing about the caustic way my mind has always painted this town and everyone in it.

But it's also honest.

Because I do feel like I'm working on it.

"I'm glad you're back, Murphy," Quinn says as we walk the short distance to where her car is parked. "And someday, I hope you're glad you're back, too."

We lean in for a long embrace, and I feel a surge of emotion rush through me as she holds me in her arms.

I don't want to be the person who lives with all this anger and resentment building to the point that I'm only ever able to talk about things with a negative slant.

I might not be the eternal optimist that Quinn is, but that doesn't mean I can't still find the good. The happy. The joy.

After Quinn heads home, I take my time wandering through the vineyard along the dirt path that leads out to the bench, trying to look at everything through new eyes.

Not just the eyes of someone remembering some of the good times from the past, but the eyes of someone imagining the good times in the future.

All the nights I'll get to sit on the bench with Wes, or snuggle up next to him in his cabin.

The chances I'll get to listen to my brother share about the things that mean so much to him.

How it will feel to watch Memphis finally solve all this financial stuff that has plagued him for longer than I realized.

And maybe . . . maybe even a time when my father and I might have a glass of wine together.

It's surprisingly cathartic, imagining all the good.

I can feel the way it pulses through me.

It feels incredible.

Like my heart, that has been brittle for so long, is finally beginning to soften.

Like this place might eventually be more to me than just the temporary safe harbor that I hoped to flee again.

Like it might eventually, really and truly, feel like home.

Chapter Twenty-Two

Wes

I didn't think I'd be making another drive into San Francisco so soon after the disaster that was my visit to the hospital, but here I am, a week later, driving back into the city, this time with a very different purpose.

"So Viv is picking me up at the airport," Murphy explains to me for the third time. "She's going to take me to lunch and then we're meeting with Todd, and then I'll be back on a plane a few hours later."

"I still think you jumped the gun in booking a return flight," I tell her as I pull up to the curb and put my car in park.

She shakes her head. "It's better this way. A quick trip, less than a day." Murphy lets out a sigh, then looks at me. "It'll be good, right?"

I reach over and put my hand on her knee, giving it a squeeze. "It's going to be great. And the good news is that you are one hundred percent in control of yourself and what you decide to do," I remind her. "So if you hate it, you say thanks but no thanks, and you come back."

Murphy nods, then puts her hand on top of mine. "Thank you. For the ride, but also for encouraging me. It's been a long time since I've gotten that from anyone but myself."

She leans across the console and I meet her, pressing my lips to hers in a kiss that is over far too quickly.

"Safe flight."

"Love you."

"Love *you.*"

And then she's getting out of the car and closing the door behind her, waving on her way through the sliding doors that lead into the airport, with nothing but a purse slung over her shoulder and her guitar case. I chuckle to myself at the fact she didn't even pack a bag, then pull away from the curb and follow the signs to exit the airport.

Last weekend, after Murphy and I discussed her going to LA and I lugged her guitar out to my cabin, she surprised me by actually opening her case and singing to me. She sang a few songs, and then she cried as she sang, and it was beautiful and heartbreaking and made me wish there was anything I could do.

She surprised me again a few days later when she said she wanted to go meet with the people at Humble Roads and hear what they have to say.

I'm proud of her for giving it a shot, even if I do think she's being a little hasty about only flying down for a single day.

Less than a single day. Ten hours at most, including her time in the air.

But she's still going. She's still pushing herself. And even though she might have to deal with some uncomfortable thoughts or feelings while she's there, I think she'll be better for it in the end, regardless of the outcome.

It's because she's willing to push herself that I've decided to do the same.

Twenty minutes later, I pull into a space down the street from Seasons, the restaurant that I worked at for six years before I moved to Chicago. It's still fairly early, and there's a chance that Chef Hines isn't here since none of his restaurants are open on Mondays.

But I know Bernard, and for as long as I've known him, he's spent Monday mornings in the same booth at Seasons, sipping coffee and doing the Sunday crossword, since his Sundays are usually too busy to take the time.

When I walk up to the building, peering through the large glass windows, I spot him. Exactly where I thought he would be.

It's always something I've admired about him, how dedicated he is to keeping his life and work simple and focused on the things that matter. He told me that once, that so many restaurants fail because they try to do too many things and end up alienating the customers that built them up in the first place.

I guess that's kind of what happened to me, in a personal sense. Instead of staying focused on the things I know and was passionate about, I decided to do too much. To be too many things to too many people.

And in doing so, I forgot who I was.

I tap lightly on the glass of one of those large windows. When Chef Hines looks up and sees me, he takes off his glasses, almost like he can't believe his eyes. Then I hear the faint sound of his shouted "Wesley!" before he leaves his booth and heads to the front.

He opens the door just as I get there, and then he yanks me in for a hug, my tall frame bending slightly as I wrap my arms around him as well.

"Wesley!" he says again, then pulls back and places his hands on either side of my face. "I can't believe you're here!"

It's only in this very moment that I realize how worried I was that he'd turn me away, and I can't help but smile, reveling in his joy at seeing me.

"I'm sorry I haven't been by sooner," I tell him. "I missed you."

Chef Hines pats me on the shoulder, then waves for me to follow him inside. Once we're both in, he relocks the front door and leads me over to his booth.

"I wish I had known you were coming today. Linus would have so loved to see you," he tells me, referring to his partner. Then he gestures for me to take a seat across from him in the booth. "How long are you in town?"

"I'm actually back in California." I pause. "I'm the head chef at a new restaurant at a winery in Rosewood."

"That's wonderful, Wes. I'm so happy for you. A better fit than the Santiagos, yes?"

I lick my lips, letting out an awkward chuckle. "Yes. Definitely a better fit."

Then he gives me a sympathetic look, and I suddenly realize . . . He already knows.

"I'm sorry that things didn't work out for you. But the best thing you could do is move on and find something else. Sounds like that's exactly what you did."

"How'd you hear about it?"

He taps his pen against the newspaper between us. "Alejandro called me. Right after it happened."

I blink a few times, and this time I'm *more* than surprised. "He *what*?"

"The way he phrased it was something like, 'I just left your little protégé on the street with a black eye. You better teach him how shit works, Bernard. Get him out of Chicago.'"

Nausea begins to rise inside me, and embarrassment isn't far behind.

"I'm so sorry, Chef," I tell him, unable to look him in the eye. "I didn't mean for you to be involved in any of it."

When I finally do look at him, I see that same sympathetic look from before.

"Wes, I don't know all the details of what happened. But it doesn't surprise me that the road you were on ended up bringing you back here. Men like Alejandro Santiago are very different from men like you, and please believe me when I say that is a compliment."

Part of me wishes that Chef Hines had been a little more forth-coming when I was considering the move to Chicago to work for the Santiagos. If I had known how much he disliked the man, maybe I would have made a different decision.

But in the same breath, I know it's not his responsibility. He did warn me, after all.

Part of me thinks that maybe he actually made the right call in letting me figure it out myself. There are definitely some lessons I learned from my experience in Chicago and working for Alejandro and Bridget that I wouldn't have learned if I hadn't made the mistake of going.

"Come," he says, a genuine smile on his face. "Let's make something together."

An hour later, we're standing on opposite sides of a counter in the Seasons kitchen, each of us enjoying a slice of an artichoke flatbread pizza that reminds me of all the incredible ways Chef Hines knows how to use veggies as a primary.

My biggest weakness has always been how heavily I lean in to protein, and I make a pointed note to myself to remember this as I'm making adjustments to my menu in the future.

We spent the entirety of our cooking time going over what happened in Chicago. There is nothing as horrible as sharing your failures with the man who trained you, pointing out all the ways you *didn't* become the person he tried to mold you into.

"I'm sorry I let you down," I tell him, wiping off my hands on a napkin.

"You didn't let me down, Wes."

He crosses his arms and pins me with a look I know all too well.

It means a lesson is coming.

"Despite everything, I am proud of you," he continues. "I'm proud of all you've accomplished and all you've *tried* to accomplish, because it means you pushed yourself outside of what is easy. So please don't rest how you feel about everything on *me* being disappointed in you."

His words ease something tight in my chest, and I give him a grateful nod.

"What it sounds like, though," he adds—and here comes the lesson, I can feel it—"is that you let yourself down. *You* had expectations for yourself, and however things turned out with the Santiagos isn't what you had hoped for."

Fuck if that isn't the truth.

"So the best thing you can do is learn from it." He shrugs a shoulder. "It's that simple and that easy. And it's also that difficult and that complicated. Because not everybody knows how to learn from their mistakes. Instead they just keep doing the same things over and over again and hoping to come out better the next time."

Chef Hines drops his arms and rounds the counter, then places his hands on each of my biceps.

"But I know you know this already. It sounds like you're already making changes, figuring out what to do next, how to do it better."

He squeezes gently, then lets his hands fall away and turns to clear the dishes we used to make the flatbread pizza.

"So what you need, Wes, is not to come to me hoping for forgiveness. You need to look inward for that. *You* are the only one who can forgive yourself for the ways that you feel like you've let yourself down. And that is one of the hardest things any of us can learn how to do."

When I pick Murphy up from the airport later that evening, I can pretty much tell from her smile that the day was amazing. I already had an idea that she was enjoying it from the dozen or so texts she sent me throughout the day, but the pure joy radiating off her is just confirmation of what I only thought I knew.

"Tell me everything."

"They offered me a job as a songwriter."

I smile as I pull out into traffic. "Holy shit!"

"I know! It was so much better than I thought it was going to be, you know? Todd is actually really nice, and he set me up in the booth and had me play some of my music for him. And he said he wants me to write music for their artists. Not just Vivian, but other artists, too. People I admire and think are insanely talented."

She sinks farther into the seat, a dreamy smile on her face.

"I can't believe this is happening."

I reach over and rest my hand on her thigh, giving it a light squeeze. "I can. When you're as talented as you are, a guy like Paul can only hold you back for so long."

Murphy gives me an embarrassed smile and hooks her hand into mine.

She tells me about her day, from the time she landed to visiting the record label's headquarters.

And all the while, I'm gearing myself up for the part where she tells me that she's moving back to LA. It makes sense that they would want her there, to be able to sit outside the recording rooms and collaborate.

She was happy there until it all fell apart, so I know she'll be happy there again.

Even if it means she leaves me behind.

"They want me to move to LA," she eventually shares.

She turns in her seat and raises her knee to her chest, then wraps her arms around it before slipping her hand back into mine.

I swallow thickly, the time I spent getting ready for this conversation doing almost nothing to truly prepare me for how it feels to hear her say it. To know she's going to leave.

The feelings swirling in my chest are much stronger than I anticipated, and it takes everything inside me not to beg her to—

"I told them no."

My head swings to the side, and I hold tightly to the steering wheel, careful not to jerk us into a neighboring lane.

"What?"

Her smile is soft, and she squeezes my hand.

"I told them that I would love to work for them, but that I didn't want to be based in LA or anywhere in Southern California."

"Murphy . . ."

"My life is here now, Wes."

"But that doesn't mean you can't rebuild a life there."

"I know that." She squeezes my hand again. "I *know* that. But it's not just my life that's here, Wes. My heart is here, too. And that's something I won't be able to find there. I just won't."

My own heart constricts in my chest, the overwhelming feeling of knowing I've found my soulmate coursing through me and out to my veins, to every part of my body.

I look over at Murphy again, and this time, I can see she has tears in her eyes.

"I love you."

It's a whisper when she says it, but her words have never sounded so loud and strong in my mind.

In my heart.

"I love you, too."

We ride in silence for a little while, the lights of passing cars illuminating her face enough for me to glance over and look at her often, and I love seeing the happy little smile on her lips.

And all the while, her hand never leaves mine.

I hope it never does.

Chapter Twenty-Three

MURPHY

I pause at the threshold to my room. My hand hovers over the doorknob when I hear the faint strum of the guitar. It's a familiar melody, though I'm unable to place it in my memory.

"I can see your shadow under the door."

I blink a few times in surprise at the sound of my father's voice, and I slowly push the door open, certain I must have imagined it. But there he is, sitting on the edge of my bed, my guitar in hand as he plucks idly at the strings.

I can't decide what's more of a shock: him sitting on my bed playing the guitar, or the soft smile on his face as he does it.

"I didn't know you played," I say, struggling to find the words to express how confused I am at the sight before me.

He nods, his body rocking minutely from side to side as he continues strumming.

"Your mom taught me. Said it was the best way to get something off your chest without talking." At that, his smile turns sad. "Words never came easy to me, even back then."

Dad has always been kind of a gruff guy. Gritty in a way I don't really understand. He's never been a great communicator and rarely talks about how he feels. Unless he's irritated about something.

I've always chalked it up to losing my mom and turning inward with his grief. It never occurred to me that the man my mother loved was always a growly bear who didn't say much, even when they were younger.

"We used to play together over on that hill where her bench is." He makes a huffing sound that I think is supposed to be a laugh, and shakes his head. "Well, *she* played. I plucked along like an idiot, just grateful to be sitting next to her."

Something tightens in my chest at his memory of their love. Of *his* love.

He so rarely talks about her. And my own memories of my mother are vague, little snippets of images and random things. Mostly memories cobbled together from the few photos I have from when I was a toddler.

But nothing ever feels real or concrete. It's a sad truth of losing her when I was so young. I envy everyone who got to know her in ways I never will.

"What is that you're playing?" I have a feeling it's related to Mom somehow, but I can't place exactly why. "I feel like I've heard it before."

Dad smiles at me then. A real one.

"Because you *have* heard it before. It's your good night song. Your mom created one for each of you." He pauses, his fingers stuttering on the strings. "Well, for you and Memphis. She hadn't written one for Micah yet."

My chest twists again. I try to imagine her playing me to sleep, wishing I had a real memory of it.

"Does it have words?"

He shakes his head, and his fingers pick up their strumming again.

"She didn't really write songs. Not like you do. Said she didn't want to write the words, she wanted to create the feeling."

I nod, understanding what he means.

That's how I feel sometimes when I'm writing music. I don't envision myself performing the song. I imagine how others will feel when they hear it. How the words and the sounds filter into their ears and ripple through their bodies, touching their minds and hearts before traveling down into their fingers and toes.

It's why the songwriting part has always felt more important than anything else, and why I'm so excited about this opportunity with Humble Roads. There are still all these words and feelings inside me that just *have* to come out, even if I'm not the one performing them.

Almost as if he heard my thoughts, my dad speaks again.

"Memphis told me about the trip to meet with that record label." The room is suddenly far too quiet as my father stops playing and crosses his arms on top of the body of the guitar. "Said it was a big deal."

My head tilts to the side as I regard him.

Something's different.

I mean, I knew it when I came in here and found him playing my guitar, which I've literally never seen him do in my entire life.

But it's something else.

I just can't put my finger on it.

"Yeah. It's a really big deal."

It's not in my nature to boast, but if my father is taking an unexpected interest in something I love—something that has divided us for as long as I can seem to remember—then I want him to know *exactly* how big of a deal it really is.

"So you're gonna head back to LA, then?"

"Do you even really care?" My words come out harsher than I intend, barbed with the pain I've felt at his constant inability to be supportive of my dreams. So I don't rush to apologize for what I said or how I said it.

My dad's head falls just a bit, his gaze dropping to the floor.

"I deserve that," he says, his voice soft. "But to answer the question, yes, I do care. I want . . ." His voice trails off and he looks toward my laundry basket, almost like he's searching for the words amid my dirty clothes. "I want you to be happy, Murph. I do. It's all I've ever wanted."

My chest gets that tightness again, though this time it prickles at something behind my nose as well.

"Just . . . sometimes I'm not very good at saying it. I've missed you a lot, Murph, and I'm glad you're here. But if heading back to LA will make you happy, then . . . Well, that's the most important thing."

I lean against my dresser, bracing my hands against the edge.

How long have I waited for something like this?

For this . . . olive branch?

Years.

A decade.

The part of me that had given up hope of ever reconciling with my father wants to lash out at him. Reject this kind, sensitive side of him that feels almost unnatural because I'm so unaccustomed to it.

But there's a little girl inside me who just wants her dad in her life. And if he's willing to let something shift between us, surely I can, too.

"I'm not going back to LA."

He blinks a few times, surprise evident on his face.

"I told Todd—he's the guy from the label—that I would take the job, but that I wanted to be able to work from here." I cross my arms. "My life in LA . . . I feel like I've finally moved on from it. And there's no reason that I can't write from here."

When my father stays silent, a thought occurs to me that hadn't before.

"That is . . . if it's okay for me to stay."

He reaches up and scrubs a hand along the edge of his jaw, his eyes aimed at the floor. Then he takes a deep breath and lets it out long and slow.

I don't know how I'll feel if he asks me to go. Especially after I've finally gotten to a point where I actually *want* to be here. Wes is here, and that plays a big part in knowing that I'll be happy in Rosewood.

But he's not the only reason.

Something in my soul has settled in a way I wasn't expecting since I moved back.

Maybe it's a result of finding love.

But I have a feeling it's just as much about finding myself.

If I hadn't moved back, I might never have worked through the emotions of what happened in LA. I might never have reconciled with Memphis. I might not have realized how much this vineyard is a part of my past and just how much I want to help it succeed and be at least a small part of my future.

And now, this conversation with my father. Unexpected and yet possibly exactly what I've been seeking.

Permission to leave, possibly even *encouragement*, if he thinks it'll make me happy.

Right? Isn't that what he said?

Because really, was I so desperate to leave because I didn't want to be here? Or because I didn't want to feel like I *had* to stay? Like there was no other choice for me.

My mind scrambles over all these little bits, trying to sort them and make sense of them. Trying to suss out all the subtle nuances.

But before I can get too lost in thought, my father finally looks back up at me, and I startle when I see his eyes are glassy.

"I'm sorry, Murph." His voice is a ragged whisper. "I'm sorry I've ever made you wonder if I want you here. I *always* want you here. But only if you want to be."

My throat constricts as emotion wells in my chest, and before I can think it all the way through, I'm crossing the room and wrapping my arms around my dad's shoulders.

I can't remember the last time we hugged. Something inside me seems to release when his arms wrap around me too, and hold me just as tightly as I'm clinging to him.

"I love you, Murphy."

I squeeze him tighter.

"I love you, too."

We stay like that for a long moment, each of us seeming to revel in this much-needed cease-fire. Eventually, I pull back and sit on the floor in front of him, cross-legged.

"Can you play me the song again?" I ask him. "And the one for Memphis, too?"

He gives me that barely-there smile and then picks the guitar back up and begins to play.

Eventually, he passes the guitar to me and asks me to play him something I've written. A song that means something to *me*.

So I play him the song I sang for Wes in the car the night of his anxiety attack.

My father has questions in his eyes when I finish, but he doesn't ask them. Instead, he just nods and tells me he thinks I'm very talented.

I can't expect him to suddenly be a completely different person. He's not the talkative guy who is going to ask a million questions, and it'll take a long time before things between us feel more natural. Easy.

But I'll take this middle ground we seem to have found.

I'll take it every damn day.

I ruminate on our interaction for the rest of the afternoon and into the evening, long after he's gone back to work and I've found myself out at the bench, waiting for Wes. I think about what my dad said about my mom, and himself.

What he said about me.

Our relationship is far from perfect, but just like with Memphis, there is a path to reconciliation with my father now. Something I've never imagined was possible in the past.

I'm not sure exactly what prompted him to come to me. Maybe it was finding out about Humble Roads and assuming I might be leaving again. It's the only thing I can think of that might be an answer.

Regardless, I'm glad he did it. And I can only hope that it was the first brick in a large wall that desperately needs to come down.

"Hey."

I turn at the sound of Wes's voice, and I can't help the smile that crosses my face at the sight of him.

He takes a seat next to me and leans in, pressing his lips against mine in a way that is both gentle and purposeful. Like he knows exactly how he wants to kiss me. It sends a shiver down to my toes, and I revel in it, to the point where I almost moan at the loss when he pulls back.

"How's the writing coming?" He props an arm along the back of the bench.

I chuckle. "I haven't written anything today."

Wes laughs, too. "I thought the whole point of you staying here today was so you could write. You mean you could have come with me?"

Shaking my head, I keep plucking at the strings. "Nope. I ended up hanging out with my dad for a little bit."

The expression Wes gives me makes me laugh again.

"I know. I wasn't expecting it, either."

I explain what happened, and Wes lets out a long whistle when I'm finished.

"Sounds like you had a different kind of productive day."

"I really did."

"Well, I'm sure that Todd guy isn't waiting by his computer for you to send him anything."

Snorting, I shake my head at him. "Why do you always call him 'that Todd guy'?"

Wes just grins. "Because it makes you laugh, every time."

It's been two weeks since I went to LA and met with Todd and Vivian and the team at Humble Roads. I've been working on music here and there, mostly in my undies in Wes's bed in the morning before I have to get ready for work.

My first deadline is coming up, and I want to impress them. So taking the day off today and giving myself permission to just enjoy the time with my dad was an active sacrifice on my part.

But I also skipped out on driving with Wes to San Francisco again to see his brother. Originally I was supposed to go, but there was a part of me that just felt like Wes really needed alone time with Ash after what happened with their mom.

Sonia's disappearance from the hospital was really hard on Wes. It brought up all these feelings from childhood, and I know he's still processing things. When Ash found her a week later, she was already wasted again and back with one of her boyfriends. She had turned Ash away after only a few minutes.

It didn't feel like a good time to try to force an upbeat, meet-the-brother lunch. So I told Wes I wanted him and Ash to have some brother time, and I planned to stay behind and work on my music.

"How did it go? How's Ash?"

Wes grimaces, his lips twisting to the side. "He always gives me a brave face, but I know the stuff with my mom is wearing on him." He shrugs a shoulder. "There isn't much we can do except continue to be there for each other."

When he doesn't offer anything else, I set my guitar aside and shift closer to him, placing my hand on his warm thigh.

"I know it doesn't make things better, but I'm here for you."

His arm wraps around me and pulls me even closer, his hand squeezing my shoulder. Then he presses his lips against my temple and just holds himself there, almost like he's breathing me in.

"It *does* make things better," he tells me, his voice a whisper. "*You* always make things better."

He kisses me again, and my heart soars.

Wes holds me closely. Reverently.

Like I'm precious.

Like I'm everything.

And I hope he never lets me go.

Epilogue

Wes

Three months later

The sound of a strumming guitar is what wakes me, and I smile into my pillow at the familiar melody. Murphy's been working on this one song for weeks now, and I'm starting to enjoy the way it brings me gently out of sleep in the mornings.

I also enjoy the fact that she normally writes music wearing nothing but her panties.

That thought is enough to push me out of my warm cocoon. I roll over, push up onto my elbows, and peer over the edge of the bed. Sure enough, Murphy is sitting cross-legged on the floor with her guitar in her lap, a notebook open in front of her, and a pencil between her teeth.

She doesn't realize I'm watching her—she rarely does when she's as focused as she looks right now—and I take advantage, tracing my gaze over her bare skin. I wish the guitar wasn't perfectly positioned to hide so much of her body, but I also like the tease of it. My morning wood begins to demand more attention as I imagine her dusky nipples pressed up against the back of the guitar.

"I can feel you watching me." Her eyes flick up to mine as she stops strumming, but then she's looking at the notebook and making a few marks.

Flipping my body around, I bring my head to the end of the bed and cross my arms, resting my chin against them.

"Here I was thinking I was being sneaky."

She giggles, and the sound twists itself around my heart the way it always does.

"Not a chance in hell. I can *always* feel you watching me."

It doesn't surprise me that she senses my attention, because I feel the same way. There have been more than a few instances over the past several months we've been together that I'll look up from what I'm doing—whether it's chopping veggies in the kitchen to prep for the next meal service, or rinsing in the shower, or just sitting on the bench in the vineyard—because I know she's there.

It's like my heart and hers are magnets, and something inside me notices when she's near. It's wild, and I love everything about it.

"What do you think about . . . this?" Her fingers return to the strings.

I've heard her play the chords so many times, I can tell she's starting in the middle. I'm proven right when she sings the last line of the chorus before moving into what I'm guessing is the second verse. It's a folky little number that she's working on for a popular singer from the nineties who has decided to jump back into performing again.

Murphy's words are soft and warm and she closes her eyes, her head falling back as she sings. I'm no music expert, but it's easy to see how damn talented Murphy is. I'm entranced. Humble Roads is lucky as hell to have her writing for them and their artists.

I think they should sign her, but in the two or three times I've mentioned it since she started working with that Todd guy, Murphy just pats my hand and reminds me she's happier with how things are now than she ever imagined. So much of her performance joy was actually in hearing her music, not about being onstage.

As long as my girl's happy, I don't care either way.

When she finishes, she presses her hand flat against the strings, her eyes finding mine.

"It's really good."

Her smile stretches wide. "Really?"

I nod. "I especially like that little yodeling thing you did at the end."

"I wasn't *yodeling*," she says, bursting into laughter.

"Well, I don't know what it's called. The part where your voice wobbled around a bunch."

Murphy falls back slightly, leaning against the couch behind her.

"It's called melismatic singing," she finally answers, wiping her eyes. "But I can't *wait* to tell Vivian you called it yodeling."

I shrug. "Like I'm going to know what melatonin singing is."

At that, Murphy lets out another laugh and then sets her guitar aside, doubling over in hysterics. I mispronounced it on purpose. I'll do anything to hear her happy.

It doesn't hurt that she's sitting there topless, either. I bite my lip, watching her tits jiggle.

Eventually, her laughter fades. Murphy gets onto her knees, scoots toward me, and presses a kiss against my temple.

"I needed that this morning," she tells me. "Thanks."

I wiggle my eyebrows. "I accept thanks in other ways, you know."

She snorts and rolls her eyes, then drops down so she's sitting on her feet in front of me. "As lovely as that sounds, you have that meeting this morning."

I groan at the reminder and shove my face into the crook of where my arms are folded in front of me. There's no way I would forget, but it's the last thing I want her to bring up when I'm in the middle of pitching some morning shenanigans.

"I remember," I grumble. "Wish I didn't."

She hums, then rubs her hands gently along my shoulders and upper back.

"It's a good thing," she tells me, her voice soft and loving. "And you get to spend the day with Ash."

Sighing, I nod. She's right, but it doesn't really make it any easier.

I push up and sit on the edge of the bed, begrudging that the cozy joy of ogling my girlfriend is over and the day has officially begun. "I'm gonna hop in the shower."

After giving her a quick kiss, I head into the bathroom and flip on the water. Then I brace myself on the counter and stare down at the sink, mentally preparing for what lies ahead today.

My brother talked me into going to Al-Anon, some sort of AA meeting but for family members of people with substance abuse problems. Part of me gets it—I have my *own* issues because of my mother. It makes sense that talking about it would be helpful. But I'm not entirely sold on the group thing, and I only agreed to it because it's important to Ash.

Now that the day is actually here, though, I'm wishing I was a whole lot more selfish. Or even that I was the type who could just text him a bullshit *sorry I can't make it* text. Because it's the absolute last thing I want to do.

I step under the water and let the scalding heat soak my tense muscles for a long moment, reminding myself that I'm doing the right thing. Then I make quick work of my shower routine and hop out, knowing that I don't have too much time to laze around if I'm going to meet Ash in the city.

We're making a day out of it. First the meeting, then lunch to chat. Afterward, we're going to stop by the apartment he and Mira just moved into, and I'll get a chance to meet her as well. Stupid meeting aside, I'm kind of looking forward to it.

When I step out of the bathroom, I find Murphy has—sadly—put on a shirt and moved to the kitchen. She's humming that same melody as she pours herself a cup of coffee, and her ass sways along.

Her eyes find mine, and I know I don't imagine it when they brighten at the sight of me. As if I didn't just see her a few minutes ago. As if I don't get to see her all the time.

Just like that, the stress about this meeting begins to abate. Not entirely, but enough that it's not clouding my entire mind anymore.

The clouds have a hard time sticking around when the sun is out and shining.

That's what Murphy is to me.

The sun.

Brightness.

A light in the darkness that the world can sometimes be.

And I love her for it.

For so many other things, too. But definitely for the way my soul feels lighter when she's around.

I take the cup of coffee out of her hands and set it on the counter before tugging her close.

"I'm crazy about you. You know that, right?" I say, wrapping my arms around her, my heart buoying at the feel of her body pressed against mine.

I know it's too soon, right now. We still have so many things to learn about each other. But someday, Murphy's going to wear my ring on her finger. It's a truth I know in the depths of my soul.

"Of course I do." Her response is muffled where she's tucked her face against my chest, and her arms tighten around me. "I love you more than anything."

I lift her face so I can see her beautiful eyes and revel in that love. Then I drop my mouth down to hers, like I have so many times before.

Like I plan to do for the rest of my life.

ACKNOWLEDGMENTS

I always thank my husband first because of everything he does to support me, but for this book, I feel it's especially important to name him first. Danny: thank you for always believing in me, for building me up when I feel like I might crumble, and for never letting me downplay the hard work that goes into writing a story. I love you more than anything, and I always will.

Thank you to Sammi for jumping up and down with me in Florida. To Julie, for the listening ear and incredible advice whenever I need someone to talk to. To Meredith, for inviting me on this crazy journey. To Kimberly, for your incredible insight that helped give this story that extra something. To Krista, for all the minutiae that we wouldn't have caught on our own. And to Maria for wanting to champion Murphy and Wes's story.

About the Authors

Photo © 2022 Sean Murphy

Meredith Wild is a #1 *New York Times*, *USA Today*, and international bestselling author of twenty-two novels. After self-publishing her debut novel, *Hardwired*, in 2013, Wild used her ten years of experience as a tech entrepreneur to form her own publishing imprint, forging relationships with major retailers and becoming one of the first indie authors to be fully stocked in brick-and-mortar bookstore chains nationwide. Both traditionally and self-published, Wild's books have hit #1 on the *New York Times* and *Wall Street Journal* bestsellers lists. She has been featured on *CBS This Morning*, the *Today* show, the *New York Times*, the *Hollywood Reporter*, *Vanity Fair*, *Publishers Weekly*, and the *Examiner*. Her foreign rights have been sold in over twenty-three languages. She resides in Florida with her partner, her children, and their many cats.

Jillian Liota is the author of more than fifteen contemporary and new adult romance novels. Her writing has been praised for depth of character, strong female friendships, deliciously steamy scenes, and positive portrayal of mental health. Jillian is married to her best friend, has a three-legged pup with endless energy, and acts as a servant to a very temperamental cat. She currently lives in Georgia. For more information, visit jillianliota.com.